SATAN'S LASH
THE COMPLETE CASES OF
SATAN HALL, VOLUME 1

THE
ARGOSY™
LIBRARY

SATAN'S LASH
THE COMPLETE CASES OF
SATAN HALL, VOLUME 1

CARROLL JOHN DALY

PRIMARY ILLUSTRATOR
JOSEPH A. FARREN

COVER BY
LEJAREN HILLER

POPULAR PUBLICATIONS · 2022

TABLE OF CONTENTS

BLACK TURNS WHITE

*He Was Little, and Some People
Took Advantage of It*

1

THE HARNESS BULL had passed slowly by hours and hours ago, it seemed. Yet I knew by the clock in the little pawnshop that he had been gone only five minutes. I had held my breath in fear that he might try the door. But he was true to form and passed it as he had passed it so many nights before—just a single glance through the dirty pane of glass. Twenty minutes, all told, since Billy Ludlow and Rattigan had gone inside.

Slinking back against the elevated pillar, I wedged myself between the heavy stanchions. I'm almost a contortionist—the tricks I can do with my small but wiry body.

It was late, and few people came along the avenue. Yet each one of those few brought my heart into my mouth and sent my back tighter against the steel pillar. Occasionally, I thought that figures moved behind the curtain in the rear of the shop. But that was imagination only, for the curtains were heavy and tightly drawn.

Billy Ludlow, the best box man in the past ten years! I sneered at that now. I wished they'd come out. I wished they'd brought soup and blown the old box open. Though old, the safe seemed too tough to crack with a can opener. Still, Billy Ludlow had said that—

My breath sucked in, and I held it a moment. Then it came out like you'd stuck a pin in a toy balloon. I didn't turn my head right away. I couldn't. And what's more, I didn't need to, I could have picked out those footsteps with my eyes closed any place.

I tried to tell myself that I was wrong—that the owner of those feet was having a night off and spending it quietly in Brooklyn.

I swung my head slowly and saw him. He was passing under the street light, his long arms hanging at his sides, his narrow twitching fingers snakelike against the blackness of his trousers legs. And his head—his peculiar head with its features all seeming to come to points—starting at his chin and making one great V, up to the brim of his wide, slouch hat. I didn't see his hair, but I knew that the jet-black, thin line began down by his forehead and widened as the dark hair thickened, into that same V.

It was "Satan" Hall, the meanest, the crudest, the most sinister figure in the police department. I sunk my finger nails into the palms of my hands. I hated him—and, yes, I feared him; not the physical presence of the man, but the deadly, sinister twist to his lips; the hidden something behind his cold, hard eyes.

I watched him now, fascinated, as he neared that door— the door with the broken lock, and the two men in the back room beyond, who worked upon the safe—the two men that I was to warn of danger. It would be too late now. It would only attract attention, breed suspicion in that mind of Satan Hall. But truth is truth. My lips were dry and parched; my tongue stuck to the roof of my mouth. I couldn't make a sound.

It was too late to run now, even if I wanted to or could have. He'd see me sure. He was at the far window—by the

door, and— He stopped, turned sharply, and bending his head forward looked straight at me.

Like a man in a nightmare, I saw him hesitate a moment as he tried to pierce the darkness. Then he stepped from the curb, and in those steady measured strides walked straight to the elevated pillar and to me.

"Hello!" He stopped directly before me. "It's 'Kid' Blaney himself—the boy criminal—the master mind." The sarcasm slipped out of his voice and a metallic hardness crept in. "Come, Kid, what's the game?"

"Nothin'." I tried to cross my feet but nearly lost my balance. "I was seein' a twist home, an'—an' sort of hung around."

"That's fine." He nodded his head and jerked a thumb back over his shoulder. "She lives over the pawnshop, and you're thinking things might happen below to disturb her, eh?" And he put his eyes on me.

They were green eyes. They were hard eyes. They were steady eyes. It was like you looked at the steel of the elevated pillars through a thin coating of ice. And they lit right on your eyes but didn't stop there. They somehow shoved themselves back into your head and jumbled up the thoughts you had there and made your tongue come out and lick at your lips.

I knew it was coming. I had seen it too often before, and felt it too, not to know. He just raised his right hand and swung his open palm against my face. And as my head jarred aside and my feet half lifted from the ground, he brought over his other hand and smacked me back on my feet.

"Come, Kid," he said very slowly, "what's the game?"

That was what he always did. That was what he always said. After that, you went down like a thousand of brick; hard pavement or soft dirt or broken glass didn't matter. I half closed my eyes and drew in my breath, and wondered if he'd hit me hard enough to crack my skull against the steel pole.

But the blow never came. His fist stopped suddenly in the air, and he muttered:

"I oughta beat it out of you—I oughta smash it out of you." He turned and walked quickly back to the sidewalk.

Twice he looked up and down the street for the harness bull, and once he put something to his mouth. But he didn't blow the whistle. He finally shrugged his broad shoulders, walked straight to that pawnshop door, spun the knob, pushed the door quietly open and stepped inside. There was no one to deny that Satan Hall had guts.

His huge figure was close to the curtain when I let out my warning cry—the purring, yodeling note, of the alley cat that prowls at night.

I saw the curtains jerk violently aside, but I couldn't tell if it was done by the dick who had entered the door, or the boys who worked on the big box behind the curtains.

There was the sudden stab of orange-blue flame, a roar, and another roar—the shattering of the window—and I was off across the street and into the alley of the warehouse, that would take me to the block behind.

Some one was calling. Windows were going up. A police whistle came shrilling through the night. Another and another, and the beat of a heavy club upon the stone pavement. From the shadow of the alley, I watched the pawnshop.

A minute passed—two, perhaps. The curtains parted again. Two figures were merged as one. They crossed the floor, reached the door, and stood framed in the light. One figure was Satan Hall and the other figure was Rattigan. Satan held him by the coat collar.

I didn't wait any longer. I ducked down the alley, through a loose board in the fence—and so came into the street beyond.

Billy Ludlow had not come out of that back room. Billy Ludlow would never come out of that back room. Satan Hall always shot to kill.

I guess panic got me when I reached my house and dashed through the tenement door and up the stairs. And I never reached the top floor and my room, but found myself pounding upon the door on the third floor and heard a voice hoarsely whispering:

"Mary, let me in. I'm in a hole—an awful hole." It was my voice.

She came quickly and opened the door and put an arm about me and led me to a chair in the living room and talked to me like I was a kid—and me over sixteen.

My hands didn't shake so much when Mary held them.

It was good just to look at her. She had the biggest blue eyes and the silkiest sort of hair, and, even though her little nose was turned up, you couldn't rightly call it a pug nose.

I was proud to know Mary Rogers and have her for a pal. Her father had been the greatest forger of all of them; doing penwork that ran at times as high as ten grand. But I'd have been proud to know Mary just for herself. It wouldn't 'a' made no difference to me whether her old man had been a scratcher or picked a pocket. Mary was class by herself.

"I'm in a devil of a mess." I blurted it out. "You gotta do something big for me or they'll send me away. You gotta lie for me or maybe they'll burn me. I don't rightly know. You gotta say I was here with you to-night—from twelve to now, anyway. You just gotta, Mary." I clutched at her hand. And before she could even ask me, I spoke my piece. "I was standing outside of Isaac's pawnshop when—when a lad got knocked off."

She turned kind of pale and went to her knees and put her arm about me. And I told her about it—that is, some of it. But I didn't tell her I had gaycatted the job for Billy Ludlow, nor that I was playing outside man. She was built funny.

"I was only walking by, Mary." I guess I turned my head. Them blue glims of hers, when they were soft and wet, were hard to look at and lie to. "I wasn't doin' nothin'—just standing there, when Satan Hall comes by and spots me, and— He socked me, too, Mary." I told her the rest of it best I could—of the killing, I mean.

"But they can't do anything to you, Kid—nothing."

"It's Satan, Mary. He hates me and I hate him. He'll frame me. I wish I had the guts to kill him."

She winced at that and talked to me for a long time. It was about right and wrong and didn't make much sense, but somehow, coming from Mary, I didn't mind it so much.

"It wouldn't do any good for me to lie for you, Kid—not if Frank Hall saw you there." She never could get to calling him Satan.

"But don't you see?" I pulled eagerly at her arm. "He couldn't go on the witness stand against me. He loves you. He couldn't make a liar out of you." And I got up from the chair and followed her to the window.

Then something come over me, or rather—come under me, for it got me inside. Not in the heart—like the books say, but in the stomach—like you were sinking. And I didn't think out no words; they just came up in my mouth and popped out.

"I couldn't make a liar out of you neither, Mary," I said. "I'd rather take the rap."

She didn't talk for a long time. Then she said:

"You go to bed, Kid." Her eyes half closed. "I don't think Frank Hall will—will do anything wrong. You're sure, Kid—certain sure that you weren't working with Billy Ludlow?

And I hung my head and looked at the queer figure in the rug.

"Yeah, Mary, I was just walking by." As I said, it was hard to lie to her.

She didn't move. She just sat there by the window, looking at her white hands. I waited for her to speak, and when she didn't I went down the narrow passage, found the door to the main hall, and stopped, listening.

Plunk! Plunk! The tread of feet on the floor above! The even tread of feet—the dreaded feet I knew so well! And then they stopped, and I waited for them to come again, and let the door slip softly closed. My room was directly above Mary's. Surely, I would hear those feet cross the floor above. Satan Hall could never walk so lightly that I wouldn't hear him. And I didn't hear him; try as I might, I couldn't even imagine a sound. I hadn't heard him at all; that was it.

And I heard the steps again, this time with relief. They were on the floor below. They were coming up the stairs. Just one of the tenants! You couldn't nohow spot them or confuse them with the steps of Satan Hall. I breathed easier and waited until they'd pass the landing, and then I'd slip right out and to my room.

The steps reached the landing, swung around it, and came directly to the door—the door I crouched so close to. Too late I remembered that I hadn't let the latch slip closed. My hand shot out and gripped at the knob, just as another hand gripped that same knob. Was it another dick, coming—coming for me?

Like a shadow, I snaked along the wall toward the little kitchen as the door swung open and a figure stood framed there. I didn't know him at first—didn't know him even when he closed the door with a click and turned the key on the inside.

"Kid! Kid!" Mary's voice came easy enough. Then, "Kid," again, this time with alarm—and finally with a little quiver, "Who's there?"

A man spoke.

"It ain't the Kid; it's me." And I knew that it was the voice of "Red" Donnelly—the mob leader—my mob leader.

"I seen your light and wondered what kept you up so late," I heard Donnelly say, as he entered the living room. "Maybe you were thinking about me, eh, Mary?" And his words were slightly thick.

Now what was I to do? For some months past, I had kept Red Donnelly from Mary. It hadn't been so hard. Several times, I'd run in on them and whispered to Donnelly that Satan Hall was on the street below—and twice, after Red had become suspicious, I'd even phoned Satan Hall and in a disguised voice told him it was a warning from a friend. He'd come, too—and Donnelly, watching from across the street, would know I hadn't lied.

First I was for slipping out the door and running to the phone in the hall below and ringing up Satan Hall. I even spun the key in the lock, when the thought struck me.

Would Donnelly be alone? Would he have left some one downstairs to warn him if any one came? Would he— And I ducked quickly into the kitchen, back through to the dining room. There was a fire escape there. The light shone beneath the curtain that divided the dining room from the living room as I crossed the floor and started to raise the window.

Red Donnelly had spoken very low, and Mary had answered him in a quivering, false voice which didn't register the confidence she tried to make it register.

"You can't make a go of it, sister," said Red Donnelly. "It's me or Satan. He's playing the friendship-for-your-father act and all the time he's a dick that your father wouldn't 'a' wiped his shoes on. But, of course, with me— It's you."

Mary sort of stifled a scream, and I looked between the curtains and into the living room. Red Donnelly had both his hands on her shoulders, and he was looking down at her. I could see those big blue eyes of hers. They were burning bright, as they were when she lay there on her back for so many days—like to die, with the fever.

I didn't want to do it. I told myself I was a fool to do it. I knew that Red Donnelly had only to raise his hand to wipe me out like a dirty mark. But I just had to do it. There was something stronger than myself that was driving me, even though I knew I wasn't big enough or strong enough, and if I was strong enough, there was a rod under the left arm of Red Donnelly—a rod that he wouldn't hesitate to use—never had hesitated to use. My hand raised to part the curtains. I stopped dead.

Every hair on my head went stiff, like you sent them up with a single snap of your fingers. Across the floor above— faintly out in the hall—on the stairs, coming down—lower and lower—nearer and nearer were those sinister, foreboding steps—the even tread of feet—the feet of Satan Hall.

Red Donnelly and Mary Rogers hadn't moved and hadn't spoken. But they didn't hear anything. And just as Donnelly's right hand swung around and pressed against the girl's back, the footsteps reached the door and stopped. A split second of silence. Then, like the pounding of a giant hammer, three knocks came upon the door.

Three breaths sucked in as one. That's why they didn't hear mine, I guess. But Mary's breath came out first, and there was a scream in it, a low cry of terror—of horror. And it was of me she thought. The single name "Kid" rang for a moment, before the hand of Red Donnelly clapped over her mouth.

Then the doorknob turned. Had I spun the key? The knob turned again. A heavy body pounded against the door. A moment of hesitation, the snap of wood—and the door burst open. The feet of Satan Hall were in the flat. I glued an eye to the crack in the curtains and saw him enter the living room.

Mean, hard, cruel, were those green eyes, and the twist to his mouth was more pronounced. Red Donnelly turned his head and tried to grin at Satan over his shoulder. But it was more a deathlike parting of the lips, such as you see on them faces when some copper makes you march by a stiff in the morgue. And what's more, Donnelly still kept his left hand across Mary's mouth, and the right one clutched at the sweater on her back.

Satan didn't speak. He just stretched out his right hand, gripped Donnelly by the shoulder and tore him from Mary with such force that a handful of wool was ripped from her sweater and stayed in Donnelly's fingers.

I wasn't scared no more. Here was the despised and feared Satan Hall. Here was Red Donnelly, who no one ever dared to cross. And now they were face to face in hatred and anger.

I wondered why Satan Hall stood so, with his hands empty, while the right hand of Red Donnelly stole slowly up his left side, the fingers almost beneath his jacket.

Satan went in for action. Oh, I had seen it many times—felt it many times. But, somehow, you never connected up such a thing with Red Donnelly. Satan lifted that right hand and smacked Donnelly across the left cheek. It didn't seem very hard, but I knew better. I saw Donnelly's body waver. Then the left hand came and rocked him back into place again.

Then Satan spoke.

"Don't let those itching fingers of yours pull out that gun unless—unless you're intending to use it," he said simply. "I don't like to go in for out and out murder."

And Red Donnelly knew that to draw a gun meant death.

A moment they faced each other. Mary was back by the wall, her face in her hands, her frightened blue eyes riveted on the two men from between her fingers. And Satan Hall did it. He just seemed to pick that fist of his up from some place below his knees. There was the flash of white knuckles and a dull crack of bone against bone. Red Donnelly crashed to the floor.

I don't know if Satan Hall lifted Red and carried him to the door and put him in the hall, or if he simply helped him there. For I had jumped back from the curtains as those green eyes glanced toward it. But I did hear Satan say, before he came back into the room:

"That's entirely personal, Red. I won't search you to pin a gun charge on you. But the next time you think of paying Mary Rogers a visit, remember the Silverman affair in Brooklyn, and remember that you know who killed Silverman, and that I know who killed Silverman—and that it's only a matter of time before twelve men, good and true, will know who killed Silverman. Think that one over, and—good night!"

Satan Hall was a peculiar man. He didn't comfort Mary

with fine words or flowery language. He didn't say he'd always protect her. Never a word of love passed his lips. He came back to the room, rubbing his huge hands with those long, quick fingers.

"You needn't be afraid of him any more," he said. And then, even before the words of thanks were out of the girl's lips, "Where's the Kid?"

"Isn't he in his room?" I guess Mary was startled out of her fright.

"No, he isn't. And you, Mary? Why are you fully dressed at this hour? Don't answer it if you don't want to. I know why. You never take your things off until you hear him go up the stairs to his room. Why do you stick to him?"

"He sat with me for nights and nights, Frank, when they didn't expect me to live. And I didn't have a job and I didn't have a penny. And, Frank, he took care of me and fed me and saw that I had broths and medicines and—"

"You've paid that back to him—any number of times. You've given him protection—protection from me." His face softened—that is, if his face could soften. Anyway, it was different. "Tonight I've got him for a good long rap."

"But you wouldn't, Frank; you couldn't. He was only passing. Maybe what he told you wasn't all true. Maybe he thought some one was inside and—and, boylike, he waited and watched."

"So he came squealing and squawking to you, because he—because—"

"Because why, Frank?" Her voice was very low.

Satan hesitated a moment, and then: "Because he knows I promised your father I'd take care of you. Your father's mind was warped, Mary. He wouldn't have fitted to-day.

I was with him at the hospital when he died. Your aunt had moved away with you. I didn't know what you went through. I never knew until I found you here. He—"

"He was shot, wasn't he?" Mary sort of turned her head.

"Yes." Satan nodded. "He was shot by a cop that didn't know any better—didn't know who it was in the dark. The Kid, now, Mary—why do you stick to him?"

"Because he's got it in him. He never had a chance. It's environment, Frank—nothing more. He's good and—"

"He's rotten all the way through," Satan said, and I gripped at the curtain. "I've given him break after break. If I sent him over now, it would be the best thing for him, and for you. He's graduated from the kindergarten of crime; he never knew an honest day. He's being sucked up by Red Donnelly's mob. It won't be long before he goes in for murder."

"No—no, he wouldn't do that. He promised me that," she broke in.

"Well, he's close to it. He lied to you to-night? He was the outside man for the job—trusted at sixteen. Then he squawked and whined to you to lie for him. I know—I—"

"No, he didn't, Frank. He said he'd rather take a rap than have me lie for him."

"Well, this time he takes it. I don't think anything will do him good, but it'll save him from burning—too soon. It'll save him from the Donnelly mob. He's no good. He never earned an honest penny—never—"

"He is good. He has earned an honest penny—many of them." She blazed in on him. "It's men like you that drive such boys down. He'd be ashamed now, if he knew I was telling you what I'm going to tell you. But it'll show you what he's had to live with—what he's been taught to think with. He knew how I felt about crime, and when I lay there sick and he had over a hundred dollars hidden upstairs, he went to work on the dock so that he could buy me things I needed, with money that would be clean to me—money that wouldn't make me ashamed afterward.

"He left here every morning at six thirty, when old Mrs. Wallis came in, worked all day and got what little sleep he could in that big chair there—for close to six weeks. And you say he's rotten! What has he been given to reason with? What chance has he had in life? He couldn't see any wrong in stealing money—money for me. But he knew I could. He thought it was silly, ridiculous, childish, probably, on my part. Yet he respected it because he respected me. Well, I'm going to stick to him. I'll stick to him even in this. Yes, I'll go on the stand and swear that he was here with me, no matter what people think." And she started in to cry, leaning her head against Satan's chest. I could have killed him then.

Twice Satan tried to put his arm about her, I think. Finally, he ran his hand through her hair and talked to her as if she were a very little child.

"I'll never speak to—never see you again," she sobbed, "if you send the Kid—the Kid up."

"All right! All right!" There was a funny crack in Satan's voice. "I'll give him a break. Mary; give him a break for you. There isn't any excuse for me to the department—unless I could use him for—"

"No! No!" She clutched at his shoulders now and shook him. "You wouldn't do that, Frank. You couldn't do that.

That would be worse—far worse. You'd never have the heart to make a stool pigeon out of the Kid."

"It's part of the system. Warn him to lay off the Donnelly outfit. Let me see some of the good ooze out of him. I've seen enough of his rottenness. He'll do you a rotten deal at the end. All right, I'll give him this one break. Warn him."

He turned on his heels. The feet were measured and the tread heavy again. But he was hardly out the door and on the stairs before I followed him to the hall, watched his figure pass down the last flight, heard the hall door, below, close, then I sneaked off to bed.

What would the mob think if they ever knew? Knew that I, Kid Blaney, had worked on the dock—worked to get money for a sick twist who was thinking backward. And—but I raised my head as I found my door. I'd do it again for her—any time.

For a long time I lay there, thinking—just one thought. I wished I had the guts to kill Satan Hall. Rotten, was I? Maybe I was, but it was Satan and the rest of his kind that kept me so. I never had no desire to work until just once. That was the job on the dock. I got to like it and the boss sort of got to like me. He saw how little and not so strong, I was, and was going to take me into the office. It was one of Satan's breed who found me on the dock and told the boss. You can't sort of blame the boss. He was white. He paid me for a full week, though it was only Thursday.

I'm not knocking the law. But it ain't for me—ain't for my kind.

I think Satan watched me a lot after that. I was mighty careful. But Red Donnelly seen how the land lay and took care of me, so I didn't have to worry. I was mighty scared, too. I know what it means to have a cop with something on you what he don't use. It drags and it drags, until the time comes when he wants to use you—make you a stoolie for him. And if you don't come across with the goods, he reaches out and rides you on the old charge.

"I don't think he's going to ride you, Kid," Red Donnelly said one night. "I figure it's that twist, Mary, who's taking such a fancy to you. She's got Satan nice and neat, but she's a queer one and we can't work through her." He stroked his chin. "Satan's closing in on me; Satan's got to get the works. Satan—" And suddenly, "It ain't myself I'm thinking of, Kid. It's Billy Ludlow; shot down like that without a chance."

Of course, the whole thing was Red Donnelly's idea. I didn't have any say in it one way or the other. He'd have killed me if I'd wanted to get out of it. And it was just between him and me. Not another one of the mob were onto it. He always spoke of it as if it was Billy Ludlow that made him plan to "give it to" Satan Hall. But I knew different. It was the Silverman affair.

Anyway, that very night I went to work in earnest to trap Satan to his death. As Red Donnelly laid it out I couldn't see no flaw in it. The thing was to sell Satan the idea that I was going straight.

It was the mission in the Bowery where I started. I even got the want ads too, and had Mary write letters for me—my writing being sort of hard to read and harder still to get down what I meant. Then I took up night school, which was funny at first, but after a bit passed the time more agreeably.

But the big thing was that I shook the Donnelly outfit.

Of course, they wouldn't have stood for that without beating me up or even knocking me off, but for the strict orders they must have had from Red. Red was deeper than I thought. I give him credit for being a schemer and a plotter. It wouldn't be long now before that sneering, twisting mouth of Satan would close forever.

Of course, Mary was pleased; and of course, as we hoped and planned, she told Satan Hall; and, of course, Satan wouldn't believe it until he had checked up on me. He still twisted his lips when he passed me, and once told me that the iron gates up at the big house were waiting for my first bust.

The day finally came. I wasn't nervous like I thought I'd be—just steady and easy—as right in front of the eyes of Satan Hall, Red Donnelly stepped out of the doorway and grabbed me by the arm. We talked so for a moment, then, with a shrug of my shoulders, I followed him into the tenement.

Twenty minutes later, I came out. Satan Hall was not in sight. But I didn't look very careful. In a determined stride, I shot right down the avenue. I didn't have to look behind me. Instinct or something tells me, I guess. I knew that some one was getting my smoke, and I felt that that some one was Satan. I've had tails put on me too often not to know.

Straight to Satan Hall's flat I went, rang the bell downstairs, and, getting no answer, turned after a bit—to see Satan standing behind me.

"I want to see you, Satan," I told him. And seeing the puzzled look on his face, I added my often rehearsed line. "I ain't doing it for you, Satan. I'm doing it for Red Donnelly.

He gave me a chance when I wanted to go straight. There ain't many big timers what'd do that."

"No," Satan said, "there aren't." And he took me upstairs to his room.

I didn't wait. I busted into the story.

"Donnelly's gone soft. It's the Silverman job... You've got 'Ollie, the Swede' locked up. Donnelly thinks he's going to talk. Donnelly didn't do the job himself. He'd—he'd like to talk first."

Donnelly knew that Ollie wouldn't talk, and that Ollie had the shrewdest mouthpiece in the city. He also knew that Ollie would be brought up on one of these habe-as-corpus writs in a week and be freed, and also that Satan knew that Ollie wasn't going to talk.

"Red Donnelly wants to turn State's evidence. That's it, eh?" Satan stroked at his chin.

"I don't know. Red asked me to tell you he wanted to talk to you. He says it's about the Silverman case. He says his conversation will interest you. I'm not asking any promise from you. He'll get that from you himself before he speaks out. He wants me to set the time with you. He wants it so only you and him and me will know."

Satan Hall did some thinking. He thought like we hoped he'd think. He'd reason that Donnelly wanted to get in his say before Ollie. And since Satan knew that Ollie had shut up tighter than a drum, it was up to Satan to listen to Donnelly.

"Very well," Satan said finally, "I'll meet him. And tell him I'm nearer to that Silverman solution than he thinks. This'll be his last chance to talk. Where does he want me to meet him?"

"Up Riverdale way," I told him. "I don't know just the place. He'll drive the car and you can keep an eye on him, and frisk him, too."

"I'll frisk him all right." Satan Hall nodded. And after I told him that Donnelly would meet him at ten minutes of one at a certain uptown subway station, he stretched out his hand and took mine.

"I never would have believed it, Kid. I've been watching you for weeks. Thanks for this break." Those green eyes searched me.

"Don't thank me, Satan," I told him. "I wouldn't 'a' done it for you. I wouldn't have turned stoolie for you. I'm doing it for Red Donnelly. He let me go when I wanted to go."

"Yes—yes. And he had this in mind," said Satan. "You can be sure of that. I always thought he was yellow. You're a straight shooter, now, Kid. Give me your hand and your word that there's nothing tricky in Red's proposition."

And I give him my hand and my word. That don't mean nothing with a dick—not a thing.

I spent a good part of the early evening with Red Donnelly.

"It's great, Kid," he told me. "Great! If this pulls off O.K. there'll be a grand for you." And after a moment's hesitation, "A grand, after the first big job we work? It's too bad you're so small, Kid. I'd make you a big guy, even now."

"If I wasn't so small, you couldn't pull this job to-night." And then, the thing popping into my mouth before I thought it out: "I think I'm going straight after this job. It's easy and restful."

But Red Donnelly was talking.

"I've never seen Satan draw a gun—never. You have, Kid. Is he quick? Fast—faster than me?"

"I seen him down by the river the night he shot 'Big Boy' Fitz," I told him.

"Fitz had him covered, but Satan went for his rod just the same. Fitz winged him twice in the left arm and the right shoulder. He wasn't shooting so good. After that, Red, it was curtains. Fitz went out funny, with his mouth hanging open, and—"

"All right—all right," Red Donnelly said irritably. "Enough of that. Fitz was a fool. It won't be that way with me. He'll never know, never suspect."

"Satan had no rod in his hand when he walked into Isaac's neither. His hands were hanging by his sides. I saw them—both of them. Yet—yet—Billy Ludlow never came out."

"Killed him like that? One shot, eh, killed him?" Red was sort of thoughtful.

"They buried him, anyway." I shrugged my shoulders. It was funny to see the yellow oozing out of Red Donnelly's spine.

"It won't matter, Kid, won't matter," he said again. "He'll frisk me—know I'm not armed. Know there isn't any place to get a gat. He'll turn his head sure—for a second even. I'm lightning quick. I'll just shove the gun close to the back of his head, so he won't have a chance. He won't have a chance."

That was the tough Red Donnelly talking. Well, it wasn't my party. All I wanted was to see Satan knocked off his spot. It was awful, knowing he'd always hold that Isaac job over my head.

Three times Red Donnelly broke open his gun and made sure it was fully loaded before he let me stow it away inside my shirt. And three times more he pulled me back out of the hall to tell me to be sure and follow every instruction. And hadn't we gone through it a hundred times up at the shack already? But when we left, he half read my mind, and eased it considerable.

"And don't bother about how Mary'll take it," he said. "I've got something on Satan she don't know—something that would make her tear her heart out before she'd talk to him again. Now listen."

He leaned down and told it to me. I couldn't hardly believe it even after I knew it was true.

"You can tell her that—after I give Satan the works," he said as I left him.

I grinned as I saw Donnelly's murder car by the door, and skipping out the rear hopped a fence to the street behind. I didn't want to be frisked with a .38 aboard me. My heart was singing, too. It was great news. It would knock Satan out of Mary's life like—like—well—nothing at all.

I didn't wait. It was only nine o'clock. Donnelly and Satan wouldn't reach the shack until one thirty. I went straight to Mary and told her the thing—the terrible thing about Satan Hall.

When I left her, things weren't so good. Her words were ringing in my head. But I set my teeth and bit my lip. To-morrow Satan Hall would be dead.

I spent a few minutes looking in the window of "Nosey" Davis' shop. Then I went inside and made a small purchase and listened to Nosey's suggestion of where a lad with a little ambition could pick up some nice stones: rocks what

Nosey would be willing to handle to every one's advantage, including his own. Nosey was a tough old fence. But somehow things didn't interest me any more. I was thinking about that first job on the dock, and how Satan and his kind—

NO ONE TOOK any notice of me when I left the subway at the end of the line and plodded back through the woods to Riverdale Avenue. I found the old shack and splashed my pocket flash about the single room.

Donnelly had done a good job in puttying the cracks and stretching the tar paper over the single window. He should have stuck at the trade he was brought up to—a carpenter. But it wasn't that which showed how good he was. It was the packing box—the three foot high box that didn't look wide enough to get a telescope into. The lid on it moved easily up and down. The slick work Donnelly did was making it look as if that lid was nailed down with huge nails—nails that actually only went through the cover, and were nipped off at the end. But if the nails alone didn't convince you that the box was nailed closed, an attempt to open the lid would. Leastwise, it would when I was inside. For there was a hook that I could fasten the lid down with from the inside—and also open the lid with. Open it and slip a .38 caliber revolver into the right hand of Red Donnelly.

There wasn't a picture, a table, a piece of furniture, nor even a bit of paper or shavings to hide a thing under, to make Satan suspicious—only that box. And I don't think, from looking at it, any one would believe a ten-year-old child could hide in it. And they'd probably be right. No, I ain't as small as a ten-year-old child, but I can do more things with my arms and legs and that body of mine than Toto, the clown. That's why the mob had used me to slip through places you'd hardly expect a cat to get into.

So a couple of hours I sat there on the floor, with the gun before me. Sometimes my pocket flash was out—sometimes it was lit—for mostly I didn't like the dark then. A half dozen times, I sprung the cylinder of that gun; a half dozen times I held the lead bullets balanced in my hand.

It was a big thing for a kid like me to face. If I didn't go through with it, Red Donnelly would do me in sure. And Satan—he was only waiting for a chance to lay that hand upon my shoulder. With Satan dead—with Satan dead— And I clenched my hands.

I couldn't nohow make myself comfortable there. When the flash was lit, great shadows appeared on the walls of the shack—shadows with long arms, twitching fingers, and features that came all to points. And when I sat in the dark, the face of Mary just seemed to set itself smack in the corner and look at me. Not in anger, you understand— not even reproachful—just sort of soft and understanding. Like she said, "You know, Kid, and I know. Whatever you do will be right."

I nodded and half said to myself the thought that held everything else down in my head. "If I don't go through with it, Red Donnelly will kill me."

I twisted the barrel of the gun again, came to my feet, spotted the time as ten minutes to one, and decided to go through with it.

So I started to pack myself into that box. It wasn't easy, alone. I had to double up my feet and keep my hands in the air. But I did it again as I had done it before: twisted

my hand with the gat in it sort of around my neck, leaving
the rod just where the lid would open. After that, I spent
the best part of ten minutes turning my head so that my
left eye would be in line with the knot hole. And my eye
would stay there; I couldn't now twist it away again. All set!
I pushed the hook into its eye with my thumb and waited.

Yes, and waited!

I didn't really hear the car pull up when it did come.
Distinctly, though, I heard the slam of the shack door and
the deadly tread of Satan Hall's feet as they followed the
soft, creaking ones of Red Donnelly across the room.

They passed close to the box, and I saw only legs and the
huge hands with the itching, snakelike fingers as Donnelly
hung the lantern on the ceiling hook.

"Well, it's private enough and lonely enough." I guess
that Satan Hall shrugged his shoulders when he spoke. I
could see his feet planted firmly on the floor but his body
was turning, and those green eyes were taking in the room.
Then he walked to the box and leaned upon it. His hands
played about the lid. But the hook held the lid and I held
my breath, and the perspiration that had been hanging on
my forehead suddenly poured down my face and got into
my eyes.

I wondered what sort of a line Red Donnelly would feed
Satan to take his mind off things. As far as the Silverman
affair went, it was generally understood that it was Red
Donnelly who shot him—shot him three times in the back.

But Donnelly talked sort of low and nervous, which I
guess would seem natural enough. Once, though, he raised
his voice and whined.

"Lord!" he said. "I can't talk if you watch me like that. I

can't talk with that hand of yours itching around your rod. You frisked me, didn't ya? You locked the door, didn't ya? You're the strongest man and the handiest with his mitts in the whole department, or out of it for that matter. You ain't afraid I'll jump ya. You ain't afraid of me physically!"

"Neither physically, mentally nor morally," said Satan Hall. "Come on, spill your story. I'm a good listener if you're a good talker."

And Donnelly talked low—talked and came close to the box. I saw the fingers of his left hand feeling along the tiny knot hole. I felt his body jar as he leaned against the box. Then, under his arm, I saw Satan Hall nearly across the room. Satan's head turned, and Donnelly's finger slipped through the tiny hole. I shoved up that lid and let the gun go out.

For a moment, my hand touched Red's. His was cold and damp, like you'd picked up a paper of fish and the paper had split. Yep, Red Donnelly was going to put a bullet smack into the back of the head of Satan Hall. Satan wouldn't have a chance. Donnelly had said that. What a dirty skunk Donnelly was! I knew it then—knew it for sure, as the gun left my hand.

Red Donnelly's body lurched forward. Satan heard him and turned with a curse. Then the moving body of Donnelly blocked my view. But I heard the deafening roar of a heavy .38. Another roar and a third one followed so quickly that the last two shots seemed as one. There was the crash of a body—of a body that must have fallen to the floor.

Things were a bit dazed after that. There was the smell of burned powder in my nose, the curl of smoke through the tiny knot hole, a choking, sickening sensation as I tried to suck in my breath, and I coughed.

I heard the feet, felt the box lurch, breathed deeply of the air. A hand gripped my shoulder, tore me from the box as if I were a doll, and set me on the floor. I looked smack at the green eyes, the twisted lips, and the powder-marked chin of Satan Hall. If he ever looked like the devil at all, this was the time. I didn't speak. I couldn't. I saw the body of Red Donnelly stretched on the floor.

"You yellow rat," said Satan Hall, and brought up that right hand and crashed it against my chin. At least, he must have done that. I ain't rightly sure. I only know that my body was falling away, my knees sagging when the thing struck. No pain—no nothing! Just a dead blackness—a gripping, sinking blackness!

Some one was calling me from a long ways off, and something was shaking me by the shoulders. I opened my eyes and looked into the green glims of Satan Hall. But they didn't seem sinister now, and his lips were parted, and his smile was sort of—well—it didn't seem right, and I closed my eyes for I thought I must be dreaming. But when I opened them again, it was there—and, yes, the smile was friendly, kindly. It was even gentle. And he was talking.

"Mary was right and I was wrong, Kid. You're white after all. I'm sorry I pasted you," And he shook me some more. "Don't you see, Kid, I'm your friend now. I know the truth. I broke open Red's gun and found that it was loaded with blank cartridges."

"I didn't do it for you," I told him. "I did it for Mary. I wouldn't 'a' done it for a dirty dick." I gulped the final words.

"Well, this dirty dick will do something for you, Kid. He'll get that job back for you on the dock—the one you liked. So you did it for Mary? And what did I have to do with Mary?"

"She loves you," I told him. "She told me so to-night."

"Yes." His eyes lit up, then the light went out of them again, like you'd thrown a bucket of water on burning coals. "Well, I won't see her again, Kid. There won't be any need now. Red Donnelly won't bother her any more. He said something to-night that will give him the chair."

"He ain't dead then. I ain't a murderer." And my head seemed much better.

"No, Kid, he isn't. I figured he belonged to the State, not me. You can tell Mary the truth. She'd better know now. I'm the—the cop that killed her father."

"She knows," I told him. "Red Donnelly found it out, and I told her tonight. But she always knew."

"What did she say?"

"She said— That's when she said she loved you. That's when I slipped into Nosey's and got myself the blanks, though I wasn't sure if I'd use them then. No, I wasn't sure until later, Frank." And somehow the name "Frank" came natural enough, and—and he was a square guy. It seemed then like I'd always known he was a square guy, and I liked him. And my words blurted right out without no thought that I knew of—behind them.

I said:

"It wasn't just only Mary, Frank. I wanted to give you a break, too."

SATAN'S LASH

He Slapped Down the Man
Who Terrorized the Law

1

THROUGH THE FOG

THE FOG WAS being slowly lifted by a sharp, fresh breeze from the west, which found its way even into that side street of the lower city. The dulled electric street lights seemed to flicker like ancient gas lamps as the wind swept the dampness about—occasionally piercing its dismal haze.

A man in civilian clothes, his overcoat collar turned up and buttoned tightly about his neck, his dark-gray slouch hat pulled down on his forehead, but his head erect to breathe deeply of the fresh breeze, turned from the avenue onto the side street. He very nearly collided with a uniformed police officer who was slowly pounding his beat.

The officer stepped aside, looked up quickly; then, turning, followed the man the few steps to the street light. Beneath the dimness of the light the officer spotted the broad shoulders, the great length of arm, and the knotted ruggedness of a huge hand with its strong, muscular fingers. He stretched out his nightstick gingerly, carefully, almost deferentially, and touched the figure lightly on the shoulder. The man swung quickly around, almost directly beneath the light. Sinister, hard, green eyes rested upon the mild, blue, Irish ones of the patrolman.

The patrolman wet his lips, tried twice to speak and

failed as he stared at the
man before him. He knew
him, of course. Every one
knew "Satan" Hall, the
hardest, crudest, and most
sinister detective on the
city's force. The officer
looked at his features again,
studied them almost as if
for the first time, though he
knew them well: that peculiar head with its features all
seeming to come to points,
starting at the chin and
making one great capital letter V, ending in the brim of
his gray slouch hat. And though he couldn't see it, the officer knew that the jet-black hair began in a single thin line
down by his forehead, widening as the hair thickened, to
make that same V again.

Even the ears, just visible below the hat, were tapering at the ends; and the curve of the lips, in tune with his
slanting eyebrows, gave a satanic expression to the entire
face. The patrolman didn't look at the man's feet. He didn't
need to. He knew that the toes of the shoes would be long
and pointed at the ends, and he wondered how Satan Hall
came to walk so heavily and so steadily in that deadly tread
which the criminals feared.

But it was Satan Hall who spoke first.

"Well, Horgan," he said, "what's on your chest?"

Patrolman Horgan rubbed his chin before he spoke.
Then he said:

"You're going—you're going to pass Chicorro's place." There was a moment of hesitation under his scrutiny; then, almost in an effort to vindicate the words he had just spoken, he added: "You've got to pass Chicorro's if you go that way. You've just got to."

"Yes?" Satan Hall waited.

"Yes." This time Patrolman Horgan spoke with emphasis and determination. "You're new in this district, Frank Hall. Chicorro's all right—a regular guy. Besides which"— Satan Hall still regarded him fixedly, coldly—"Al Handley is in Chicorro's. Hall, a cop hears things, though this is gospel on the avenue. You've snooped into Handley's affairs. He's going to shoot you on sight. Don't sneer like that. It isn't all bluff. Maybe he feels you've got the office to stay out of Chicorro's. You're new here. Handley has got—"

When the patrolman hesitated for the right word, Satan Hall cut in:

"Got protection. That's the word, isn't it? He's to be let alone."

"He's a regular. He's close to Chicorro, and Chicorro's the Old Man's friend. The Old Man won't like it. Of course, Al Handley won't expect you around here to-night. It's just his way of showing the boys how big a guy he is. But he shot off his trap, madlike, when he'd found you'd searched his rooms. He says you'll know where to find him if you want him. At Chicorro's. And you'd better come armed. He's just making good to the boys. He'd have to make good if you came."

"You mean—murder?" Satan Hall said quietly.

"Call it what you like; the name won't help you none."

"There's the chair; the hot seat up at the big house." Satan Hall smiled—at least, his lips curved up a bit more at the corners. Most people thought it was meant for a smile, though his eyes never changed. Just hard and green—and cold!

"Roasting one guy won't stop another guy from murder," said Patrolman Dorgan. "A lad don't fear burning until he's in the death house. But I've tipped you off. Al Handley is not a fool. He wouldn't underrate you. He might hide out down the block, and your passing Chicorro's be misunderstood. He's got to make good if you force him. You understand?"

"Yeah, I understand." Satan Hall stuck the end of a match between his teeth, chewed it a moment, then flicked it into the gutter. "You mean it's Al Handley or me. One of us has to eat dirt."

"Well, now—I wouldn't call it that." The soft, persuasive Irish voice that was famous for patching up neighborhood quarrels came into play. But as those green, sinister eyes stared steadily at his blinking blue ones, Dorgan groped aimlessly for words. "I don't know—something like that, maybe; though I wouldn't rightly call it 'eating dirt.'"

"I never ate dirt," said Satan Hall slowly. "I wouldn't know the taste of it. It would make me sick. But Handley—" He stopped suddenly. "You don't like me, do you, Dorgan?" When no answer was immediately forthcoming, he continued! "Be a man this once, and not a ward-heeling cop."

The Irish blue eyes of Patrolman Dorgan flashed for a moment and gave back stare for stare.

"No," he said, "I don't like you. That's flat."

Satan Hall nodded. His lips parted again; white, strong teeth showed.

"Then why did you tell me this?"

"Because," said Dorgan honestly, "after all, you're just a cop like me."

"I see. Not a case of dog eat dog, eh?"

"Well," said Dorgan, as if he studied the thing out for the first time, "I guess it's because you're part of the police. It would be like crossing one of the system."

"Yet," said Satan, "the system crosses its own every day. Crosses millions—crosses the people—the people who pay its salaries." As Dorgan straightened and anger shot into his eyes, Satan said: "Oh, that's not personal. It's the system as a whole I'm thinking of. I don't want to be part of it. I don't want— Good night, Dorgan!" Satan Hall turned suddenly and continued in the direction he had been going when he turned the corner.

Patrolman Dorgan had him by the shoulder.

"You'll—you'll be passing Chicorro's after what I just told you?"

"Don't worry," said Satan Hall slowly. Then, over his shoulder as his heavy tread beat upon the still, wet pavement, he added: "I won't be passing Chicorro's. Believe that, absolutely, Dorgan. I won't be passing Chicorro's to-night."

2

THE MAN WITHOUT FEAR

SATAN HALL TOOK the business of man hunting very seriously indeed. If he wasn't the best detective on the city's force, he was the most feared by the criminal classes, and the most persistent in his work. It was accepted almost as a great universal truth, both in the police department and the underworld itself, that Satan Hall did not know what the word "fear" meant. But perhaps that was not strictly the truth; for a certainty, he appreciated fear in others if he did not recognize the word as connected with himself.

To him fear was a habit, something born of lack of understanding—an uncertainty of life that, cultivated, became part of the individual. He couldn't understand that; at least, in a way acceptable to himself. The most timid man, forced to ride often in airplanes, ceases to fear them, accepting as part of his daily routine that which previously had been an overwhelming fear in his days—a nightmare of horrid dreams in his nights.

But it was not just the knowledge of Satan Hall's lack of fear that made his name a dread thing in the underworld of a great city. Many servants of the law stuck as doggedly to their jobs and faced the dangers of flying lead with the same courage as Satan Hall. It was the eerie air, the steady tread of Satan Hall's feet, but most of all, the uncertainty of the man himself.

He was reputed to be lightning quick with a gun. Reputed, only, for few men were alive to tell of that single motion of his right or left hand, the flash of a pistol, and the spurt of flame. Those who had seen that single movement and heard, perhaps, the roar of that deadly gun, could not—at least in this world—tell of it.

Satan Hall knew that Al Handley was a racketeer, a gunman, a killer. He knew that more than one murder could be laid directly to Al Handley, as did a dozen or more officers on the police force. But they knew also that knowledge, even certainty, is not evidence in a court of law. So Al Handley went his way, more admired, more feared, and if the term can be used—more respected by the denizens of the night.

Now, hands sunk deeply in the pockets of his great coat, Satan plodded heavily down the street in the direction of Chicorro's so-called night club. It was fairly early. No tin-pan notes of a piano came up to him as he reached the dreary old house with its tightly drawn curtains, its massive doors, its bleak silence. Slowly, but without stopping, Satan turned, descended the three steps to the basement, passed beneath the little shedlike protection, and tapped upon the door—once, twice, in quick succession. A moment's pause, while he counted ten, then four quick knocks, followed by three slow ones.

A bolt shot heavily back; the door opened slightly, and Satan Hall pushed his way in, forcing the door wider to admit his big body.

"Oh," said a hawk-faced individual. "I was expecting some one else."

"Pleasant surprise, eh?" The corners of Satan Hall's lips curved quickly, to straighten again almost at once. "Here, hold my coat. I won't be long." He swung his coat off quickly, knocked the man's arm away from a white push button on the wall, and tossed the coat over his arm. "I wouldn't do that," he said gently. "I haven't any particular reason not to like you, Romano; don't give me any."

"But," the sharp-featured little Italian stammered, "hadn't I— Let me tell Chicorro you're here. He's—he's in his office upstairs."

"No!" Satan took the man by the arm and led him down the hall toward the bar in the rear. "Don't tell Chicorro. There's no need for him to be disturbed. I'm welcome, of course?"

"Of course." Romano got the words out with difficulty, and as they approached the swing doors which led to the bar, he dragged Satan to a stop. "Better see Chicorro up in his office." A moment's hesitation, and then, very low and in a faltering voice, he added: "He's in there, in the bar."

"Chicorro? I thought you said he was—"

"Not Chicorro." Romano held the arm tightly. "Him— Al Handley. Satan, you're—"

"My name is Hall—Frank Hall." One of Satan's huge hands tightened on the little man's arm until his face blanched.

"Don't do it, Satan." Romano spoke huskily despite the pain of those viselike fingers. "I'm telling you friendly. Handley is bad—a bad man to-night. At the best—"

"At the best?" encouraged Satan, loosening his grip.

"Well, Chicorro won't like it. The Old Man won't like it. Al won't— You're new, Sa—Hall—new down here."

"I'll soon get acquainted." Satan Hall pushed the little man from him and stretched a hand toward the swing doors.

"Handley is bad!" Romano said again.

"Yeah, I heard that." Satan nodded. "That's why I'm here. I want to find out just how bad he really is."

Romano eyed him sharply now, grasped at his coat and spoke quickly, desperately, but also warningly. He knew Al Handley, and had heard much of Satan. It was his duty to protect the house. Nothing ever happened in Chicorro's, because Chicorro permitted nothing to happen there. Chicorro was "right." Any one who knew the Old Man realized that. The Old Man himself wasn't above smoking a cigar in the privacy of Chicorro's office.

"Listen, Hall." Romano spoke rapidly, letting the words slip out through hardly parted lips. "There's bad blood between you and Handley. Every one knows that. Handley said he'd be here to-night. You've got nothing on him. That ain't law and order. That's personal, your coming here. You're taking a chance. A dozen men could easily be convinced that you came looking for trouble—trouble which you'll get if you go through those doors. Handley ain't no common gunman." Satan Hall still looked at him. "Handley can draw, aim and fire in just one second. What do you say to that?"

"That if that's the best Mr. Al Handley can do, he'll be just one half second too late."

Satan Hall stepped forward, rested a huge hand on one

of the doors, flung it quickly open, and stepped into the room.

The hour was early—early at least for the night life of a big city; especially the big city as Chicorro's knew it. A half dozen men, perhaps, were in that room. Three stood at the bar, two sat at a small table, and a single individual in the corner was going over the racing sheet of an evening paper.

The bartender, Louie, saw the detective enter first. His right hand raised, paused in mid-air, and stayed there, the bar rag clutched tightly in his knotted fist. Then he turned blue, fishlike eyes to stare at the middle man of the three who stood by the bar. He didn't speak at first. He couldn't. As Satan entered the room and his heavy feet pounded slowly upon the hard wood, the bartender found his voice.

"Satan—Satan Hall!" he said, and found immediate employment beneath the bar.

3

AL HANDLEY, RACKETEER

THE THREE MEN before the bar turned as one. The man farthest from the swing doors and nearest the end of the bar moved first. Two or three quick, sliding steps and he was around the end of the bar and hidden from possible gunfire by the bar itself and the protecting ledge of shelves behind it.

The weak-faced man nearest Satan Hall, with the blinking, dull, frightened eyes, let his mouth hang open and his cigarette slip to the floor before his muscles responded to the frantic, confused orders from his brain. Then he half turned, backed quickly across the room, and stumbled over the outstretched feet of one of the men at the table; he recovered his balance and continued his backward movement until he was flat against the farthest wall.

There was a smothered curse as the two men at the table raised their eyes, jerked at once to their feet, and stood gripping their chairs—held so by the impending drama. Though Satan Hall's eyes looked straight ahead, each man in that room felt that those sinister green eyes could see his every movement, perhaps read his every thought. At least, after the first shock of surprise, all hands were conspicuously prominent—and empty.

Not one of those men had ever seen Satan Hall's gun, but they knew that he had one. Silent friends, with sightless eyes and stilled mouths, had all too often bore witness to that fact.

Satan Hall walked slowly down the length of that room to the single man who stood by the bar—facing him. There was no sound but the beat of those heavy feet—a slow, methodical beat that the criminal knew so well. "Killer of men," one enterprising newspaper columnist had called him. All the time his arms hung at his sides, his huge hands with the hard, muscular but supple fingers reaching almost to his knees.

Al Handley, gangster, gunman, hijacker—and now one of the biggest lights in the city's latest menace, the racketeer—had faced death many times. But, mostly, it was the other man's death he faced. His face was hard and coarse, his lips thick, and his eyes thin slits that were more a cultivated habit than a natural make-up of his features. His nose, too, was not the original gift of nature. It was flat and broad, as if in youth a horse had playfully kicked it, so that his slitlike eyes between narrow eyelids did not fit in with its encroachment upon the rest of his face.

There was no fear in his eyes as he faced Satan Hall— more a surprise, a doubt, the uncertainty that all criminals felt in the sinister presence of Satan Hall. But his ratlike eyes lowered quickly from Satan's green ones, rested for a split second only upon the huge hands which were free of weapons, then returned again to the face of Satan Hall.

As a rule, Al Handley was a man of action, not a man of thought. But he thought now; quickly moving, kaleidoscopic, mental ideas that were hard to put a finger on. He had spoken out his mind when he threatened to "get" Satan Hall and hinted for, if not actually dared, Satan to come to Chicorro's if he wanted him. Yes, he had meant it when he said it, of course. He couldn't deny that to himself even now. But Chicorro had heard him. Chicorro had smoked a cigar with the Old Man only this same afternoon—and they wouldn't want trouble—at least, trouble at Chicorro's. And Chicorro had smiled and patted him on the back and told him, Al Handley, it would look good to the boys when Satan didn't show up.

Now, he wasn't afraid. No, not him! Not Al Handley! He only had to narrow his eyes a bit more, tap his hip pocket suggestively, though he carried his gun beneath his left arm pit, to bring one of his unruly boys back in line or stop at once the activities of some rival racketeer who was muscling in on his territory. He wasn't afraid. He was perplexed, that was all. But Satan Hall's hands were empty, well down by his sides. Al Handley jerked down his vest, straightened the flower in his lapel, then picked gently at the corner of the purple handkerchief which protruded from the breast pocket of his one-hundred-and-fifty-dollar gray suit with the white stripes in it.

He smiled now as Satan Hall drew nearer. The breast pocket was close against his left armpit. His right hand, which caressed the handkerchief, was very close to the butt of a heavy-caliber automatic. Just a second to reach, draw and fire! After that it would be up to Chicorro to fix it with the Old Man. Self-defense, and that sort of thing! For there was no reason, no legal reason, why Satan Hall should be interested in him, Al Handley. The only man who could have talked was that dirty little rat—the slimy, yellow stool pigeon who had been picked up in the lake that very evening. No, Bertie wouldn't talk now, and—Al Handley's hand crept a little closer to that gun—neither would Satan Hall talk if— Handley half turned his head and spoke, just as if the bartender was still standing behind the bar, facing him.

"Chicorro's ain't what it used to be, Louie." He tried to make his voice indifferent, but despite his effort, a tremor crept into it. "Most any sort of a guy comes here now. But maybe I'm wrong, and it's just the need of ventilation."

"Hello, Handley." Satan Hall stood directly before Al Handley. The gunman had to turn square around and face him. There was no smile on those thick lips of Al Handley now; no flicker of amusement through those thin slits that hid the color of his eyes; no light banter to his voice when he spoke, either. He knew that every word he said would be repeated; every action he took would be vividly pantomimed by those who watched. But for the life of him, he couldn't get the scathing words out—the words which would make Satan Hall slink from Chicorro's; the words that would dog Satan's days—haunt Satan's nights. He finally simply said:

"What do you want, Hall?"

Al Handley would have given a pile of jack to recall the name "Hall." He meant to say "Satan," but it just didn't come. He knew the detective hated the name on the tongues of others—on the tongues of his enemies, at least. And Al Handley was surprised to find that his lips were dry and the temptation to moisten them with his tongue was irresistible. It was something he despised in others— something that he always waited for and watched for—and recognized as fear. And now, was Satan Hall watching for that very thing with him? Well, he'd bite his tongue off before he wet his lips, but they were so dry and it was so hard to find words. Fear! No, it wasn't that. Al Handley and fear! The thing was silly. It was unexpected; that was all. Satan Hall to defy the powers that be and come, like— But Satan Hall was talking.

"Why, you invited me to come. Come—and come armed. That was it, wasn't it, Handley? Come and come armed! Well, I'm here." Leaning forward, but never moving his hands from his sides, he said: "Now, Handley, are you going to eat dirt—eat dirt, here, right in front of your friends, or are you going to make good?"

This time Al Handley's tongue did come out and lick his parched lips. But, strangely, he didn't speak. His shifty, narrow lids blinked, and he took in the questioning, startled—yes, maybe even expectant faces of his friends in the corner of the room. And their presence gave him courage, or if not courage, a sort of desperation born of hurt pride, and maybe even a touch of fear. After all, there was something vulturelike in the watching, eager eyes of his friends. If he didn't make good now—

If Satan only had a gun in his hand! If he'd only make a threatening gesture toward one! Did he stand like that, with his hands by his side, because he knew that Al Handley would not dare shoot down a man who was not using his own gun? No, it couldn't be that. Satan Hall would not be such a fool as that. There were five witnesses who would swear that Satan shot first. It would be a simple matter to take Satan's gun and fire a shot from it after he was dead— dead, there upon the floor.

Satan must know that, and yet—yet how could he stand there so, with his hands at his sides—empty, and facing Al Handley, the most dangerous man along the avenue? The man who even Chicorro feared was trying to take his place! But then, Joe Raymond had been a good shot—and Jerry Gandie—and there was "Paul, the Wop." None better than Paul, the Wop! And Al Handley wondered if Satan had stood like that, with his hands at his sides—empty—before those three had died—died with a tiny hole almost smack in the center of each one's forehead. Yes, exactly in the center of their foreheads, Al Handley thought now. Just as if Satan had taken an instrument and measured it out before he fired! Al Handley tried to pull himself together. Satan was talking again.

"Just as I thought," Satan said slowly. "All mouth and no courage. You yellow bum! You're only good to shoot a real man in the back from behind a garbage can in a dark alley. A bad guy! A racketeer! The feared gunman of the avenue! So it took me, Frank Hall, to walk in and show you up to your friends for what you really are. Just a four-flusher. Just a small-time crook, posing as a big-time racketeer. Why, you're just one big bust."

Satan's head shot forward, and his green eyes glared in hatred—a hatred of such intensity that Al Handley stiffened. But as he stiffened, his right hand moved slightly and the fingers half slipped under the lapel of his jacket, just below the breast pocket with its gaudy, purple-edged handkerchief.

"And don't pull that gun, Al, unless you're really intending to use it." There was a new hardness in Satan's voice, and an elation, too; but it was the elation, and not the hardness that reached Al Handley and stayed his hand. It seemed as if Satan were encouraging him to draw his gun. That was it. That was what Satan wanted. Al Handley was sure of it. And why—why? Surely Satan couldn't reach up, draw, and fire in the time it would take Al Handley to get out his gun, for Satan Hall's hands still hung at his sides, listlessly, almost lifelessly.

"That's right, Handley." Satan nodded his advice when the hand stayed close to the lapel of Handley's jacket, only his fingers lost to view beneath it. "Don't let them knuckles of that right hand of yours disappear. I might misunderstand, you know. Remember that, Handley. Remember that I don't play with firearms. I was brought up better."

There it was—the uncertainty of the man. Every bit of mental energy in Al Handley's being cried out for him to draw that gun and fire. But he couldn't. His fingers just stayed there; already the tips of them barely touched the cold surface of his automatic. Nothing to do but clutch it, jerk it out, and fire! Satan's hands still hung by his sides. But Al Handley didn't draw the gun. He couldn't. It was as if his hand were frozen there on his chest. Everything he had ever heard about this man, Satan, raced through his frantic mind now.

"What are you going to do, Satan Hall?" Al Handley heard the words. They seemed to come from a long ways off. Then, with a start, he realized that the voice was his. But that wasn't at all what he wanted to say.

"What am I going to do?" Satan's lips curled at the corners now, but no one would have thought for even a moment that it was a smile. "I'm going to do what I'd do to any cheap gun—any bum that would threaten a copper because he thought that copper's hands were tied up with the red tape of the system. Al Handley, eh? Feared racketeer, eh? The worst man on the avenue to cross, eh? Well, you're just a bum. And like the bum that you are, I'm going—yep, Al Handley—I'm going to slap you down."

To the horror and amazement of Al Handley's friends, Satan did just that thing—the thing he was famous for. That he did it was the "horror" to those men standing in the room; that Al Handley took it was the "amazement."

Satan Hall suddenly raised his right hand and smacked Al Handley across the left cheek. To the watchers, it didn't seem like a very hard blow, but one of them who had received just such a "slapping down" from Satan, knew better. Al Handley's huge frame trembled visibly, his head jerked sharply, and his whole body seemed to tilt toward the bar. Then Satan's left hand came up, and the open palm of this hand rocked Al Handley back on his feet again.

For a moment the detective and the racketeer faced each other. Al Handley grew tense in body and mind. And Satan did it! He just closed that right hand into a huge fist. There was a single upward movement, a dull crack—like a heavy hammer upon hard wood—as Satan's fist caught Al Handley flush on the point of the jaw.

Just for a split second Al Handley clicked his heels together, like a soldier on parade, then crashed back and landed heavily upon the floor.

4

THE DEAD MAN IN THE LAKE

SATAN LOOKED DOWN at the fallen man a moment, then turned to the bar, and, leaning over it, called to the bartender, who was on all fours behind it.

"A little drink, Louie," he said, almost pleasantly. "A trying evening. Something to straighten my nerves." And when the trembling Louie came to his feet and reached for a bottle on a shelf behind the bar, he added: "Not one of them, Louie. It wasn't as trying as all that. Just something to wet my throat after so much talking. A bottle of ginger ale and an opener. I'll be opening it myself. It might prove healthier."

All the time that Satan stood at that bar, leaning his elbow on it, the silent men in the room felt—despite the fact that they did not see his eyes—that those sinister green eyes watched them. They noted, too, that at no time were Satan's hands dangerously, or even remotely, near his guns. The two guns they had never seen; but, as gossip had it, they were tightly strapped beneath either armpit.

Easily indifferent, almost nonchalantly, Satan Hall sipped his ginger ale. Only once did he give any tangible, or at least audible demonstration that he was interested in what was going on behind him. That was when

Romano, who had stood with his back against the swing doors, opened one slightly and took a short step backward. Then, though Satan never turned his head and though his back was almost to that door, he said:

"No, I wouldn't do that, Romano. Al Handley will tell Chicorro all that will be necessary." As the doors swung back and Romano's feet set squarely together on the floor, he added: "As for you boys, you better give your dear colleague, Al Handley, a hand. I didn't hit him very hard. He's just soft."

Whether it was a desire to help their friend or whether they took the suggestion of Satan Hall as a command, the two men nearest the bar assisted Al Handley to his feet, wiped the dust from his clothes, and held him as he leaned against the bar, his eyes rolling.

Finally Handley began to talk, incoherently at first, threatening as his head cleared—and in a burst of uncontrollable passion when he fully realized what had happened and looked into the face of the man who had so humiliated him before his friends.

"I'll kill you for this. I'll kill you for this," Al Handley cried out over and over as the two men, aided now by a third, held his arms as he frantically tried to break loose and reach for a gun.

Satan Hall still leaned easily against the bar, his right hand hanging by his side, his left hand raising the glass of ginger ale slowly to his lips as he watched the struggle—the desperate, real struggle of the infuriated man to get at his gun. And he encouraged him to greater efforts—even goaded the friends who held him.

"Why don't you let the big bum go?" Satan sneered as

another man came up from behind Al Handley and gave a hand in holding Handley's arms.

"Come on," Satan mocked them. "He's been shooting pickpockets and frightening women and children by making funny faces. Now he thinks he's a cop killer. Thinking of going over to headquarters, maybe, and giving the boys a laugh. Yeah, a cop killer! Let him go. Maybe he's even thinking of pulling a gun on me."

"Easy does it, Al." One of the men spoke soothingly as Handley struggled helplessly. "Don't you see what he's doing? He's goading you on. Trying to make you go for a gun, so he can— Don't you see, Al. There was Joe Raymond and Jerry Gandie and Paul, the Wop. Don't be a fool, Al. Your time will come."

"He's got no gun. I'll kill him. He's got no gun—no gun in his hand. I'll kill him." And Al Handley, thoroughly obsessed with rage, redoubled his efforts to break free.

"See how his mind runs," Satan sneered on. "Give him a break, boys. Let him loose. See the feared Al Handley go into action, or maybe some of you want to give him a hand." Suddenly leaning forward and boring the men who held the struggling racketeer with his sinister, cruel, green eyes, he said: "Stand aside, you lads. Stand aside or—"

And he stopped dead. A telephone rang sharply behind the bar. Louie hesitated a moment, then looked at Satan Hall.

"Sure!" Satan nodded. "Don't let the little difference between Handley and me interfere with business."

A moment's pause while Louie picked up the phone. Then came Louie's soft voice. "Sure, boss." Suddenly the receiver clicked back on the small house telephone behind the bar.

"It's the boss—Chicorro." Louie directed his words to Satan Hall. "He wants Romano up in his office at once."

"O.K." Satan spoke back over his shoulder at Romano. "Just see me out and let me have my coat first. Good night, boys. Take good care of Al." As he reached the swinging doors, he said: "If soft words won't quiet Al, just slap him down."

The men still held Al Handley. His struggles ceased somewhat now, though he still strained hopelessly against the detaining hands. All eyes were on Satan as he backed from that room. Although unspoken threats hung on their quivering lips and the lust to kill flashed in their burning eyes, no hand moved toward a gun and no lips spoke a single word.

For a moment Satan hesitated; then, backing quickly through the swing doors, pushing Romano with him, he took his coat, went down the hallway, thrust back the bolt, and, opening the basement door, passed out into the night. But before the door closed behind him, he heard Romano mutter:

"Slapped him down, he did. Slapped Al Handley down. Who'd think it possible?"

Stepping into a drug store, Satan found a telephone booth and called police headquarters. It was a minute or two before he got in touch with Inspector Fisk.

"Frank Hall," he said. And then: "I know who killed Detective Linden, and I've got a witness. He'll need protection, though, and I've promised him that. He'll slip into headquarters and talk to you right away. Should have been there by this—"

"Fine," cut in Inspector Fisk. "I'm glad, now, I got you the assignment with Captain Rogers. It looked good because you and Rogers are old friends. What's the name of the witness, and where can we find—"

"Haven't you seen him yet?" said Satan Hall. "He promised to show up at headquarters and ask for you by five o'clock. I tried to get you before. Bertie said—"

"Bertie? Bertie who?" Inspector Fisk cut in again sharply.

"Bertie Ramovitch. I—"

"Tough break, Satan." A few words were mumbled that Satan's dancing brain didn't get, then the inspector added: "Some boys saw the body in the upper part of the lake."

"What body?" Satan just shot the words into the mouthpiece.

"The body of Bertie Ramovitch. I'm trying to tell you that he was murdered sometime this evening, carted up to the park, and thrown into the lake and—"

"I should have killed him."

"What was that you said, Frank?"

"Nothing," said Satan Hall. "But you're not going to let the lad get away with that. I know who killed Linden. Linden was my buddy, inspector. We worked together for years. He was shot in the back. Bertie told me. The fact that Bertie was murdered shows that he spoke the truth. Al Handley shot Linden in the back, without giving him a chance. We've got to drag Al in."

"That's sentiment," Inspector Fisk said briskly. "And sentiment doesn't fit you, Satan. Linden was your buddy.

Go out and get evidence. They don't want unsupported knowledge in the district attorney's office, in the court of law, or in the jury box. Yes, yes—I know Handley killed him. But it would be the height of folly to arrest him and bring him to trial now. Handley has big friends. They have money, influence. They'd force a trial, and then—well—he'd be acquitted, and you couldn't try him again for the same crime."

"But there's no evidence. Bertie was the only witness. You can't let Handley get away with that killing. Linden was shot in the back. And I know Handley killed him. I know absolutely."

"Of course you do," said Inspector Fisk. "That's why I put you down there. Linden was your partner. I knew you'd do all possible. Stick to the thing until it gets hot again."

"It's cold—colder every day. There was nothing but Bertie."

"Well," said Fisk, "that's your trouble. You know Handley murdered Linden, shot him down in cold blood. If you can't hang that murder on him, hang another on him. So long as he burns."

"You mean frame a—"

"I want evidence of murder. The district attorney wants evidence of murder. The jury wants evidence of murder. And none of us care whose murder it is so long as Al Handley is roasted."

"But I care," said Satan viciously. "I want Handley to die—die for one reason alone. I want the whole underworld to know that he died for one reason alone—he died because he killed Linden—because he killed my—"

"And that's sentiment," Inspector Fisk said again. "But

suit yourself, Satan. I want Al Handley for murder—any murder. No, no more talk. I've given you a pretty free hand. Go back and talk with Captain Rogers. You two started in on the force together—same precinct and all that. He knows a lot. But take it easy with him. He's slated for an inspectorship and don't want to make any bad friends just now. It's the system."

"The devil with the system." Satan Hall listened a moment, heard the inspector chuckle, then slam up the receiver. "I should have killed him," Satan murmured to himself. "Yes, I should have killed him. I wonder what Billy Linden is thinking of his buddy now." As he left the drug store and plodded heavily across town, he mumbled: "But Billy would have called it murder. He was one of the system. It can't be murder. There must be some other way."

A plain-clothes man lounging beside an oil heater in a room empty of furniture but for a few wooden chairs, came to his feet as Satan Hall entered the precinct police station. He hesitated a moment, tossed his cigarette on the floor, and ground it out with a heel of his shoe. As Satan passed to the little door in the back of the room, he made up his mind to speak.

"Hall," he said suddenly and half apologetically, perhaps, when Satan paused and looked at him—for Satan worked alone, was taciturn and silent, and had little in common with his fellow officers. "I guess you ought to know. The Old Man came in a couple of minutes ago. I'm not aiming to make a hit with you—be friends with you. It just seems you ought to know. The captain wants to see you as soon as you come in."

"Yes." Satan waited. There was no expression on his face.

"Yeah," said the other. "The Old Man was polite and friendly—too friendly. And it came over the wire five minutes ago that you—well—that you slapped Al Handley down—slapped him down." Despite the man's apparent unfriendliness toward his brother detective, there was a certain admiration in his voice.

"Yes," said Satan. "He had it coming to him." He turned briskly, sought the door again, and stopped as he passed out into the little hall and to Captain Rogers's private room. "Thanks," was all Satan finally said, and even that single word seemed to the plain-clothes man to be given begrudgingly.

5

THE OLD MAN

SATAN HALL PASSED into Captain Rogers's room, closed the door softly behind him, and stood with his back against it. He nodded to the captain, saw the worried look on the round, good-natured face, noted, too, the droop to the cigar and the slightly open collar at the neck. It was a sign that Captain Rogers was worried. But it was not to Captain Rogers that Satan's keen green eyes gave their attention.

Satan knew who the fleshy man in the big wooden armchair was, even if he had never met him. He was the power of the district—politician, fixer, and vote-getter.

His face was soft, flabby, and very white but for the purple lines only partly hidden by the generous powder of the barber shop. The Old Man always looked as if he had just left the barber's chair. His dark hair, starting far back on his forehead, was nicely combed and recently oiled, and gave the impression of being carefully touched up, though that was only an impression, for no gray showed in its smooth, silky blackness.

Though his face and head were massive, his features were small. A little mouth, which puckered slightly when he wasn't talking, made his lips seem thinner than they actually were. His nose turned slightly at the end, and the blue, mixed with the red of it, gave it also a purplish color which lent truth to his often-repeated words that it was caused by high blood pressure. His eyes were small, beady, blinking, brown affairs that might have been attractive in a smaller face. But the whole face was one of placid ease—a calmness of bearing that could not be ruffled. Yellow gloves were held tightly in his left hand, and his right hand grasped the top of a light-brown cane, the gold head barely visible through the pudgy, short fingers with the pink, clean nails.

Captain Rogers looked at Satan and spoke in a tired, strained voice:

"I want you to meet—"

"The Old Man." The squat figure came to his feet with an agility that was surprising in a man of his build. "Just the Old Man. My friends all call me that, and you're going to be my friend, of course. All the boys on the force are friends of the Old Man." He chuckled now as he gripped Satan's hand.

"Hall! Frank Hall! Satan Hall! That's it. No offense," he said as the green eyes regarded him steadily. "You and Captain Rogers worked together years back, I understand. We welcome you to our district. We need men of your reputation for courage and fearlessness. Fortune seems to have smiled on the captain and passed you by. But that's uptown, Hall; decidedly uptown. Here we take care of our own, and see that they are rewarded for their good service.

"They know that, appreciate it, at City Hall, and at times find it annoying. But we have our way. We always have our way. Only yesterday the mayor said"—he paused and looked at Satan like a skilled actor letting a particularly effective line sink in—"the mayor said: 'Joe, it's no

wonder you're so well liked down your way—and your
way is getting bigger every day—beginning to take in the
whole of the lower city. When you're right—when you
want something for some one, you go after it until you get
it. Yes, you're a man of likes and dislikes—and mayor or
no mayor, Joe, I'd hate to be the man you were down on.'

"Just the mayor's joke, that, Hall, for it's seldom that I
have anything but good words for our boys. Because they
deserve it. Captain Rogers sees to that. You take Captain
Rogers's advice and it won't be long before we have the
shield of a sergeant for you. First-grade detective, with your
accomplishments! Oh, we've heard of them. No, sir; we're
all for building up this department to be the envy of the
entire city. We reward the deserving and crush the—yes,
sir, crush the undeserving. For we must weed out the bad
to protect the good. Captain Rogers will tell you that we
have use for none but the best down this way." The Old
Man snapped out his watch, glanced hurriedly at it, and,
sticking it back in his pocket, arranged his muffler tighter
about his neck. Buttoning his coat, he lifted his hat and
stick down from the chair where he had placed them.

"But it's time I was home. Just dropped in as I was passing." He patted Captain Rogers gingerly on the back,
gripped Satan Hall's hand again, shaking it vigorously. It
was a cold, moist hand. Something like shaking the fin of
a seal, Satan Hall thought. Then, just before he left, he said:

"You're new down here, Hall, and we want to help you.
Listen to Captain Rogers. He's the best police captain
in the entire city, bar none, and even now is slated for an
inspectorship." He winked once at the captain. "I don't
mind telling you that was what brought me to city hall

to-day, and that the powers that be were favorably—very favorably impressed. Good night, captain. Good night, Hall. It's been a pleasure to meet you. I sincerely hope that nothing untoward will happen to take—take you away from us, and lose for the captain that inspector's shield he so rightly deserves."

The Old Man went, humming a tune, nodding a cheery good night to the lieutenant on the bench outside, and stopping for a short chat with the uniformed man at the door before he slipped on his yellow gloves and tucked his gold-headed cane beneath his arm.

"Close the door," Captain Rogers said in a tired voice. When Satan did that, he murmured: "Sit down. We need a talk." Another moment until Satan took the chair the Old Man had vacated, and then: "You know why he came, Satan?"

"Yes," said Satan. "About Handley. I slapped him down to-night. He had it coming to him."

"Yes, I know. That's what brought the Old Man here." Captain Rogers jerked a thumb back over his shoulder at the door. "I wonder, Satan—after all these years, what made them shift you down here—even temporarily. Oh, you're not a fool. You know as well as I know that trouble follows you—official trouble."

Satan straightened slightly in the chair; his green eyes blinked.

"You could have put up a holler," he said. "The Old Man could have fixed it."

"Yes, he could have fixed it. But I couldn't do it. Not with you—not after what we went through together—those first few years." He laughed sort of harshly. "And I'm the captain and you're the first-rate detective. You were always a better officer than I—a better hunter of men. A go-getter. But you hated the system. Now you're down here, and with half a break I'll be an inspector by the first of the year. Why did they send you here, anyway? Trouble up the line after your— It was Billy Linden who was killed. Have you been different, Satan, since your friend was killed? A little harder—a little colder—a little more against the system? Was he closer to you than I used to be?"

"You and Billy Linden were pretty much alike, cap. Maybe he sort of held me in check, like you used to. But, like you, he was one of the system. He let the man who killed him shoot first. He didn't want to embarrass the department—the system. And at the end the system got him. They killed him."

"I see." Captain Rogers nodded. "But that has nothing to do with your trouble at Chicorro's. I heard what Al Handley had said—his threat to you. There was no need for you to go there. Just a hothead. You could have ignored the threat, and I would have seen that it was not repeated. Despite your views and your ethics, this precinct is run straight. Its captain is honest. I could make trouble for Chicorro, of course. He sells liquor, like a thousand other speakeasies, but there's no trouble in his place, and there's no law on the statute books of our State which forbids it. That's for the government to attend to."

"Other places are raided." Satan's lips smiled.

"Yes, I suppose so. That's part of the system." Captain Rogers smiled rather sadly. "Tell me, Satan. You've worked pretty much alone. I've understood that right of yours, from higher up. Now, have you anything particular against Chicorro?"

"No." Satan shook his head.

"Or Handley?"

Satan hesitated a moment, and then:

"No. Nothing—nothing in the way of evidence against Handley."

"Because if you have"—Captain Rogers closed his mouth grimly and let his hands slip far apart—"no one— no one guilty of a crime can—can fix me, inspectorship or no inspectorship. Of course, there are favors given and favors returned. Chicorro stands in right with the Old Man. Chicorro's the biggest bootlegger in the district. But his liquor won't poison you. And if I ran him out, another would come in. Chicorro don't make trouble for me, and I—well—maybe we sort of see that people don't make trouble for Chicorro.

"There will always be illicit liquor as long as prohibition lasts and the people want the liquor, whether it's Captain Rogers who runs this district or another. I can't say that there isn't graft handed out now and then, but there's none to me. My bank account can show that. It's—yes, it's the system. I protect the innocent and the honest against crime. There's nothing in it for me but the job."

"And an inspectorship," Satan said softly.

"Yes, and an inspectorship." Captain Rogers leaned over and lifted a photograph framed upon his desk. "I'm older than you, Satan—a good twelve years, I guess. That's my daughter, there. Looks like her mother used to." A moment's gulp, and then: "She graduates from high school this February. An inspector could send her through college. I don't think that a captain could. Not a captain whose savings—and more—were eaten up by operations, doctors, and hospital bills before her mother died. Take a good look at that picture, Satan. She's all I've got—all I work for—all, maybe, I live for. I promised her mother I'd send her through college, and now—now, if you've got anything on Chicorro or Handley—yes, or even the Old Man himself—give me the facts and I'll see them in jail if it's my last official act. I'm still—still an honest copper."

6

THE SYSTEM

SATAN REGARDED THE outburst calmly, took a cigarette, put it between his teeth, and, striking a match, slowly lighted it.

"It's the system," he said. "It'll get you, maybe, in a different way, cap. But it will get you just the same, as it got Billy Linden. I suppose I can take all the Old Man said as threats—personal threats."

"Yes," said Captain Rogers. "The Old Man has a habit of saying exactly the opposite of what he means. And you slapped Handley down." There was just a glint in the blue eyes of Captain Rogers. "Bad for the system, maybe, but it took courage to slap Al Handley down. It's a wonder he didn't kill you, Satan." And when Satan's lips turned decidedly up at the corners, he added: "It's a wonder he didn't try to kill you."

"A wonder." There was a slight question in Satan's voice. "But it was a disappointment, cap; a big disappointment that he didn't try to kill me."

Captain Rogers sat quietly a moment and removed the cigar from his mouth. He looked at the ash upon the edge of it, saw that the steel basket had been kicked well away from his desk, and finally deciding against the effort, tapped the ashes onto the floor.

"It isn't Handley. It's that it happened at Chicorro's that makes the trouble for me. The Old Man is interested in Chicorro, and therefore has to be interested in Chicorro's right-hand man." He watched Satan sideways, to be sure the significance of the thing sank in. "If you—if Handley had pulled a gun on you and fired—and you got him— things might have been better. That is, if it all happened outside of Chicorro's. For there's more than a rumor that Handley would like to take Chicorro's place and that Chicorro knows it."

"Look here," Satan said suddenly. "Let's have plain talk, cap. Suppose I had dragged Handley in tonight—suppose I wanted him for murder—what would you do?"

"If you can get him for murder, bring him in." Captain Rogers turned sharply. "Friends would have to stick to him, of course, while he's alive. He knows a lot. But bring him in." Bending forward and trying to read something in Satan's green eyes, he asked: "Is that why you searched his room? Lay your cards on the table, Satan. I'll do every- thing—and every man under me will do everything—to convict him."

"And the little girl and the college—the system?"

Captain Rogers's face flushed suddenly. "You don't think I'd send her through college on an inspector's salary that was bought at the price of human blood! Why, I couldn't look her in the eyes. But tell me the truth. What have you got on Al Handley?"

Satan answered quickly enough.

"Nothing—absolutely nothing. It was just a theoretical

case. You see, I've never fully understood the system. I don't know for sure how far it goes."

"Well, you know, now, how far it goes with me." Captain Rogers came to his feet. "If every wrong-doer was locked up, there wouldn't be enough jails in the entire country to hold them, let alone in the State. You know that as well as I do. If you've got anything on your chest, get it off right now. But don't get mixing yourself up in common brawls that are of your making, and for your own personal satisfaction. There was no excuse in the world why you should have gone to Chicorro's. You went, looking for trouble. And you'll get it. Al Handley is a gunman and a killer, but mostly his victims—or, to be real legal, his reputed victims—have not been citizens the city can't spare. Now— well—he'll go gunning for you. He'll act quickly. He'll have to. A thing like that travels fast. And each day you live—each hour, even—Al Handley's grip on his associates weakens. After all, Satan, a man is only as bad as another man's mind pictures him."

"And if he gets me, what?"

"Then I'll move heaven and earth to convict him."

"And if I get him?" Satan asked very softly.

"That"—Captain Rogers set his jaw grimly—"depends entirely on how you get him. You have nothing against him but his threat. A common grudge of the individual, not the—"

"The system," sneered Satan.

"Exactly," said Captain Rogers. "Police officers are hired by the taxpayers to protect them, not to eliminate undesirable citizens. Because there's a shield presented to you by the city, pinned inside your coat, that doesn't give you the right to shoot a man down in cold blood. There's a law that calls that murder; there's a law that makes a punishment fit that crime. It's for a judge and jury to pass upon that—not you, as an individual. Oh, you're not a murderer, Satan. Not even a killer, in the full significance of the word. But your law is not the law as laid down in the regulations. You believe, with the criminal—get your man before he gets you! Good logic, maybe, but not the law of—well—of the system."

"I'm to let Handley have first shot. That's it, isn't it?"

"That would give you provocation to kill him, of course." Captain Rogers nodded. "But that's not the point."

"But the point or not, that's the fact, isn't it? That's the system, isn't it? That's the system as you know it, as Billy Linden also knew it."

"The law is made to protect the police officer just as it's made to protect the civilian. If you've been threatened, you have access to the law."

"Sure!" Satan curled his lips. "I could swear out a warrant and get a city magistrate to bond Al Handley over, for five hundred dollars, to keep the peace."

"I suppose you could." Captain Rogers yawned slightly.

"But it's my life or that of Al Handley. You've practically said as much. One of us must die."

"It isn't that bad, Satan. I've promised the Old Man to pull you in line. He'll get Chicorro to pull Al Handley in line."

"You believe that he can?"

Captain Rogers hesitated a long moment, looked at his cigar, put it between his teeth, and drew on it several times before he was thoroughly convinced that it was out. Then he said:

"No, I don't believe it. That's why I warned you."

"So"—Satan stroked his pointed chin—"if Al Handley shoots at me, and I live long enough to fire back, that's the system. It's not his rotten heart or black soul that counts with the jury. It's his rotten marksmanship, eh?"

"It's no use, Satan. You've made up your mind not to understand. Your trouble with Handley is personal, not police work."

"So the only solution—the only hope for me, is to take my medicine or take my job back uptown, or—" Satan paused and smacked his lips.

"Or what?" said Captain Rogers.

"Or protect myself to the best of my ability after, not before, I'm attacked. That's it. Play the system."

"Self-defense is the right of any man." Captain Rogers was on his favorite subject now, and, leaning back, let the tips of his fingers come together. "If Al Handley attacked you, fired on you and didn't make good"—he smiled at the word "good" and lingered over it—"why, the broken faith would be on the other side. The Old Man would admittedly not have brought Handley into line. Besides, there would be no need of protecting Handley and no need to fear that he would talk. You would have then acted in self defense, and if you have not changed since your former days and the records do not lie about you, Al Handley would be dead."

"And that," said Satan, "would be according to the system."

"According to the system." Captain Rogers agreed.

"And your inspectorship would not be in danger."

"And," Captain Rogers said, smiling, "my inspectorship would not be in danger."

"And," Satan continued, still in that hard, cold voice, "your daughter would go through college."

"And—enough!" Captain Rogers cut in harshly this time—the hard, severe police captain. "There is just one thing wrong with your argument, Satan. Al Handley does not miss what he shoots at."

"I don't know," said Satan Hall. "You see, he's really never fired at me."

The door opened, brass buttons glittered for a moment, and a policeman spoke.

"A letter for—for Detective Hall."

Satan Hall took the letter and tore open the envelope. He read it through twice. It was short enough.

> If you want to learn absolutely positive, with evidence that'll stand up in a court of law, who killed your buddy, Detective Billy Linden—come to No. 1067 ½ East Second Street. But you gotta come at once. Apartment 3B—top floor—rear. Come alone, and don't tell no one until this bird who murdered your friend is cooked up good—because I'm afraid of getting kicked off.
>
> From One Who Wants To Get Even.

Satan Hall let his green eyes rest on Captain Rogers. Then he crumpled the note up in his huge fist, raised his hand, poised—to throw the note in the steel wastebasket. Then he thought better of it and stuffed it into his pocket.

"I'll toddle along home, cap." He walked to the door and

then asked: "Do you think the Old Man will be able to put the checks on Al Handley?"

"Maybe by to-morrow, when Al cools off. But what do you think, Satan?"

"Me?" There was a sound in Satan's voice which Captain Rogers at first thought was a laugh, but after looking at Satan's somber, stern, hard face, decided against that thought. "Me?" said Satan again. "I don't think. I know he won't be able to—in time."

Captain Rogers heard the door close; and heard, too, the heavy pounding of those feet—that steady, even beat. He nodded and thought that he knew why the criminal feared them. But he sighed as he looked at the picture of his daughter again. He wondered if, after all, there wasn't something radically wrong with the system—something on which he just couldn't place his finger.

Finally he shrugged his shoulders. Satan had been right. The system and his daughter's college education were very closely connected—in fact, inseparable, he guessed.

7

THE HOUSE ON EAST
SECOND STREET

OF COURSE, SATAN could not be absolutely sure that the note was a trap. He thought it was—hoped it was. But trap or no trap, he recognized it as a duty to investigate anything connected with the business of crime, especially with the one particular crime—the murder of his side-kick, Detective Billy Linden.

If all clews, anonymous notes, or even well-meant information given by individuals proved correct, the business of the man hunter would be an easy job indeed. But it was necessary to run down anything that gave the slightest possibility of success, or even if it gave no possibility. Satan remembered when—

He dismissed such thoughts now as he walked out under the green light and stood on the broad stone steps of the station house. The note, of course, was a trap—perhaps such a note as Billy Linden might have received when he was shot down in the dark hallway of an apartment house uptown. Shot down in a district far from Al Handley's usual activities. Shot down because he had picked up a thin lead, the long and tedious ramifications of which might ultimately lead to Al Handley and a bit of murder that had

74

not been committed with Al Handley's careful eye to detail and native American love of personal liberty.

A trap! Satan Hall nodded. He liked traps. They were generally enlightening, instructive as well as—he thought for a moment—destructive! Yes, he guessed that was the word. Anyway, he liked the taste of it in his mouth.

Just one doubt! It had been just such a note which had brought him to Bertie Ramovitch's musty, ill-smelling room over on the East Side. He had thought that a trap, too.

A moment of hesitation as he stroked his chin, let his eyes involuntarily narrow and slant upward; then he swung on his heel, reentered the station house, and crossed the hall. Stepping through the open door, he approached the desk of the lieutenant on duty and obtained an envelope. With a nod to the lieutenant, he smoothed out the note he had received, placed it in the envelope, and ran the flap across a protruding tongue; assuring himself it was tightly sealed, he scribbled the name of Captain Rogers upon it and turned to the lieutenant.

"Give this to the captain in a half hour." He shot the envelope along the police desk which stood on the two-foot platform. "Not before then." He looked at the clock. "He'll be busy now, but it's important."

"O.K." The lieutenant picked up the envelope, turned it over several times, then stuck it against the inkwell before him, after marking the time of delivery upon it.

"Been hearing things about you, Satan," he said pleasantly, in a mood for conversation. "Heard about how you—you—"

Satan suddenly cut in in a mechanical voice.

"Slapped Al Handley down? Yes, that's it. He had it coming to him."

"We'll be hearing more about that, I guess." The lieutenant nodded emphatically, and seeing in Satan's eyes that he was not in the proper frame of mind for enlightening conversation on that subject, repeated rather lamely: "We'll be hearing more about that, I guess."

"Yes," said Satan very seriously, "we'll be hearing more about that. Good night!"

He turned quickly, and this time he did not hesitate beneath the green light, but descended the stone steps, walking rapidly but evenly and heavily toward the east.

Satan was a lone worker, had long been recognized as such by Inspector Fisk, who took a tolerant and rather paternal attitude toward his "peculiar views" regarding the system. But Inspector Fisk knew that Satan was a valuable man to that same system—a system which Satan abhorred with a passion that was almost an obsession.

As Satan walked eastward now, he wondered if he had played the game squarely with Captain Rogers. It wasn't lack of trust. It was that very trust in Captain Rogers's honesty and sense of duty which made him keep his mouth tightly closed regarding the fact, not the evidence, that Al Handley had murdered Billy Linden.

Satan knew that Captain Rogers would have acted at once had Satan told him who killed Billy Linden. It would be like Rogers to forget, then, the influence, the power, the forces that would stretch out their hands and—well—take the college education away from that little girl of his.

Yes, Satan knew exactly how Captain Rogers would act. Al Handley would be dragged in before even his friends could know what happened to him. All but one chair would be removed from that little basement room downstairs, and Al Handley would be given a chance to talk, confess, tell the truth about the murder.

And he might talk, too; that is, if a keen lawyer with influence in one hand and a habeas-corpus writ in the other didn't beat them to the confession. Confessions of that kind were part of the system—part of the old system, Satan thought, when the criminal had no friends, no influence, no money. But now such confessions were only too often repudiated at the trial, and maybe rightly so, too, for Satan knew of more than one innocent man who had confessed to a crime he had not committed.

Satan shook his head. That was another fallacy of the system—the system which he felt was wrong, knew was wrong; the system which didn't give a cop an even break with a killer—which strained the widow's pension fund and let nine murderers out of ten walk the streets of the city—free men.

But there was Captain Rogers, and the motherless daughter who must go through college. College! Satan Hall wasn't strong on colleges. An education of that kind would never take a bullet out of a cop's stomach and put it back in the murderer's gun again. And Satan Hall never thought except as a cop.

Captain Rogers would get that note in time to find a body. Whose body?—Satan wondered. He had never given the system a break. Why should the system give him one now? But he shrugged his shoulders and plodded on.

He was well over on the East Side now, walking more

slowly, with measured strides down East Second Street, watching the numbers.

As he neared No. 1000 he nodded his head. He was right in coming alone. His keen, hardly moving green eyes had detected the figure across the street that moved quickly back in the shadow of a doorway as he approached. Satan understood. That moving figure had been placed there to assure the writer of the note that Satan did not lead a parade. But it didn't matter, anyway. The man who killed Billy Linden was still at liberty and alive. And the man who knew it, and was Billy Linden's friend, still permitted him to be at liberty and be alive. It was with such a thought in his head that Satan turned into the dismal, chilled dampness of No. 1067 ½ Second Street.

A dim gas light flickered in the musty old entrance, barely illuminating the dirty, ill-smelling hallway. Satan shoved both his hands into the pockets of his great coat, clutched a gun in either one, and started up worn stairs. He mustn't carry his guns openly in his hands. That was part of the system, and Satan was playing the system tonight. A cop mustn't make trouble. He must let some one else make it. But he must expect it and be ready to cope with it once it forces itself upon him. Yet the system took no account of a figure that might now be lurking in a dark corner, waiting to shoot him in the back as he climbed those stairs.

Where was the "even break" to it? If his keen eyes saw that figure, the law gave him no right to shoot. He must call out his warning. If the other was susceptible to the fear and majesty of the law, well and good. But if the other decided to shoot, the officer's only protection was the inaccuracy of the criminal's aim. The system was not right in that, Satan thought.

Satan pictured as he went up those stairs the same scene some few months back, the only difference being that it was laid in an uptown setting. Billy Linden, then, had mounted stairs as Satan mounted them now. He knew Billy's way—Billy's courage. He sensed the fact that Billy must have paused on the stairs—maybe even seen the figure over his shoulder, maybe even called out. Then the roar of a gun, the quick feet, and the slamming of the front door as Billy Linden rolled to the foot of those stairs, a bullet in his back!

Satan grimly climbed those stairs. The boards were old; they creaked dismally in the silence of the tenement. He tried walking on the edge nearest the wall. But it was no use. The old stairs gave up their dead, groaned like a sick child, or snapped out sharply like an irritable woman.

8

—

THE VOICE BEHIND THE DOOR

WHEN HE REACHED the first landing, Satan stopped and peered through the dimness, up and down the damp, stuffy hallway. Then he listened. He thought that a door closed softly on the floor above, but he couldn't be sure. He didn't like the sound of it just the same. To him it meant one of two things: some one had stepped out in the hall above, closed the door behind him, and now lurked at the head of the stairs, watching—waiting—for the top of Satan's head to appear as he came up; or some one was listening for him, had received a signal of some kind or other that he was already in the building. Behind that closed door, the stage was being set for his arrival—being set, perhaps, for murder.

Whether he liked it or not, Satan went on now, and he didn't try to deaden his footfalls any more. He rather liked the sound of them. Whoever waited above knew that he was coming. But if it was Al Handley, he couldn't know that Satan Hall intended to play the hand of the system to-night. The steady tread of his feet would be heard above; appreciated, too. There was a psychological effect to them. Satan knew that Al Handley had a yellow streak. He had seen that at Chicorro's. Now he counted on that yellow

streak to broaden with each step he took upon that second
flight of stairs—each footfall to register fear in the racketeer's scheming, shrewd little brain. Satan nodded grimly.
But most of all, he wanted that fear reflected in the trigger
finger of Al Handley's hand.

Steadily, slowly, he made the second landing. He didn't
stop and listen now, but, turning to the left, plodded down
that hallway. His green eyes narrowing in the darkness, he
searched and finally found the door with the number 3B
upon it.

Satan paused before that door and tapped lightly on it.
There was a moment of silence, and a voice said: "Come in."

Satan straightened. It was a low voice, hardly audible
through the closed door. But Satan thought that it was
not the voice of Al Handley. Still, he turned the knob and
pushed the door open wide before entering the room. Then
he stepped briskly through the opening and faced the man
before him. He was surprised. The thing was unexpected.
The man before him was Chicorro. He was to one side of
a cheap wooden table, his right hand resting upon it, the
fingers plainly gripping it. His left hand hung by his side,
extended slightly forward, awkwardly. But it was clearly
evident that both hands were empty.

"You!" Satan said. "You wrote that note?"

"Yes." Chicorro nodded. "I wanted to talk to you. Wanted
to call you off a—"

Satan knew. That note hadn't been just a plot to have him
open that door so that Al Handley could blaze away at him
before he could go into action. He had expected that—was
willing to chance that; was willing any time to face a man
with a gun. But now— He didn't need the sneering laugh

behind him to tell him the truth. The hard, round surface that bored into his back was enough. He knew the feel of a gun, and knew, even before the words were spoken, that Al Handley had stepped out from behind that open door and stuck a heavy-calibered automatic into his back.

He heard the door close as Al Handley spoke.

"You were a fool to come, and this time you'll take it in the back, like any yellow dick should."

Satan's eyes were straight on the face of Chicorro. The swarthy features of that well-known racketeer had turned pale. He wet his lips with a tongue before he spoke.

"None of that talk, Al," Chicorro said huskily, as if the truth had dawned on him for the first time. "We're here to—you said to fix things with Satan—that he'd listen to me and take the—the money. Easy does it, Al."

Al Handley laughed as the gun bored harder into Satan's back.

"A wise dick, Satan Hall. Thought you could slap Al Handley down and get away with it. And then you walk into a trap like this!" Satan sensed that the gloating was near an end, and the lust to kill was creeping into the man's voice. "Well, here's where you take a bit of lead to the grave with you."

Satan's right hand simply raised slightly. He spoke quickly but calmly.

"It's no go, Al," he said. "I've got your boss, Chicorro, covered now. My finger's pretty tight upon the trigger. Your first shot might not kill me, and Chicorro would go out. Or even if it did get me, I might get that single press of a trigger in first."

"Cut it, Handley!" Although Chicorro's voice rang with

command, there was fear in his eyes. Suddenly, after looking over Satan's shoulder, he cried: "Al, I believe you want
him to do it. I believe— You dirty, double-crossing rat, you
want to run the racket! Satan, I didn't— Let me—"

"No." The nose of Satan's gun peeped over the edge of
his pocket now. "You keep your hands steady and empty,
Chicorro."

Somehow he felt that Chicorro spoke the truth and that
he didn't have any hand in this.

"I don't know," Satan said, "if you're in it or not in it. But
it's your racket, Chicorro. It's up to you to handle it. One
thing you can be sure of. Your life snaps out with mine."

Al Handley cut in:

"You don't feel like slapping Al Handley down now, do
you, Satan? Satan, eh? Well, you'll be meeting your name-
sake in a minute, and you—"

Satan wasn't listening and more. He was thinking. Al
Handley was much cleverer than he thought. Here was
Handley's chance to rid himself of Satan, and perhaps of
Chicorro, too. In the natural course of events, Al Handley
would take Chicorro's place, have Chicorro's influence.
Chicorro's money. But suppose Chicorro didn't die? What
then? Chicorro was bad. Al Handley might try to convince
Chicorro that he knew Satan wouldn't kill him. And since
they were tied up so closely in the murder of Satan Hall,
Chicorro would not dare to talk about the events in that
squalid little flat. But if Chicorro feared to talk, he wouldn't
fear to act. Al Handley would be found very shortly with a
body full of lead at the end of an automobile ride.

Satan saw a chance—not much of a one, but a chance,
anyway, of meeting Billy Linden and explaining to him

that he didn't die without paying Billy his debt—without taking Al Handley with him. And the system? It would be satisfied for once. There would be a dead cop beside a dead racketeer. And—but he felt Al Handley's hand stiffening, the rod going deeper into his back.

Satan spoke quickly.

"It's possible, of course, that your first shot will kill me cold and I'll not get Chicorro," Satan said. "But if—if it don't kill me, I swear this to you, Handley: your boss, Chicorro, goes over the hurdles with me. I swear it."

Was Satan right? Was Chicorro, after all, a victim of this meeting, just as he, Satan, was? He was right. Al Handley wanted Chicorro to die, and he wanted Satan to kill him. Handley was also afraid that Chicorro might lift a gun and be ready to shoot him before the dead body of Satan had fallen to the floor between them.

Yes, Satan was right. For, almost as soon as he had finished his words—this threat to kill Chicorro—Al Handley had moved his gun, brought it up higher, so that it rested close beneath Satan's shoulder blade. Handley was going to make sure that his first shot wouldn't kill Satan. He was going to give him a chance to make good his promise to kill Chicorro. Satan's back was to him, so there would be time for a second shot.

"Slap Al Handley down!" Handley couldn't keep from gloating over his kill as he kept his eyes riveted on the pale face of Chicorro. "Now, then! What was that?" He straightened—listened.

9

THE YELLOW STREAK

FROM SOMEWHERE ON the street far below came a shrill whistle; not a police whistle—more as if the little fingers of either hand had been shoved into a human mouth.

That was the break, and Satan acted. He simply jerked his gun up and twisted quickly.

Al Handley's gun roared; a bullet tore into Satan's left shoulder. But instead of preventing his quick turn, it switched him around perhaps a bit more sharply.

Yellow? Yes. Like all his kind, Al Handley was yellow. Now, although Al Handley had the time to aim and fire, he didn't; that is, he didn't aim. He looked into those burning green eyes and fired wildly. Satan jarred back against the table from the force of the heavy lead as it tore a hole through the side of his chest.

Almost with the roar of Al Handley's second shot, Satan's fingers had closed upon the trigger of his gun. His green eyes, now beginning to dim and take on a dull, filmy look, narrowed in satisfaction. In a misty way he saw the little, round purple hole in Al Handley's forehead, slowly widening and turning a vivid red—just before the body of Al Handley slumped to the floor.

"Billy—Billy Linden would sort of like it that way,"

Satan murmured as he sank into a chair, his arm resting on the table, his smoking gun still firmly clutched in his hand.

In a hazy way he knew that Chicorro faced him, and that Chicorro was talking. Chicorro was saying something about not shooting—that he didn't have a hand in it, that Handley had double-crossed him, that it was a "good job that dirty skunk was dead."

"Not me, Satan. Don't give me the works. That would be murder now. I'm not Al Handley's kind. I didn't—"

Satan looked at Chicorro in amazement. He seemed so far off, as if Satan looked at him through the wrong end of a telescope. It seemed, too, that his hands were stretched high in the air, and that there was fear in his eyes.

Suddenly the truth dawned on Satan. The gun was still in his hand—gripped there tightly, the nose of it picking out a spot on Chicorro's chest. A finger still caressed the trigger. Satan laughed. A finger that was not his—at least, to all purpose and intent not his! For he could not move his fingers, his hands, or his arms. He tried to lift the left hand that hung by his side, but made no go of it. His brain seemed fairly clear. It could give orders to his body, but those orders could not be executed. The muscles would not respond to any demand.

He tried to talk, guessed that he did. Then he found that the words came back to his ears, but only after a long interval—as if he whispered them too low to hear, and some one later repeated them to him.

"All right, Chicorro." He tried hard to keep his eyes open. "I guess it wasn't your racket. You—can explain this to—to—" Maybe his head cleared a bit or maybe it got more cloudy. He didn't know which. But certainly it seemed to him that this little affair didn't need any explaining. It was part of the system. He carried a chunk of lead in his body—two chunks, in fact; little souvenirs of the system—things that would lift a cop from the stigma of homicide to the glory of heroism. But Chicorro. That was the trouble. It would bring the Old Man into it. It would be like Captain Rogers to hold Chicorro. But Chicorro wasn't guilty. Chicorro was talking again.

"All right." Satan interrupted Chicorro's flow of words. "You weren't in it. Just police business. Part of the system. You weren't here. Understand, Chicorro. You weren't here at all. And it's a good thing he's dead—that fellow on the floor—the dead one. What's his name again now?" Things weren't quite so clear.

Chicorro was talking.

"Handley. Yes, it's a good thing he's dead. The dirty, yellow two-timer. What do you mean I wasn't here? What—" A moment's wait. The slam of a door below. Then: "There's some one coming up the stairs. That was the whistle; that was the signal. It's the cops. What do you—"

"There's a window; there's a fire escape. I—I'd never say you were here if the Old Man was to think that it was a credit to Captain Rogers that he—well—that that fellow got killed."

"The Old Man will. He will. No one will miss that yellow bum. Don't keep that gun on me. You ain't aiming to shoot me trying to escape? I—" A jerk of his head. "That's Rogers's voice on the stairs."

One quick look at Satan, one quick look at the door, and Chicorro turned swiftly and sought the window. There was a dull scraping of feet on rusty iron supports, then silence. The next moment the door burst open, and Captain Rogers, followed by two uniformed officers, was in the room.

"I found that note on the desk and knew it was a trap, Satan, and"—Captain Rogers half stumbled over the body on the floor—"you beat him to it. Thank Heaven for that, even if— Satan, you've been hit!"

"Yeah," said Satan when Captain Rogers came close to him and began issuing orders to one of the men. "You see, it was the system, cap. I gave the system a break—and—and I guess it gave me one."

BACK BY THE little white bed in the hospital, the best surgeon in the city allowed the nurse to help him on with his coat. Before leaving, he lifted Satan Hall's wrist with his long, strong fingers. Then he said cheerfully:

"He's too hard to kill, Captain Rogers. One bullet was very close to the right lung, though. For a moment I thought of leaving it there, but—" The doctor broke off suddenly, listening.

The man on the bed moved, rolled his head once, and said:

"Funny, too. And me never having much use for a college education."

"Just the effect of the ether," said the eminent surgeon. But Captain Rogers shook his head. He didn't believe that. Didn't believe it at all. And he could not understand why the Old Man, Chicorro's friend, should send flowers to Satan—Satan Hall, who had just killed Chicorro's right-hand man, Al Handley.

SATAN SEES RED

*He Hunted Men—His Law Was His
Own—and Police and Gangdom Alike
Feared and Hated Detective Satan Hall*

1

BETWEEN THE EYES

DETECTIVE SATAN HALL dropped to one knee and fired twice. His movements were so quick—just that sudden, dropping twist of his long body—that the sharp staccato notes of the Tommy gun died almost before it had begun to play its tune of death over the edge of the galvanized ashcan at the end of the alley.

A black touring car, with curtains tightly drawn, which had been moving slowly along the deserted street, suddenly increased its speed; reached the scene of hostilities and slowed down, the high-powered, high-priced motor purring softly.

The thick-set man hidden behind the ashcan came to his feet, tottering slightly. The Thompson machine gun balanced for a moment on the edge of the can, then toppling forward fell with the clang of metal to the sidewalk.

The gunman, his left hand dripping red, his right clutching a heavy automatic, half backed, half ran toward the slowly moving car. His gun wavered slightly—uncertainly and menacingly—toward the little hallway where his intended victim had taken refuge. Twice he squeezed lead toward that hallway. A side curtain of the car flapped

Hall fired twice

back and other guns roared in the same direction as that of the wounded gangster.

Then, with a quick dash the killer ran into the street, clutched frantically at the nickel handle on the rear door of the get-away car, slipped once, and with an audible groan of relief pulled himself to the step. He turned then, as a hand stretched from between the curtains and held him, his back pressed against the side of the car. Evil, ratlike eyes pierced the darkness; and taking careful aim as the car increased its speed, he fired at the face he now saw peering from the hallway.

Two guns roared as one; two spurts of orange blue flame split the blackness of the night.

The killer slumped against the side of the car, his knees sagged, and his heavy body was held only by the clutching fingers of a hand.

Another hand came from behind those curtains; fingers

His gun wavered
toward the hallway

grabbed at a gray jacket. The car swung suddenly. The gunman sank to his knees on the running board—hung so a moment. Then, as the car swerved back, his body twisted, broke loose, and plunging to the pavement turned grotesquely over and lay in the gutter. The black touring car turned a corner and was lost to view.

There was the shrill blast of a police whistle and the distinct pounding of heavy feet. Detective Satan Hall stepped from the hallway, brushed the dust of the sidewalk from his right trouser leg, and mumbling something about "the street cleaning department," faced the patrolman who came running up.

"Hall. Satan—Frank Hall." Patrolman Leary corrected himself as he remembered Detective Hall's lack of enthusiasm for the title "Satan." "They didn't get you then." And with a shake of his head that bespoke long and observant duty in the lower city, "They will though. That's sure."

"Maybe." Satan Hall's green, slanting eyes narrowed, giving the peculiar cut of his hair an even more pronounced V shape upon his forehead. "But *there's* one lad who won't get me." He jerked a huge hand, with long, strong fingers, toward the inert form in the gutter.

For the first time Patrolman Leary saw the body of the gunman. He snapped erect, and raising the service automatic that was already clenched in his hand stepped carefully toward the silent figure.

"Is he dead?" he asked in a whisper. Despite his years of service Patrolman Leary had never lost his superstition—or, as he would have explained it, his first feeling of reverence in the presence of the dead.

"That's for the medical examiner to decide." Satan shrugged his broad shoulders. "My duty is only to produce the body. His, to permit the burial."

"HE'S STIFF AS a mackerel." Leary came to his feet after kneeling for a moment by the body. He whistled softly as he saw the round hole almost directly in the center of the dead gangster's forehead. He looked at Satan again, trying to make out in the darkness those pointed features which gave him his name. And they seemed clearer now. The sharpness of the chin, the decided points to the ears—or at least, to his left ear, which Leary could see plainly because of the tilt of Satan's soft black felt hat. Yes, it was all there. And Leary gulped. There was a tiny hole in the dead man's forehead. It was more than a rumor, more than just a superstition, then, that Satan's bullets were generally found right between his—well—his "dead men's" eyes.

People were on the street now. Windows were going up. A sergeant had joined Leary, and with his hat in his hand was scratching his head and looking down at the dead, white face.

"It's Ed Graff," said Sergeant Clifford, as Satan came to him and looked indifferently down at the man he had killed. "He was Bowers' man. It'll raise an awful smell."

"Won't it!" Satan nodded.

"I wonder," said the practical sergeant, "what Bowers will say."

"I wonder," said Satan, just as slowly, "what Bowers will do." And he smiled to himself. "Maybe I'd better go and ask him."

"Maybe," said the sergeant, very seriously, "you'd better go and report to Captain Mullery. Oh, I know you're sort of the lone wolf of the Department. But, after all, you're working out of his precinct. I've sent Leary to call in. But maybe Mullery ought'a hear it from you."

"Maybe he ought to." Satan pulled at his pointed chin.

"It will be a surprise to the captain," offered the sergeant.

"Yeah, it will," Satan agreed. "And it'll be a surprise to John Bowers—a disappointment, too," he added with a grin.

"Don't underestimate Bowers." Sergeant Clifford laid a kindly hand upon Satan's shoulder. He liked Satan's direct way of doing things. He liked the easy indifference with which Satan cut departmental red tape with a few well directed shots from his service automatic. But he knew, as well as every cop on the force soon learned to know, that being a part of the system meant promotion, and promotion meant more money for an underpaid policeman.

2

THE SYSTEM

DETECTIVE FRANK HALL walked down two blocks, turned left, did another block and a half, and passing under the green light entered the station house. The lieutenant on the desk looked at him and nodded toward the room in the back.

"He's in there, Hall." And then, as Satan passed to the door to the left of the desk. "It was Ed Graff, wasn't it—he's dead, isn't he?"

"Uh-huh." Detective Satan Hall stuck the end of a match in his mouth. "It was Graff—and he's dead." And swinging on his heel he thrust open the little door and stepped, with that even, measured tread of his, into the presence of Captain Mullery.

Captain Mullery took his cigar from his mouth and laid it carefully on the edge of the flat desk behind which he sat. Then removing a bit of tobacco from his lower lip he looked at the detective. But it was Satan who spoke first, and his words were not the desired apology or the explanation that Captain Mullery hoped for, but did not really expect.

"Did the warrant come?" Hall asked lazily, as he threw himself into a chair.

Captain Mullery leaned far back in his seat, tucked the cigar into his mouth, took several draws upon it before making sure it was out and then as carefully placing it upon the desk again said abruptly exactly what was on his mind.

"You had to kill him, eh?"

Satan shook his head, then grinned. At the best, his grin was unpleasant. To Captain Mullery it seemed even sinister.

"No," he said, "I didn't. I could have let him kill me. Might have saved you a lot of embarrassment. I did my best to let him live." Satan shook his head. "It was wasted effort. Ed Graff didn't have any nerve, besides being a remarkably poor shot."

"I hope you had to do it." Captain Mullery shook his head. "Bowers is a powerful man in the district. And don't grin, Frank Hall. There always has been and always will be politics and influence. You can't afford to offend people, make trouble for the big boys, if you want to wear the stripes of a sergeant."

The captain came to his feet, and passing around the desk looked down at Satan Hall. "And you should be sporting the shield of an Inspector. Look at me! Not half the nose for crime you've got. Not half—" His hands came far apart. "You've got to play the system if you want to get anywhere. You grin—and you're mighty proud of yourself. But you haven't others dependent on you. I've got a wife and kids, and I've got to swallow certain irregularities."

"I'm not criticizing you." Satan pulled himself erect in the chair. "And I don't expect you to criticize me. I've lived a flat-foot and I hope to die a flat-foot. Maybe, if I had a wife and kids, I'd excuse—" He came to his feet suddenly. "I've known you for years, Mullery; pounded a beat with you in the old days. We can't all think alike. Did the warrant come?"

"Yes." Captain Mullery gulped. "It's a mean break for you, Satan. The murder ain't hot any more, but every so often it bobs up that Ferago is back in town. One lad has been killed who saw that murder, and a cop that—"

"Yeah," Satan said impatiently. "But Ferago is in town now. You know, as well as I know, who committed that murder. Ferago had only a small part in it. Bowers beat in that old man's head five years ago. It was a brutal affair. Now—Bowers is a big shot. He's got money, so he's got friends and influence—and he's got votes."

"You can't do anything to Bowers—get anything on Bowers. That's just talk—and five years is a long time, Satan."

"Ferago's yellow. Ferago will talk before he fries. And if Ferago talks, Bowers burns—money, friends, influence, and what have you."

"But the rumor of Ferago being back is just gossip."

"Bowers knows it's true. Ferago's here under the name of Randolph. Bowers knows I want him—and Bowers is afraid I'll get him. More afraid, now that Ed Graff got kicked over."

"Anyway"—Captain Mullery shook his head—" the Commissioner, or whoever shoved that Ferago warrant on you, gave you a bad break."

"Maybe." Satan stretched his hand out for the envelope the captain lifted so reluctantly from the desk. "But I asked for it."

"You asked for it!" Mullery gasped, as Satan dug into the envelope, unfolded the warrant and nodded his approval.

"Yeah," said Satan. "I don't like Bowers."

"No." Mullery pulled at twin chins. "No, you don't. It's that girl then, Mary Rogers—that you—that all the—that they—" And Captain Mullery stopped dead.

SATAN HALL WAS leaning over the desk now, his green eyes points of flashing steel, his long tapering fingers twisting spasmodically, his thin lips a single straight line, but for the sinister curves at either end.

"I knew her father," he said almost viciously. "The girl's straight. She has no friends. The police see in her only the daughter of a dead crook."

"Bowers likes her," Captain Mullery said reflectively. "Your trying to drag in Ferago won't help you none with Bowers. He'll find out, and—"

"He's already found out, else why the shooting tonight?"

"Look out he don't take it out on the girl to get even, if you—if you live. And if you die"—Mullery spread his hands far apart—"she won't have you then. It's helped her, Satan—the boys knowing you take an interest."

"If he harms the girl," said Satan slowly, "I'll pop him over."

"That," said Captain Mullery, "would be murder."

"Sure," Satan agreed. "Bowers is welcome to what comfort he can get out of that thought."

Captain Mullery followed Satan Hall to the door.

"Well," he said, "I wish you luck. At least, as to your physical well being. It's a big city for a cop working alone, without the Department at least officially behind him. How do you propose to start hunting for Ferago? Where will you look? If he is in the city they'll smuggle him out quick enough."

"I'll start tonight. Now!" Satan's V-shaped jaw set tightly. "And I'll look exactly where you'd look. Where every dick in the city, who's paid attention to underworld gossip or stool pigeons, would look. Right smack in the John A. Bowers Club, or whatever the official label is for Bowers' speakeasy and gambling joint. Goodnight."

"Just a minute." Captain Mullery stretched out an arm and fastened it on Satan's arm. "You're not going there now. Listen, Satan"—when Satan would have shaken him off—"Bowers is still mighty fast with a gun. The place simply reeks with high class racketeers. If you did get in, if you did get Ferago—why, any one of the dozen might kill you. There would be ten witnesses to swear that you drew a gun; a lad without a record who'd take the blame for knocking you over. Bowers' political friends to help him beat the rap. I wouldn't—"

"No, you wouldn't." Satan shot the words through set lips. "But you know, as well as I know, that Ferago is there. That he plays cards with the boys, drinks at the bar, struts in and out of the game rooms—and the only compliment he's paid the police force is to shave off his mustache. It's a disgrace to the force. He's yellow, and he'll talk. Talk, as soon as he realizes Bowers can't spring him."

"But the evidence?"

"A man and a woman who both saw Ferago at the time of the killing. You didn't know that, eh? But Bowers must know it, or guess it—though he don't know who they are. Not even the Commissioner knows who they are."

"I'm not thinking of Ferago or Bowers, but of you,

Satan." And as Satan jerked his arm free: "I could send a couple of cops to stand out front. Nothing official, under-stand—but they'd act as a—well—a sort of a restraint if Bowers decided to give you the works. More, I can't do. It's the infernal system, Satan. Bowers knows big guys—politicians."

"Yeah. I know. I'm working alone and won't embarrass you. The Commissioner's a straight-shooter. If Bowers has anything on you, put your house in order. I'm going to get him."

"Me? Good Gawd!" Captain Mullery was more surprised than offended. "I only know that big people told me he was 'right,' and to lay off him; leave him alone."

"Good!" said Satan as he jerked open the door. "Leave him alone, to-night, then."

And he was gone, pacing slowly and evenly across the floor before the desk. At the outer door he hesitated, turned back, and approached the lieutenant on the desk.

"You've had occasion to visit Bowers. Yeah, John A. Bowers," he added as the lieutenant stiffened. "Oh, I don't aim to accuse you of being over friendly. But they say he always sits a lad under a lamp, in a big overstuffed chair, so he can watch him. Is that right?"

"Why—I— So I've heard."

"It's truth, isn't it? Isn't it?" Satan was leaning over the end of the desk now, his face very close to the lieutenant, his hot breath upon his cheek. His hot breath! And the lieutenant straightened. Like the man himself—the uncanny resemblance to that gentleman from hell. Yes, even the breath.

"Yes," said the lieutenant, "that's true." He realized too

late that he was a lieutenant and Satan simply a first grade detective, he watched the tail of Satan's coat disappear through the door.

"There goes a man to his death," said Captain Mullery, coming from his private room. "He's going to Bowers' to arrest Ferago."

The man behind the desk whistled softly and felt for the phone.

"Better," he said, "give Bowers a jingle."

Captain Mullery hesitated, then shook his head.

"No," he said. "Not this time. After all, Satan is working out of this precinct, though we're not officially cognizant of it." He stumbled over the word he had culled from the Commissioner's short note that the official messenger delivered, together with the warrant for Satan.

SATAN HALL'S MEASURED, even tread was well known in the underworld. But, contrary to general opinion, it was not slow. It moved his long angular body quickly.

Now—he walked two blocks uptown, three across, and another up town again. His steps became slow only when he approached the John A. Bowers Athletic Club. That he could gain admission to the club he knew. But he knew also that his entrance would be delayed; that a bell on the side wall would be pressed, and Ferago quickly smuggled from the place.

Bowers didn't know—or, couldn't know yet, that Satan carried a warrant in his pocket for the arrest of Ferago. But Bowers would know before the warrant got cold. Bowers had a way of knowing what went on, even within the department itself. But Bowers did know that Satan was hunting up information on the killing five years before.

And Bowers had shown his knowledge, at least to Satan's satisfaction, when early in his investigation Satan had stood in the City Morgue and looked down at the dead face of a young girl—a girl who had promised to talk.

Satan set his lips grimly. A girl who wouldn't talk now. And his thoughts, somehow, went to another girl, Mary Rogers, the shabby tenement, and her fight against the odds of a dead father who had been a criminal.

To one side of the little hallway which gave entrance to the John A. Bowers Club Satan waited. Several guests passed in—knocked on the unsuspicious and simple looking wooden door which was lined with steel, and after passing the inspection of the man who peered through the square in the center, entered the club.

Honest folks, many of them. Satan nodded his satisfaction. That was good. That was John A. Bowers' cupidity. There were not enough high class crooks to make the place pay. Besides this honest public lent the club an air of semi-respectability.

Satan let several couples—two groups of four and one of six—pass into the club. Then he shoved a hand far into his overcoat pocket and stepped briskly from the shadows as a single individual climbed somewhat unsteadily from a taxi and passed into the darkened hall.

Wood moved, a small square opened in a broad door, a white face appeared for a moment in the light beyond—and as the door swung open Satan took three quick steps down that hallway and was through the doorway before the astonished attendant even realized that something had barred the closing of the door.

Mean eyes glared at Satan, trying to peer beneath his

slouch hat or above his turned-up coat-collar. Thick lips parted, yellow teeth showed.

With a single movement of his right hand Satan swept the slightly inebriated customer back out that door, closed it and shoved the bolt into place.

Though his sudden entrance was entirely unexpected, the experience was not without precedent to the efficient watcher at the door. Instinctively he sensed his visitor was a detective. If it was a hold-up, the man would not have come alone. His right hand slipped slowly beneath his left arm-pit, his left hand shot swiftly toward the button on the wall—and Satan acted.

Satan's hand came from his pocket; steel flashed by the astonished attendant's arm. He felt a sharp pain, and red showed on the knuckles of his left hand as it fell to his side. He felt his right hand gripped in vise-like fingers; and as he opened his mouth to shout, Satan raised his head—and the man on the door looked straight at those slanting green eyes, that sharp nose with the slight hook to it, the thin lips with the curve at the corners—and the shout died to a gurgling sort of a whisper in his throat. He was close to death, and he knew it. Satan was a killer.

3

THE JOHN A. BOWERS CLUB

JOHN A. BOWERS, in the luxury of his private office, leaned far back in his over-stuffed chair and tried to keep the end of his cigar from getting in the telephone mouthpiece.

"Yeah? He did! Uh-huh! You don't know what judge signed the warrant?" came at intervals to the attentive ears of Carpey Marks, his first assistant, who sat and waited for the conversation to end. "Judge Quailey, eh? Yeah. No, I never did business with him."

There was no expression on the thick jowls of Bowers as he put the phone back in its cradle and eyed Carpey Marks from small round pink eyes, that seemed even smaller, set in such a large face.

"Know Judge Quailey—Francis X., I think? Anything stirring his way?"

"No." Carpey Marks pulled at a tightly set jaw. "He ain't regular. I know that. We've kept out of his court. All the boys do. They say he's straight. A sap!"

"Yeah?" Bowers let his huge head roll from side to side. "Well—see that mouthpiece, Jacobs. Tell him to get after Quailey. There must 'a' been somethin' fishy, to set him on the bench. He always was a stench. But he let me alone and I let him alone. Now—"

"Yeah?" Carpey Marks leaned forward eagerly.

"Satan Hall's got a warrant for Ferago. There's been many warrants for Ferago, but this one reads, 'alias Randolph.' What do you think?"

Carpey Marks cleared his throat and spat in a corner.

"If Satan's got a warrant, he'll serve it. That's what I think." Then more slowly: "If he's got anyone to serve it on. Even Satan can't serve a warrant unless he's got someone to serve it on."

"And you suggest?"

"The same thing I suggested when I heard Ed Graff got it. You're trying to give it to the wrong guy, chief. A dozen Satans might bob up who'd like to hear Ferago talk." And leaning far over, "But there's only one Ferago to talk, chief—just one."

"Huh—huh." John Bowers spread his huge hands across his ample front. "If there was a reason, Carpey. Not a personal one." He raised a hand when Marks would have cut in. "John A Bowers takes care of his boys—none better. You know that. They all know that. Ferago counts on me—trusts me. Knows no harm can come to him while I—"

"Yeah. He goes up and down the Avenue, buying drinks as if he were running for office. He's yellow. He got into trouble down in South America and came prancing home, scared stiff. Now look here, chief. If Satan gets him and puts the screws on him, he'll squawk. Oh, don't shake your head. That cop ain't human. I'm telling ya truths. He'll lay a gun against my belly. Yeah, and your belly."

"Not me—not me." Bowers shook his head.

"Yeah—you. Your belly, and pull the trigger—and explain afterwards. And if he wants Ferago he'd come here and get him, and—"

"Not here—not to the John A. Bowers Club."

"Yeah—here. The John A. Bowers Club, and—"

"I see." Bowers' little eyes got smaller. "Look here, Carpey. Satan will come here with that slip of paper—that warrant. You might wait in the hall, and— What's the matter with you? It's dark at the end. He'll come in under a light. Oh, hell!" Bowers came to his feet and paced the floor. "I'm always thinking of the organization, Carpey. I've got to. It bears my name and all that name stands for. If Ferago, now—if there was anything that would affect the organization, why—why—"

"Ferago takes dope," said Carpey for about the tenth time that night. "You've often said that a lad who sniffs the powder ain't to be trusted. If they put the screws on him he'll wilt. He'll squawk for a whiff of snow. He'll— What's the matter, chief?"

"Carpey"—Bowers stood above his assistant now— "I understand your feeling of loyalty to a fellow member, but your loyalty should be first to the organization as a whole. You have seen how I put aside all personal—thoughts of personal danger with regard to Ferago. I thought only of the organization. No, don't explain." Bowers raised a huge hand as Carpey's mouth fell open. "A drug addict is a menace to the whole organization. I like Ferago—you like him. We must both be above that. We must sacrifice individual friendships for the good of the whole. You may—"

"Yeah, chief." Carpey Marks, who had no illusions, nodded vigorously. "I'll attend to everything."

"It's unpleasant," said Bowers with a frown. "And unpleasant things are best quickly over with."

"Sure, chief. I'll tell him about the warrant and Satan and that we're moving him up town. I'll tell him about some girls; nice personal ones, that you picked yourself, and—"

"Do—do." But John A. Bowers was already thinking about something else. "And, Carpey, there's that Mary Rogers. You've spoken to her?"

"Yeah. And she ain't the type. At least she ain't—yet. You'll have to make her the type, if you—"

"Me?" said John A. Bowers. "I wasn't thinking of myself. She'd fit in nicely downstairs. Pleasant sort of a girl—wistful smile. I was thinking she'd be an asset downstairs."

"Better to have her keep the books—up here with you. You need someone, chief, and she does that sort of a racket—or did."

THERE WERE TIMES when Carpey Marks was a valuable assistant. John A. Bowers smiled all over his huge, heavy jowled face.

"You're very thoughtful, Carpey—very thoughtful. You say she *did;* did keep books and that sort of thing."

"Yeah." Carpey nodded. "She lost her last place. I thought it for the good of—of society to tell them a little something about her old man."

"How's she fixed for money? Satan Hall, now. It's true she's Satan's woman?"

Carpey Marks grinned.

"True enough for those that want to believe it. But it's gospel that she ain't. She wouldn't take a cent from him. She's that way."

"I see—I see. And her father being a crook—even a dead

crook. Dead!" He swung his head suddenly and looked straight at Carpey Marks.

Carpey nodded.

"The finger's on Ferago." He was quick to sense the change of subject. "Don't worry, chief." He came to his feet. "It's a bit of a drive, but in an hour I'll dump the body out by the old reservoir up Kingsbridge way. I'll take along a couple of—"

Carpey Marks paused. Both men turned toward the little glass inclosed indicator on the wall. There had been a sharp buzz, and behind the soiled glass a tiny light showed Ted.

John Bowers started toward the door and paused.

"Trouble downstairs, Carpey." His little eyes were like two round holes in a blanket. "Better go down and give it a look. It'll look better if I'm up here. Much better, if it's a big shot."

But after Carpey Marks had left the room, John Bowers paced restlessly up and down. One killing—one murder out of the past that might come back on him. Ferago! He should have put him on the spot long ago. It was Ferago who had held the old man when he—Bowers—beat in his— Bowers shuddered slightly. He was younger then. A fool for "courage," he thought. But the old man had looked straight into his face and called him by name. No one else knew. It was Ferago who had raised his head almost directly beneath the street lamp, and been seen. And now—

Why the hell didn't Carpey Marks come back? Why the hell hadn't he done for Ferago long before? He was too soft-hearted. That was John A. Bowers' trouble. Ferago had been a brother to him; they had gone through the racket together. Those that said he let Ferago come back so Ferago could see what a swell guy—what a big shot he had become—were liars, dirty liars. But it was pleasant to talk to Ferago. Ferago was a good pal. Wouldn't stick at anything. Wouldn't— But that was before he took to snow. A dope! Carpey was right. Never trust a dope.

Besides, Ferago was younger, much younger. And Bowers looked in the glass at himself. There were wrinkles down to his mouth, heavy pouches under his eyes, and his jowls were— He leaned forward and ran a finger across the ridges in his face. That wasn't age. That was his early living—hard living. Now—well, an hour in the barber chair, and any woman would look at him twice.

He wasn't really old. On the good side of forty. He had fought his way up in the racket. Any woman—even a girl—even Mary Rogers— Damn it! What did he see in that little white face, that frail delicate body? Spirit, that girl had. The name John A. Bowers must mean something to her. She was class. Destined to be a big shot—for a big shot. Well, John A. Bowers was a big shot, and it wasn't the name that made him that. He used a gun in those days—could still use it.

He jerked a hand beneath his armpit and a heavy German Luger snapped into it. Quick that! He wondered if Satan could do any better, and he bit at his lip. Satan, eh? He'd knock off his men—he'd kill Ed Graff! He'd— But what had become of Carpey Marks? And the door opened and Carpey Marks burst in.

The easy indifference of the man was gone. That nonchalant carriage and the drawl to his voice were missing when he spoke. He simply shot the words through his teeth.

"Satan—Satan Hall has been here. And he knocked Ferago on the side of the head and dragged him from the place."

4

A FIX

JOHN A. BOWERS stopped his pacing and looked straight at Carpey Marks. There was nothing to read in his face. No sudden twitching of his lips, no tightening of his eyes—no rise to his voice when he finally spoke. Nothing to show the emotions of the man; except perhaps the sudden color that came to his cheeks, to vanish almost at once and leave them that soft powdery white.

"And what," Bowers said, very slowly, "was Henderson doing? What was Longman doing? Where was Richards—and Prague? Even Gunner Rant was downstairs tonight. What were they all doing?"

Carpey Marks shrugged his shoulders. But it was not a movement of indifference. More, of resignation to the inevitable.

"I suppose," Bowers still spoke very slowly as he stood in front of Marks, "the memory of Graff—Ed Graff—was with them when they saw Satan."

"It ain't that, chief." Carpey Marks read wrongly that calm before the storm. "It's Satan. It's his face—his eyes. The slant of his eyebrows, the cut of his chin. Most of all, his walk. That slow, even tread when he comes for a man. There's death in it, chief. Them boys ain't yellow. They never expected he'd dare to come here. To the John A. Bowers Club. They had faith in—in—in the name of the organization, the pull you pack, the—"

"They knew—maybe, not as you know—but they suspected or guessed what Ferago is—and they knew that to lose Ferago was to lose me. I told them that—you told them that. Ferago, the lousy little skunk, told them that. Seven or eight of them. All 'guns.' All heavily armed. All seeking the patronage and protection of John A. Bowers. And not one, Carpey, even to pull a rod. If you had been there—would it have been the same?"

"Me? Well, I knew, chief—and I'd of gunned Satan out like *that*." Carpey snapped his fingers and shoved out his chest. There were few who could stand up to Satan like he would, or like he told himself then that he would. Besides, the boys weren't altogether to blame. Bowers had taken too long to see things in the right light. Bowers should have— But Carpey explained it, or started to explain it in detail.

"You was slow to act, chief." He stuck his thumbs in his vest. "Don't say I didn't warn you—advise you. Ferago should 'a' been put out before. Yesterday—a week ago—even a couple of hours ago, when Ed Graff was croaked. And I put it up to you strong. The trouble is, chief, you don't think fast, like you used to. You don't strike when—"

"No!" Bowers' roar of rage shook the room. For one instant all the fury that the big man held pent up in his body broke loose. Little eyes popped, great blue veins stood out on his forehead and cheeks, thick lips opened. Then his great body half turned and a huge right hand swung through the air, the back of the great knotted hamlike fist striking Carpey Marks on the side of the face and across the jaw.

Just the single crack as bone hit bone, and Carpey Marks hit the soft carpeted floor with a suddenness of a steer in the stock yard.

When Carpey Marks first opened his eyes Bowers was placing the phone back in its cradle. When Carpey Marks next opened his eyes it was from the splash of water in his face. John A. Bowers was standing above him, and he was talking.

"Get up!" he said. "I've had Satan on the phone, and he's coming over to see me."

"Yeah—yeah?" Carpey Marks staggered to his feet, felt of his aching jaw and wiped the blood from his lower lip. "I'm to tell the boys? We'll gun him out, and—"

"You're a fool!" John A. Bowers went to his desk and sat down behind it. He raised a pen and pointed it straight at Carpey Marks. "Satan put Ferago in, and Satan can get him out. See? It's not guns now—it's brains. And brains is money. It's a 'fix.'"

"BUT SATAN CAN'T be fixed. That's why he's still a dick. That's why— Gawd! chief, I ain't trying to tell you how to run things. But I know. It's been—"

Bowers waved his hand.

"I know. Every man has his price. Everything in the world is for sale if the price is met. I'm going to meet Satan's price."

"And if he won't—"

Bowers came across the room and took Carpey Marks playfully by the shoulder.

"Then," he said, "we'll change positions. I'll be the seller and Satan the buyer." He whispered for a long minute in Carpey's ear. "Mind you—the men I name go with you. If I press the bell here, act—and act at once. This time, you see, it's for the good of the organization."

"She's a nifty dame," Carpey nodded when Bowers straightened again, "and Satan would give his life for her."

"Just so." Bowers nodded. "And he'll give my life for her, too. So you see, Carpey—after all, Satan's getting all the breaks in this visit. I—"

Again the buzzer on the wall rang. This time the light through the glass showed green.

"That," said Carpey, "will be a copper. Satan!"

"Exactly. Bring him up personally. And, since I'm doing the inviting, it would be stupid to try and enforce my rule— that no man to see me enters this room armed. Still—you might try it."

"Yeah. I see." Carpey smiled, and then grimaced and felt of his lip. It was like the man, that he held no animosity against his chief for that blow. "You ain't losing none of your—your strength, chief."

John A. Bowers patted him affectionately on the shoulder.

"Nor you none of your lip." He looked down at the deep cut. "I'm speaking theoretically now," he grinned.

"Are you? Yeah, chief?" Carpey Marks smiled, but as he left the room, he frowned. That last doubtful humor of Bowers' had been entirely lost on him. But Bowers knew that, and didn't care. He didn't mind enjoying one of his little jokes alone.

John A. Bowers stood in the center of that room. Then he moved the big over-stuffed chair slightly to the right and straightened the shade of the electric lamp so that the light would fall full upon the face of the man who sat under it. Not that John A. Bowers was a great student of men. It was simply that he thought he was. He had read somewhere that great men—at least, some great men whom he had admired—did study men under a brilliant light. But the bright light had at least one practical purpose. It helped him to read men's hands—watch men's hands. Brains are all right. But they won't help you much if a man can move his hands fast; has a keen eye for distance and a steady finger upon a trigger.

John A. Bowers owed more to physical action than to mental power. It was the brute in the man that led him to the top. The shrewd brains that he had which kept him there. He didn't need to have proof of a man to "get rid of him." Suspicion was enough.

Now—Satan was coming to see him. Coming armed. There was little doubt of that. He'd never think of looking on any other copper as a danger. Bowers frowned. That was the trouble. He never had looked on Satan as a copper, as an upholder of law and order. He looked on Satan as he would have looked on any gangster—racketeer—gunman. Bowers didn't respect or fear the police. They never shot a man down—just like that. But Satan was different. Satan was a killer. Like any gunman, he killed ruthlessly. There were times when Bowers felt that Satan even killed for— for pleasure. What a man he would have made in the racket!

And the boys talked about Satan's feet. That slow, measured tread of his. Well—Bowers never watched a man's feet. Never feared a man's feet. Even in the days when he was winning his spurs by the quick and accurate use of a gun, he watched a man's hands. That was it. Feet? Hell! A child wouldn't be—

5

HUNTER OF MEN

JOHN A. BOWERS raised his head and listened. Plainly he heard the steady tread of feet. Slow and even, just like the boys already said. Measured, too, as if Satan had practiced it. As if— Bowers grinned. But he listened nevertheless, and caught that unexplainable eerie something that others had caught. Footsteps of Doom those feet were called. Footsteps of— Yes; they were like the slow tread of the last march—through the little door to the electric chair. Just like that. Just like— But it couldn't be. Bowers had never heard a man walk to the chair. It was like—like he thought those feet must be—those final steps to death. But, why? They were too steady for a lad going to the hot seat. Such steps would falter—must be uncertain. Of course! But yet they were like those last steps to death. Like he thought—

And the door opened—and Carpey Marks said:

"Hall. Detective Frank Hall, chief. And he's—well—he's got everything on him he had when he came in."

"I'm sporting a rod, if that's what he means," Satan said easily. And as Carpey Marks closed the door and stayed on the outside: "This isn't another of your warnings, is it?"

"Warning?" John A. Bowers' smile was friendly as he motioned Satan to the big chair beneath the light and watched him drop into it. "Well—maybe a hint or two was dropped your way. For your own, benefit, Hall." And after a moment's pause, while he went and sat behind the desk, "You didn't benefit by such friendly hints. I see you're still just a detective."

"Always likely to be. Just a flat-foot." Satan's eyes narrowed and his lips curved at the ends. But Bowers couldn't tell if it was meant for a smile or not. If it was, it was a most unpleasant one. But then, beneath the light Satan's whole expression was unpleasant. Bowers shook his head and ran his hand across his mean little eyes, as if to clear his vision and change the picture before him.

"Well—" Satan said, after a bit, when Bowers drummed on the desk and made a pretense of studying the detective, "let's not waste time. You want to see me. It's about the Ferago pinch, eh?"

"Randolph!" And when Satan's lips parted again, Bowers went on, "We'll call him Ferago, then. You've got a clear case against him, eh? What's the charge? What are you holding him on?"

"No charge—just suspicion. No charge—yet."

Bowers' thick eyebrows seemed to thin.

"You know, of course, I can have him out with a habeas corpus writ in less than twenty-four hours. A great thing—habeas corpus, if you don't make a formal charge—a real charge."

"Yeah," nodded Satan. "If I don't. But somehow, Bowers, I don't think you'll try any habeas corpus this time."

"No?" Bowers hesitated. Satan was no fool. Habeas corpus is the poor man's greatest protection against injustice. But it is also the racketeer's greatest weapon against

the law. And Bowers had used it many times. Now—
Bowers stroked his chin and said, "No?" again—and let
it ride.

"No." Satan shook his head. "For the moment you
do, I'll make a formal charge of murder against Ferago.
Listen, Bowers." He leaned forward, both his huge hands
with their long slender fingers upon his knees. "As soon
as Ferago knows that turning State's evidence will save
him—as soon as he knows that his own life will be saved
if he names the man who beat in that old watchman's head
five years ago, he'll talk. I've got no warrant for you now. I'm
naming no names now. But you and I know who Ferago
will name. You can't help him—you can't save him. All your
influence; all your pull; all your bribes won't beat this rap.
Bowers, I've been on your heels for years. Now—I'm going
to see you fry. Get that! You're going to burn."

"Yeah?" John A. Bowers tried to smile, but it was a sickly
grin. A dry tongue came out and licked at drier lips. His
thick jowls turned a dull white. He coughed once and put
his hand over his mouth. He laid both his hands on the
flat desk and came slowly to his feet.

"Hall," he said, in evident great frankness, "you've been
straight with me, and I appreciate it. You've got me wrong.
You've got Ferago wrong. But there is some danger of—
of—" And suddenly leaning forward, "You put Ferago
in—how much do you want to get him out?"

Satan shook his head.

"It can't be fixed," he said.

BUT JOHN A. BOWERS only smiled at that. He had heard
the same line before. From big men in the city—big shots

in politics. Big bugs on the police force. And yet— He spread his hands far apart.

"You've been trying to put the finger on me for years. And—well—you can get Ferago out, can't you?"

"Yes," said Satan," I can."

"And you've come to see me, to talk about it. You've come to warn me—to give me an out. All right. Ferago goes free tonight—and it will be worth just five grand to you."

Satan laughed, and John A. Bowers laughed with him.

"Just my fun—my little joke." He rubbed his hands together. "Come—we won't quibble. We'll make it ten grand. Cash on the spot. No checks—just bills. And after that. Well—you've been a long time on the force. We'll make you a lieutenant—a captain. Six months or a year would cover it. You've got a good record—too good a record. We could make an inspector out of you in time—make you a rich man."

Satan shook his head.

"It's not enough," he said quietly.

"Ah!" Bowers was in his line now. This was talk—this was putting the screws on him. This was the sort of thing he understood. "So you want to squeeze me, eh? You think you've got me in a jam and I'll have to pay. You've gone straight all these years—waiting, watching for the one big haul. Just one, and out! Others have thought that. But you can't do it. Money! It'll get into a guy's blood—into his mind. He can't get enough of it. I— There, there—" Bowers changed suddenly as he saw those narrowing green eyes of Satan. "I might double it for you. But it wouldn't be nearly as much in the long run as standing in with John A. Bowers. There's gravy enough for all of us. Just let me pin the shield of a captain on you, and then— Gawd! Satan, with a man like you in the racket, I could point out—"

"It's not enough," Satan said again, and his lips curled. "You see, Bowers, it isn't in my blood—or in my mind. There's nothing I want that money can buy. It's not honesty—not morals. I just don't get a kick out of money. That's why I'm a detective—just a common dick. It's my racket—my kick—to hunt men. And, now"—he leaned forward—"one man, Bowers. Just one man." Satan came to his feet, and taking two slow steps, leaned over the flat desk and pounded a long finger against Bowers' chest. "I've waited some years for this. You understand—the finger on you!"

Bowers had seen what he thought was viciousness in a man's face before. Bowers had seen the threat in a man's eyes—the hate, and lust to kill far back behind glaring orbs. And he had nodded his head and jerked a thumb toward such departing enemies. They died later—the finger was on them!

Now he thought he read that same lust to kill—that same hate in behind the green shining globes. He had never seen it in a copper's eyes before—he never expected to see it. The look that he feared in men's eyes; the look that made him kill—and kill quickly.

His lips trembled slightly and his lower one hung down. His right hand moved toward his left armpit. He didn't think of money then—he didn't think of a fix then. He thought only of drawing a gun—and using it. His fingers were on his chest now; almost beneath his coat—not far from his shoulder holster and the German luger it contained. And Satan's hands never moved from his side;

just hung listlessly there. Yet, Satan must have known of Bowers' quickness with a gun, his reputation, and—

God in heaven? Why didn't Satan move his hands? Was he a tool, or—? And little beads of sweat rolled out on Bowers' forehead, hung so and dripped slowly down his face. Satan's lips slipped back and his eyes narrowed slightly, and—he was laughing. Or was he? Was he just marking Bowers for death, as Satan had marked others for death—others, who had been mighty fast on the draw—as fast as Bowers? Witnesses had said that Satan's hand had never moved before that sudden burst of flame came from his gun, and the tiny hole appeared in the forehead of the dead man—the dead man whose gun hung clutched in his hand. A gun that was never fired—never—never—

BOWERS' HAND DROPPED limply to his side. Someone spoke. A voice that sounded hollow and distant said:

"You—you devil, you—you've come here to murder me." And the words were out and dully registering in John A. Bowers' mean little brain before he fully realized himself that he had spoken them.

Bowers was careful now to turn his side and gently take a handkerchief from his breast pocket to mop his moist forehead. But as he stood erect and faced Satan again, the thumb of his left hand slipped below the desk and pressed the button there three times. Peculiarly, it took an effort to do that—and he wondered: whether the effort showed on his face. He wondered that as Satan spoke.

"If you've rung for help—if someone walks in that door in a way I don't like, John Bowers, it'll be just too bad for you."

Bowers nodded very slowly.

"Our talk is over," he said in a husky voice. He had no more thought of bribing Satan. He had only one thought now. To see him go. "I wondered why you came, but I—I never guessed. It's personal, then."

"Very personal." Satan nodded. "You're a wise man, if not a brave one. You had your chance—if you had any nerve." Satan's shoulder moved up. "The State would have been saved an electric bill. But you were right, Bowers. I came here—well—if not with the purpose, with the hope of killing you."

"I see," said Bowers. "Hunter of men, eh? Hunter of just one man now—that's it."

"That's it. You've given me many warnings. I'm giving you a warning now. Just one man!"

"Sure—sure." John A. Bowers was relieved as the door opened and one of his bodyguard stood there. "But you can't help—" He hesitated, with the name of Mary Rogers on his lips—and decided not to use it. "You can't help the girl if you're dead, you know."

"No, and you can't harm her if—if you're not alive. That's a nicer way of putting it, Bowers. At least, I think Ed Graff would appreciate that. By the way, I knocked Ed Graff over tonight."

"Graff! An impetuous youth! He didn't—didn't attack you?" John A. Bowers' eyebrows went up. There was nothing vindictive in his voice—in his face. He was himself again now and on his guard.

"No—no." Satan shook his head. "I wouldn't go so far as to call it an attack. Perhaps 'annoyed' me is a better way to put it."

"I see. I see." John Bowers spoke now with the steel lined

doors half closed upon Satan. "Glad you called, and one bit of final advice. Don't do anything about Ferago until tomorrow. If he's as susceptible to violence and as yellow as you think—" Bowers shook his head before withdrawing it, "well—if he talked tonight, you might be just as sorry about it as I'd be. Good night."

"Good night," said Satan lightly.

But he was a bit worried as he carefully descended the steps to the hall below, and passed down it and out onto the street. There had seemed something ominous in John A. Bowers' "Good night." Just what, Satan couldn't lay a finger to. It was queer how it got him, though. And Satan was not given to conjuring up queer psychic warnings. But he was glad that, unknown to Mary Rogers, he had placed a private detective in her tenement house that night. His name was Finneran, and he was a good man.

6

SATAN'S DUTY

BACK AT THE precinct Captain Mullery was pacing his room when Satan walked in. He didn't wait.

He blurted right out with it.

"It's happened," he said. "Quicker than you thought. A private dick called Finneran was gunned out—"

"And Mary—Mary Rogers. What of her?" Satan fairly shot the words at Mullery.

"First thing I asked when the report came in. Ginsburg, on duty there, went back and had a look-see. The shooting took place on the stairs. All the tenants accounted for but—"

"But Mary, eh?"

"Well—she wasn't in her rooms." And getting up, Mullery took Satan by the shoulders. "No use to lie to you," he said evenly. "Her bed had been slept in; her room was— Well—she's gone, Satan. You've crossed the big boy, Bowers, just once too often."

"All right," Satan said very slowly. "Now—I'm going to kill him."

"That won't bring the girl back. Besides, you can't—won't be able to even see him, armed. There, there—Frank.

Things are not so bad. It wouldn't be to Bowers' interest to harm her, for you've got Ferago."

"Yes." Satan, was trying to think, and failing miserably—except for thoughts of violence, sudden death, and the huge body of John A. Bowers sprawled upon, the thick-rugged floor, with a purple hole in his forehead.

"Well"—Captain Mullery stroked his chin—"they've got the girl, that's certain. You've got Ferago. It's the very system that you object to. You've got to give as well as take, Satan. I've preached it to you for years." And more kindly, as he reached up and put a hand on a broad shoulder, "Sometimes, Satan, it's a guy like me, wanting to be a captain; wanting to give a girl a good education. Maybe another guy wants a high-priced car. It's the system. It's the racket that crooked politics, stupid laws, and human nature caused.

"Sometimes it's just an ambitious lawyer digging out coin for a judgeship. Now—it's a man for a woman. You let Ferago go, and Bowers returns Mary. It's an even break, Satan. There—there, I know you've watched over her since she was a kid. I'll see Bowers. Oh, he won't admit it, of course—but we'll come to an understanding that Mary goes free when Ferago goes free. I'll fix it for you."

"Fix it for me!" Satan suddenly jerked his shoulder free and faced Mullery, his green eyes flashing like thin points of sparkling steel beneath an electric drill. "I don't need a 'fix.' I never had a 'fix.' I'll get Bowers, and I'll—"

"Yes, I know," said the older man quietly. "You'll kill him. That's all right if you see him—see him, armed. He's fussy about that." And when Satan only grinned evilly: "Oh, that's all right—when he wants to see a guy. But when a guy wants to see him, it's another matter again. This time, Satan, you've got to make a 'fix.' If you killed Bowers it wouldn't help the girl any. If Ferago stays in, Bowers gets the juice. You ain't aiming to give him any choice—except how he dies." Captain Mullery shrugged his shoulders. "Besides, you've got to get him before he gets you, and either way Mary— It's a tough spot for a cop—a cop with an honest record."

Satan looked up quickly. If he had suspected sarcasm in the captain's voice, he found none in his face. But Captain Mullery was studying Satan carefully. The man of iron. The man who lived for nothing but to hunt criminals. The man who could not be bought, frightened, or swerved by any influence from his duty! "Duty." Well—Mullery had always thought, with others, that that word did not fit Satan Hall at all. "Passion," would have been a better word, or perhaps "obsession." But the real word was in none of these. The Commissioner had called it a "fetish."

"Well," said Mullery, "what are you going to do? Let Ferago go?"

"I can't—I can't." Satan's voice was very husky, and then very low. "I want to. I should. But I can't."

"WHY NOT?" MULLERY stuck his thumbs in his vest. He had never seen Satan suffer before. Had often wondered, when the big moment came, just how it would hit the man. Now—well—he had always half hoped for such a time, when he could talk to Satan as man to man—show him how his ideas didn't always fit, and let him know how the shoe felt when it pinched the other fellow. And Mullery was surprised.

It wasn't a question of honor—duty—loyalty to the force

or the citizens he was paid to protect. No, Mullery had never looked on Satan as an honestly scrupulous man. He could picture Satan right now as shoving a gun against the back of Bowers' head and pulling the trigger. It was something else. It was—well—just as Satan said. He couldn't do it. And Mullery wasn't sure if he was facing a great strength or a great weakness—or perhaps, after all, a simple superstition. But he tried to make Satan see the thing right—make it look good to him.

"It isn't as if you were betraying your trust," he said. "You were going to let Ferago go if he squealed on Bowers. What's the difference whether he talks now or later?" And when Satan looked at him sharply, "Maybe he won't even talk at all. Anyway, there's others that may know about the murder of the old watchman by Bowers. You'll only be delaying things a little." And as Satan shook his head and looked blankly past him, "Well—hell! It ain't my job to argue with you against your duty. I hardly know the girl. If she ain't worth doing a little irregular—"

"I think more of her than I do of my own life." Satan threw out the words. "You can't understand. I can't understand, myself. I want Bowers for murder. I've got him. I've— Don't you see? If he was to kill her tonight, I'd have to go through with it. And I love her as much as you love that kid—that daughter of yours."

"Maybe." Captain Mullery shrugged his shoulders. "But you've got a damn funny way of showing it. If it was my kid, I'd have Ferago out in five minutes. 'I could not love you half so much, loved I not honor more' may make a damn nice song in a drawing room, but it won't do Mary Rogers any good in Bowers' hands." And suddenly standing on

his toes and almost shouting the words at Satan, "Well—
what the hell are you going to do, instead of standing there
making grimaces?"

"I'm going," said Satan very slowly, "straight to Bowers
and ask him just where Mary is." And seeing the sneer of
derision on Mullery's face, "And he's going to tell me."

"Tell you! You're a fool and a conceited ass. You love
the girl and won't sacrifice a little personal glory to save
perhaps her life—or more than life. And Bowers—Bowers,
who controls half the lower city. Bowers, who fears neither
man, woman nor devil!" A jeering note came into Mullery's
voice. "You're going to make him tell where the girl is—tell
you nicely, so you can take him up to the Big House and
fry him. You're going to make him tell, so—"

Satan was walking toward the door when he turned
suddenly, took two quick steps and stood before Captain
Mullery. Mullery's words died on his lips, his jaw fell
slightly and his left hand clutched at his throat, while his
right felt fumblingly—uncertainly—almost involuntarily
toward the drawer of the desk that held his service automatic. And that hand trembled. He was looking into a face
of such diabolic fury that for a moment he did not think
it could be human. A hatred so intense that it seemed to
take on life, as if it darted out of those green malignant orbs
and was a tangible, living thing in the room before him.

Captain Mullery's eyes bulged, in—well—not in fear.
Probably—more a horror than anything else. The thin
straight lips of Satan moved evilly—yes, evilly, to the bulging eyes of Mullery. And Satan spoke.

"Wouldn't you tell me—wouldn't you tell me, knowing I wanted to know!" For a moment Satan's hands went

into the air. For a moment Captain Mullery felt that two threatening talons were sweeping toward his throat. And Satan turned suddenly and was gone.

For a long minute Captain Mullery stood by the desk. Then he drew a hand across his forehead, snapped the moisture from his knuckles, and taking a deep breath threw open the door and walked into the main room. The lieutenant behind the desk spoke.

"What you doing to Satan, Cap? He just left. No fooling about his name. The devil's in him all right."

"You're telling me, Mac." Captain Mullery's laugh made the lieutenant look up. It was like a coal shovel scraping the cellar floor.

7

SLOW STEPS

JOHN A. BOWERS was rubbing his hands together as he sat behind his shining flat desk. He smiled confidently at Carpey Marks.

"Satan will be along to see me, Carpey. There's no doubt of that. But this time he'll be wanting to see me—not me, him. Search him. Strip him to the skin if necessary, but be sure he enters this room unarmed. No sleeve gun; no tiny automatic in the trouser leg. Even make sure of his fountain pen, if he carries one."

Carpey Marks nodded his approval, then frowned.

"If he puts up a stink, tries to shoot his way in, will we let him have it? You've got to have him alive for the Ferago spring."

"No—no." Bowers closed his little eyes and tapped the telephone pointedly. "While you were slipping the girl across town I did a little phone work. No one but Satan knows the two witnesses who promised to put the finger on Ferago. Satan promised them not to tell anyone. He's kept that promise." Bowers frowned. "If he had even told the Commissioner I'd know it. My information comes from a reliable source—a lad who has to talk to me. A lad who made one slip. A well thought of lad. But that slip would give him a mighty long stretch. These honest guys, Carpey—these church guys are like us, only they ain't got the nerve and they ain't recognized as public enemies. Now—"

"Then Satan gets the heat. That's it, eh?"

"That is just it." Bowers nodded. "But he don't get it downstairs. He gets it here—right in this room, see? I want to talk to him first. I want—"

"You want to see him die, eh?" Carpey nodded. He could understand that and appreciate that. Satan had been a thorn in Bowers' side for some time. Besides, there was the girl.

"Right!" said Bowers. "I'll take his life and his woman. No—no, it ain't so dangerous. He's talking all over his mouth right now about knocking me over. I'm a big man—a strong man. There'll be a struggle, and I'll shoot him with his own gun. See?"

And when Carpey's eyes went up, and he did not see:

"Hell! You'll bring me up his rod. I'll get him to talk, name them witnesses. I'll ride him with what will happen to Mary Rogers if he don't talk—which won't be no kidding. Then, after he talks, I'll go over and shoot him through the stomach—close like—maybe twice. If we can plant his body uptown, all right—we'll let it ride that way. If we can't—well—then the story of the struggle and—"

"Why in the stomach?" Carpey was of a practical turn of mind.

"It hurts like hell, in the stomach," said Bowers simply. "And I want it to hurt like hell."

"You think he'll come up here without a rod?"

"Sure—" said Bowers. "It's his woman. He'll want to make a deal."

"Okay, boss." Carpey stroked his chin. "I was only thinking that—that Satan might not come, and—"

Both men turned together. The little light was flickering. **"THAT," SAID BOWERS,** "is Satan. Go fetch him up. No hardware—and slip me his rod at the door." John A. Bowers rubbed his hands together. Things were working fine. Satan never would suspect, at least the full significance of his reception. Just a "fix" was what he'd think; a little deal. The girl free for Ferago free. As for the killing. Well, that would be a natural outcome. It wouldn't be hard to find witnesses who'd swear Satan was looking for a chance to get Bowers. Good witnesses. It wouldn't look so bad along the Avenue either. Bowers beating Satan to the kill! Satan, the fastest, the most ruthless. A killer. A—

And Bowers stepped quickly to the door.

"Carpey," he said, "be sure about that gun. Be sure he ain't—"

"Don't worry," Carpey threw back over his shoulder. "He won't come up here armed. Not him."

"And Carpey." Bowers clutched at his lieutenant's arm. Despite his assurance he wiped tiny beads of perspiration from his forehead with a large linen handkerchief. "It looks sure, doesn't it? You'll stay in the room, hand on your gun— just as a witness to the attack, you know."

"Yeah, I know." Carpey nodded. And what's more, he'd keep a hand on that gun. "Satan'll be a fool to come up."

"Other guys have been fools over a woman. Go on." And unconsciously stating the fear in his own heart, "There ain't no other way. It's Satan's life or mine."

"Yeah," said Carpey, as he started down the hall. "If you'd take my advice you'd let me plug him in the back on the stairs."

"No—no." Bowers shook his head. But after Carpey had disappeared around the bend in the hallway he opened his mouth twice to call him back. Then, with a shrug of his shoulders, he returned to his private office, rearranged the light over the big overstuffed chair, and opening a small cabinet took out a bottle of whisky.

It was a long drink and Bowers took it neat, shook his head, blew out his cheeks and shook his head again. Somehow, Satan got under a guy's skin. That charmed life of his—those slow, measured steps—his quickness with a gun. He'd had the breaks, that was all. Yet Bowers did himself another drink and straightened slightly. Quickness with a gun, eh? That wouldn't do a lad much good if he didn't have a gun.

John A. Bowers laughed a bit at that and paced the room. He guessed, in his day, he was as quick as Satan ever was—maybe quicker. And now—his right hand shot under his left armpit and out again. He looked now at the flat bit of blue steel. Pretty fast that. Damn good and fast, when the other lad didn't have any rod.

No—the thing was in the bag. Satan, the feared Satan. Satan, the killer. Just like *that,* he'd go out. He'd die as others had died. With a bellyful of lead. Satan, the same as others. Yeah—all guys with a bellyful of lead die. No difference. But would he come? That was it. Wouldn't he—? But he couldn't guess the truth. Still—

And Bowers stopped pacing the room and listened. Down the hall, outside, was coming the steady tread of feet—even, slow beats. Just a single pair of feet. What about Carpey? What the hell did Carpey mean by letting him walk that way? Was it possible that Carpey wasn't with him? Could Satan have—? John A. Bowers dabbed at his forehead.

One, two, three more steps—then silence. And a rap on the door. Just a single rap, but a peculiar one. Bowers sighed with relief. It was Carpey Marks.

"Yeah!" said Bowers. "Okay, Carpey. Come in."

8

UNARMED

THE DOOR OPENED and Satan Hall stood in the doorway. Bowers' little eyes slipped over his shoulders and his tenseness slackened somewhat. Behind Satan was Carpey Marks. Bowers nodded, but involuntarily his right hand played across his vest, his fingers just under his jacket.

And Satan walked across the room and straight to the big chair with the light over it. And the feet were still slow and measured. Bowers felt a desire to count—one, two, three—but he didn't. He liked the way Satan dropped into the big chair. He was going to be peaceful then. Follow the custom that everyone who visited Bowers knew about.

"Well—" Bowers crossed to Carpey, took the gun he slipped him, and going to his desk sat down behind it. He looked at Carpey and nodded when he closed and locked the door. He liked, too, the way Carpey's right hand was sunk into his pocket. He even rubbed his hands together after he carefully laid Satan's gun in his desk drawer.

Satan didn't speak for a minute, then he jerked a thumb toward Carpey.

"Is our talk to be private, or do you want that punk to listen in?"

Carpey Marks straightened and his right jacket pocket bulged. He was not an imaginative man. He blurted out:

"Can that stuff, Satan. Can that stuff."

Satan put slanting, green orbs on him.

"I'm marking you, Carpey," he said. "You see, when Mary Rogers disappeared Bowers was right here with me, and you're his—" Satan bit at his lip and gripped at the arms of the chair, but he didn't speak further.

"Come—come!" Bowers didn't like Satan's hostile attitude. It didn't fit in with his idea of things. He tried his dignity; a line he culled from the life of—well—some lad he'd read about. "Why am I indebted to you for this visit? We've closed up downstairs and I was just—"

"All right," said Satan. "I want to know where the girl is—where Mary Rogers is. And I want to know now."

"Rogers—Mary Rogers?" Bowers raised his eyebrows and looked at Carpey. "Not— She isn't the girl I wanted to help; offered the cigarette job downstairs to. Don't tell me she's disappeared. But then, that's youth; that's—"

"I'll come to my point," said Satan slowly. "If you don't tell me where she is, I'm going to kill you—Bowers."

"Really!" Bowers tried to smile, but it was not very successful. There was such a deadly earnestness about the man; a feeling that he spoke the truth despite the fact that he sat there unarmed. "You don't think I know where the girl is. But, I see—and you're right. I meet a lot of people— see a lot of people, and it's just possible that I could learn where she is. You want a favor, eh?" Bowers leaned forward now. "You want me to do something for you, and in return you'll do something for me."

"No—" Satan shook his head. "If you don't want to die—tell me where the girl is."

"And, of course, Ferago goes free. That's it, isn't it?"

"No!" said Satan, "that is not it. I know you had the girl taken and I know why. To make a deal with me. And I know Carpey did the actual kidnaping, because he's the one you trust—and he wasn't here when I left, earlier. I know."

"If you know so much, it's a wonder you didn't call a cop; a real cop," Carpey sneered from the door.

Satan turned his head slowly and looked at him. Then he looked back at Bowers.

"What goes for you goes for the punk, too, Bowers. I haven't much time. Where's the girl?"

"I think," said Bowers, who liked to cloak his words, "that Mary Rogers is disappointed in you. She told me you won't see her again until Ferago is free, and you tell me the names of the two witnesses who saw that—that killing five years ago. I want a good lawyer to question them, and see who paid them to lie. I"—and as Satan would have cut in—"no—no, you want plain speaking. The price of the girl's freedom is just that."

Satan's hands dug deep down at his sides. His fingers seemed to clutch spasmodically at the heavy upholstery of the chair. At least, it seemed that way to Bowers, who couldn't see that far down from behind the desk. When Satan spoke, his voice seemed tired, yet there was a certain under-current to it—as if, far back, an obstruction held back pent-up force. A force that Bowers could feel, but could not lay a name to.

"You misunderstand me, Bowers. I'm not threatening to watch for an opportunity to kill you—hunt you down like a rat, in some alley. When I say I'm going to kill you, I mean just that. On the open street—in the lobby of a hotel—at Forty-second Street and Broadway. In plain words, the first time I see you, no matter what the place. Even in this room here."

"So that's it, eh?" Bowers looked at Carpey Marks and moved his right hand nearer to the open drawer. "So that's it."

"Yes," said Satan, "that is it. That's why I came to see you. I wanted to let you know. It will be the first time I ever shot a man down in cold blood, but it's fact just the same. I'll give you time to talk—while I count ten."

BOWERS LEANED OVER his desk now, his left arm upon it, his right hand in the drawer, clutching Satan's gun. His little eyes blinked evilly, his thick lips slipped back—and he spoke half through his teeth.

"So you'll count ten, eh? Well—begin. You're right, Satan. There'll be death at the end of it. Death for you. You've tried to hang something on me for years. You've made it personal because of a woman—a girl. Well—I always get what I want. Now—you're just a fool, like any other dick. You've threatened me. Every cop along the Avenue knows that. Mullery knows you came here tonight. They'll know you came to threaten me—to kill me. Get that! Understand that! But they won't know that you were fool enough to meet me unarmed." He waved Satan's gun across the desk. "This is your rod. There's a struggle—a shot or two. See?"

Satan nodded his head very slowly as he looked at Bowers. There was no fear in Bowers' face now. Just elation, hatred—and perhaps the lust to kill. John A. Bowers, the big racketeer, was simply Johnny Bowers again. Johnny Bowers, the gangster and gunman, who had hunted his enemies in the dark alleys of the city.

Satan looked at the gun in Bowers' hand and spoke very slowly and very distinctly. Bowers was rising from behind the desk. The gun which he held in his hand was dropping slowly from a line on Satan's head to a line on his chest—to his stomach.

"It won't work." Satan half shook his head. "You see, I sort of suspected you'd work it this way—with my gun. And since I knew you wouldn't want me up here, heeled—why—I took the cartridges out and—"

"You did, eh?" Bowers sneered. "Well—I won't have so much trouble finding another gun around here." He half glanced at Satan's gun, in his own right hand. "You're on the spot, Satan. You're going to get it right through the stomach. And then—Mary and me—or Carpey, if she don't—"

And it happened.

Satan's whole face changed suddenly. He threw himself out of the big chair. The green eyes had again become malignant, burning things of hatred. Bowers saw a claw-like left hand darting across the space before him. He dropped the gun he held and shot his right hand to his left armpit. Then he saw Satan's right hand, and the thing in it. He screamed to Carpey. Hope, fear, uncertainty—and, finally, stark terror made the words a screech in his throat.

"Give it— Let him have it, Carpey."

Bowers' little eyes bulged till they nearly popped out of his head as the shot came. He saw Carpey jerk the gun from his pocket, heard the shot—two of them, almost at once. He saw too the spit of orange blue flame close to his face, saw Satan's body half twist and his arm move across his chest. Then he saw the tiny hole in Carpey Marks' forehead; saw it widening before Carpey spun and crashed to the floor.

It seemed to Bowers that it all happened in a split second; in that fraction of a second when he dropped Satan's gun and clutched for his own, under his armpit. Yes—clutched for it and reached it—and held it—held it just so, tightly in the shoulder holster. For at the very second he gripped his Luger, he had seen the blue steel in Satan's right hand—the blue steel and snub nose of a rod, and even the belching flame as Satan swung his hand across his chest and "got" Carpey.

Bowers cried out once more as he saw in that face before him all that Captain Mullery had seen a short time before. Then Satan's hand had gone up and down, the barrel of the gun cutting deep across Bowers' forehead—across the bridge of his nose and down to his mouth.

Bowers squealed out something as the gun struck again, then sank slowly to his knees. The next instant Satan was around the desk. Fingers were reaching for Bowers' throat. Satan was talking softly, as if to himself.

"Mullery said you wouldn't tell. Mullery said you wouldn't tell—and burn. Somehow, Bowers, I think you're going to be very glad to—to burn."

Then long talons sank deeply into Bowers' thick flabby throat—and Satan laughed hoarsely.

9

BEHIND THE DOOR

IN ANSWER TO Satan's call Captain Mullery sent a detail of police to the house on East Eleventh Street. Then he burned up the tires on the police car driving to the John A. Bowers Athletic Club.

A few waiters and the club manager pointed hysterically to the floor above. None of John A. Bowers' strong-armed men were present. Above, where the men pointed—just a great silence. A young waiter sat down on the lower step and put his head in his hands and wailed:

"Oh, my God! Oh, my God!"

Captain Mullery looked up the dimly lit stairs, hesitated a moment, then waived his men to stay below as he slowly mounted the stairs—his gun drawn in his hand, his feet moving as if by a motor he did not control. The silence of the men below had been more terrifying and suggestive of what had happened in that room above than if they had spoken for hours.

Captain Mullery shuddered slightly as he reached the door to John A. Bowers' room, raised his hand to rap—then pushed his body to one side before he brought his knuckles softly against the highly polished wood.

"It's me—Mullery," he said, and was surprised at the hollowness of his own voice.

A moment of silence from within. Then the tread of feet. Not the measured tread, but uncertain, faltering steps. Captain Mullery raised his gun, then dropped it again as Satan spoke from behind that door.

"The girl—Mary—she was there? She's all right?"

"Yeah. Sure Open the door, Satan. Come—come! Now open the door," Mullery said again, as he heard a body lurch against it.

Twice Mullery called again before Satan answered him.

"You gave the cops the phone number here—the private phone?" And as Mullery cut in with a torrent of words, "Wait!"

Captain Mullery pleaded and Captain Mullery cursed, and talked of police discipline—and went downstairs and told a story that he could never remember afterwards to the medical examiner, and for once took the lip of a young interne.

But Captain Mullery did "wait," until—listening at the door of Bowers' private office, he heard the telephone ring.

After that he thought that he heard someone talking, but he could not be sure. Then feet crossed the room— stopped—and a chair fell over. Then feet again; lurching feet. A body against the door. The lock was turned—then Satan was in his arms—and blood was on his uniform. Mullery could not see exactly where Carpey's bullet had gone through the side of Satan's neck.

The medical examiner took one look, and said sarcastically to the young interne as he stood over Carpey Marks:

"This one is mine—and the other, yours. As for the big

guy with the hole in his neck, if he don't get attention quick there'll be—"

And forgetting his anger as he recognized Satan, whom he had always greatly admired, he crossed the floor hurriedly and went to work to stop the flow of the blood.

"Five minutes more and you'd have bled to death," he told Satan as he turned to the interne. "As for Bowers there—well—there was quite a struggle, and he got very badly handled—no worse than Detective Hall, though."

"No, perhaps not," said the interne as Bowers was placed on the stretcher. "But Detective Hall was just a little more systematic in—in his battle."

SATAN HALL FELT better the next morning, when Captain Mullery sat at his bedside and told him that Mary Rogers wanted to see him.

"And Bowers?" asked Satan, "He'll live—live to—?"

"Yes—" Mullery nodded. "He'll live—to burn."

"To burn!" Satan licked his lips. "That's part of the police system. The system! It don't seem worth the expense to keep a man alive to—to kill him. I could have saved the State a lot of money."

"You nearly did," said Mullery. "Now—tell me just what happened. Oh—I don't mean afterwards—after Carpey died. But before. It seems gospel that you went up there unarmed. How—?"

"Well," said Satan, "Bowers was to kill me with my own gun they took from me downstairs. And I told him the gun was unloaded. That gave me a moment's chance—and I took it. Shot Carpey; struck down—"

"Yes—yes, I know all that. But that gun of yours was found fully loaded where Bowers dropped it. How did you get another gun? On the level, Satan, I can't believe the story that you grabbed it from Bowers' hand. It's all right for the record—but for me— Somehow or other you got a gun in there with you."

"No." Satan shook his head, but he smiled. "They searched me too well. I went up those stairs and into that room unarmed. You see, I wanted to see Bowers—not Bowers see me. I had to see it his way. That is, the last time. Earlier in the evening he wanted to see me, so things were different. That time I went in heeled, but—"

"But—" Mullery leaned forward eagerly.

"But I came out unarmed, Subconsciously, maybe, I had it in my mind—when I asked Lieutenant Mac about that light and the big chair. But I don't think I planned it until—well—I thought that maybe the next time *I'd* want to see Bowers, and have to be searched. So I shoved that gun down behind the cushion in the big chair under the light."

"You took a chance," said Captain Mullery. "It must have taken nerve to jerk that gun out, with two covering you. It must have been a tough moment."

"Not then," said Satan wearily, "not then. The tough moment was—was— It was hard not to kill Bowers when I had him like that—the hole in my neck, to go on the witness stand with. But I didn't kill him—and I don't know, Mullery, if that was strength or weakness on my part. Send Mary in."

SATAN'S LAW

When Detective Satan Hall Hunted Crooks,
He Made His Own Law. And Under That
Law the Sentence Was Always—Death!

1

DETECTIVE SATAN HALL sat in one of Captain Logan's stiff backed chairs and cleaned his service guns with methodical care. His green eyes seemed even brighter; the slits they looked through even narrower as he clicked home the cartridge clips and laid the guns with a sigh upon the table. Then he smiled, but the smile seemed rather to accentuate the V shape of the hair upon his forehead, the sharpness of his ears, and the decided sardonic point to his chin.

Satan was still staring with satisfaction upon his work when Captain Logan walked in. Logan was a big man, whose shoulders had crept up—or his head settled down—so that his neck was lost somewhere between the two. He had a huge head, a large, coarse mouth, and a great, thick nose. But his eyes were small in contrast to the rest of his features. They were two round, mean little brown balls, which—if you were to accept Logan's word for it—threw abject terror into those they settled on.

Logan shot a bit of cigar from between his teeth, eyed the guns upon the table and spoke in a deep, throaty voice.

"Business, eh?" And when Satan did not answer, he jerked a thick thumb toward the two guns and repeated. "Looks like business."

Satan fired once

Detective Hall nodded slowly, stuck a cigarette into his mouth, put a match to the end of it, and finally said:

"You might call it that."

"Rattigan?" Logan's voice was affable enough, but his eyes were rounder and smaller and meaner.

"Maybe," Satan half agreed. But there was nothing to read in his face, and Logan prided himself on reading faces.

For a minute or two Captain Logan paced the room, then he paused before Satan, spread his heavy legs far apart, took the cigar from his mouth, and pointing it at Satan's middle, said:

"You've got one thing to remember, Hall; one thing to keep in mind. You're working out of this precinct now—out of my precinct. We have no favorites here—no pets here. Them that know Logan know that. You're working

*The sharp, staccato notes of
the machine gun ripped out*

out of my precinct now." Logan felt that the show-down
was coming and was willing to force matters.

"Sure!" Satan smiled, or at least his lips parted, and
Logan imagined it was meant for a smile. "I'll remember
that, Logan. You remember it, too. I'm working out of the
precinct—not in it."

"Yeah." Logan stroked one of his flabby chins. "The
Commissioner's pet, they call you. One precinct after
another." A sneer came into Logan's voice. "The hard boiled
dick makes good where the system fails! The Lone Wolf
of the Department the papers call you. But if you knew
what some of the boys call you! A dirty, rotten spy. A two
timing—" Logan had leaned over the desk now; his thick
lips had parted and were quivering; his eyes were round
points of twin steel. When Logan started to have his say
he had it out. He was a hard man; a tough man; a brutal,
unrelenting man—yet he paused.

THERE WAS SOMETHING in Satan's face that stopped
him. For the life of him Logan couldn't tell what it was;

wouldn't admit it if he could tell. But for a moment he saw all that he had heard about Satan; all that had given Satan his name on the Force. He didn't think that Satan's face had changed, though it must have. He couldn't see that Satan's lips had moved any. He thought it must be Satan's eyes. Not the outward, physical appearance of them, but something back in their sinister, green depths. But Logan knew that he had looked through and behind those eyes and seen something that he had never seen in a man before.

Logan was a brave man. There was nothing behind those green balls that struck him with fear. Logan feared no man. At first he couldn't lay a name to it, then he thought it must be horror. Anyway, Logan drew back with a soft curse, and rubbed a hand across a moist forehead. He felt as if he had looked down into the depths of hell. Sinister, cruel, malignant, unnameable things had glared out of those eyes at him. And now Satan was coming to his feet. Very slowly he was stretching his six odd feet above the floor.

Then a great hand with long, delicate fingers shot out, rested for a moment on the guns upon the table. Logan's eyes bulged. Satan seemed to make a single motion from the table toward his coat—just a single quick motion—and both guns were gone and Satan's arms hung at his sides. But Logan knew—knew, just as if Satan had thrown back his coat and shown him, that both those guns were now parked beneath each armpit.

Satan was speaking.

"So that's what some of them call me, eh?" Satan was slowly caressing a pointed chin. "Some of them, Logan—some of them." And leaning suddenly forward—"You, for instance."

"I'm only repeating what I've heard," Logan said, somewhat stiffly. He would have given a month's pay to say that they were his thoughts, but the words would not come.

"I see. Well—I'll be moving," Satan went on slowly, as Logan, somewhat recovered, set those gimlet eyes upon Satan in a final half hearted effort to stare him down.

As Satan turned toward the door Logan stretched out a hand and placed it on his shoulder.

"After all, you're a cop, Satan. Like Patrolman Shay, myself, the Inspector, even. You got certain privileges that the rest of us can't quite understand. You've got information through the Commissioner's secret channel, that I don't have access to. I've given you the run of the house, all the information you wanted. It wouldn't help me or the boys none if you pulled off a—a stunt right under our noses. You might—might—" Logan gulped, "give a guy a break."

"All right." Satan nodded very slowly. "I'm a cop—just a cop, and it isn't pleasant or profitable to step over authority. I'll tell you this. It's Rattigan and Gunner Swartz, and someone—someone else."

"SOMEONE ELSE!" LOGAN let his little eyes wander about the ceiling. "You can't do anything with Rattigan. I've raked him over the coals a dozen or more times. He's got connections; got a good mouthpiece. He's a high class racketeer."

"You didn't get him for the right thing."

"And the right thing?" Logan was slightly sarcastic.

"Murder. An accomplice to murder."

"And the real murderer?" Logan was puffing on his cigar now. There was indifference in his voice, but his little gimlet eyes never left the green, sinister ones of Satan. He felt that the long awaited break was coming.

"It isn't pleasant," Satan spoke very softly, "but you've asked for a 'break' and I'll give it to you." A long finger came out and pounded slowly against Logan's chest. "Captain Logan, put your house in order."

Logan laughed hoarsely.

"You're not referring to those apartments that I easily explained before the commission!"

"Your rich brother." Satan sneered. "But there are some things your rich brother won't be able to shoulder for you."

"And they?"

"A rotten conscience, Logan. The dead eyes of the women who killed themselves. The living accusations of mothers and sisters. Oh, don't grin. You've been a copper long enough; you've played the game long enough to know the truth. You can't get away with it."

Logan gripped Satan by the shoulder and swung him viciously around. He didn't think of what was back of the green eyes now. Anger shook his whole body. Hate blazed in his little brown eyes. He shot the words through the side of his mouth. He didn't bother to deny Satan's accusation. He didn't try to laugh it off. They were alone in that room. He spoke out his mind—at least, enough of it.

"It's not a new story." He had hard work making the words articulate. "But it's the first time it's been spoken out like that. It's been hinted before; gone into before. There was—" And Logan stopped short, biting his lip.

"Yeah—" said Satan, "I know. Clarey and Cohen. Honest cops, both of them—and they died hard. Cohen, the night you were dining with Inspector Frank. Clarey, while you were at your sister's in Peekskill. Rattigan and Swartz gunned him out. All very clever, Logan. But, in the end, all very futile."

Logan had stepped forward now and fastened the thick fingers of his left hand tight into the lapels of Satan's coat as he put those little round eyes hard on Satan's green ones. His voice shook when he spoke; every word breathed a threat—a threat that Satan must know was not an idle one.

"Suppose it were all true—every word of it, what then? What would you do? What could you do? Knowledge and evidence are two different things. I'm marking you, Satan. I'm looking at you, Satan."

"Well—you can keep those eyes for frightening women and children. You asked me to talk out, and I did. There'll be evidence. A witness who saw Cohen die."

"All right. All right." Saliva ran over the edge of Logan's thick lips. "Remember, Satan, I'm often asked to dine with Inspector Frank, and my sister at Peekskill is glad to see me any time. She entertains a lot. Good, sound, substantial country people. I don't know why you talked. You're just a fool, I suppose."

"Maybe," Satan shrugged his shoulders, "it isn't pleasant for the Force. It gets me in the stomach every time I read about a copper gone wrong. It shouldn't, because there aren't an honester bunch of men as a whole in any profession." With a single downward motion Satan knocked Logan's fingers from his coat. "You know the racket, Logan—you know the law. Not the law of the State, but the law of the criminal." Satan jerked a hand forward and pounded a finger against Logan's chest. "The finger's on you, Logan," he said simply. "The finger's on you. I'm out to get you, Logan."

Then he turned abruptly on his heel and passed out of the little rear room and by the police desk.

Logan hesitated a moment, wiped his forehead with a big linen handkerchief, looked at the phone once or twice and finally, lifting the receiver, gave a number to the operator in a low, hollow voice.

"It's me, Rattigan," he said softly. "He's leaving now. Is Swartz ready?"

"Ready, boss," came a whispered answer. "The car's around the corner."

Captain Logan sighed easily as he dropped the receiver back on the hook. Detective Satan Hall would be attended to.

2

MACHINE-GUNNED

SATAN STOOD FOR some time chatting idly with the lieutenant on the bench, then he passed out under the light, to the street. He cupped a hand and felt a few drops of rain spatter into it. Turning up his coat collar he proceeded slowly down the street.

Just why had he tipped his hand to Captain Logan? There were two reasons. One was the hope that Logan might pack up and leave the country. The Department could smother that, and perhaps, after all, it was the best. Satan's life was the Force—the hunting of men—loyalty to the badge which he wore. Neither friendship, money, nor threats could drive him from his purpose. That was why, after ten years as the most relentless hunter of men in the system, he was still a first grade detective. The other reason! Well—Logan might be frightened into some kind of action. Action! Satan's right hand slipped beneath his coat. He liked action.

At the corner Satan ran into Patrolman Shay—three years on the Force. A young man soft of skin, the enthusiasm for his job still sparkling in his clear blue eyes, still in the strong eager fingers that gripped his night stick. And now Satan saw the shadows beneath those eyes; noted the way teeth drew in the lower lip. He stretched out a hand when Shay would have passed on; held him so a moment; looked straight into the soft blue eyes. Satan was like that once. New—enthusiastic—raw. Ready to rush any place for the honor—the glory of the Force.

Patrolman Shay reddened slightly but did not speak.

"Anything to say?" Satan said abruptly.

"About what?" The red deepened and the upper teeth again took in the lower lip.

"About Cohen," Satan said almost viciously. "Stabbed to death in a back alley. A fine fellow, Cohen. A straight shooter, Cohen. A guy who knew too much. And you were off your beat; dragged off your beat by Logan."

"Afore God, Hall, I didn't know." There was a touch of horror in Shay's face. "Logan took me off. It was his order—his authority. I had to go, and now—"

"Now—" said Satan, "are you willing to go on the stand and swear to that?"

"I can't—I can't," Shay stammered. "I reported as on duty. Logan fixed it on the books. When Cohen 'went out' Logan thought it would look bad, my being off the beat. He told me to say nothing—more than hinted he'd deny his part in taking me off. They wouldn't believe me, Hall. They'd break me. I can't do it! My father was killed on the Force. My mother couldn't stand the disgrace that—"

"You can't hide a yellow streak behind the name of your mother," Satan said brutally. "You may be broken and you may not—but you'll be a man. The hooks are in Logan. I need your testimony. Your father wanted you to be a cop; your mother bred it into your bones. And now what? You're one of twenty thousand—twenty thousand of the

finest men that ever walked the streets. Twenty thousand
fine men, whose names stink to high heaven because of a
few—a few like Logan—a few like you, who are puppets
in Logan's hands."

"Don't—don't!" Shay half turned his head. "It's too late.
I'm in it now. And, Hall—" Shay looked furtively up and
down the street, "they've been watching you. They're afraid
of you. They're marking you." And in a voice that Hall
barely caught, "Logan's going—going to kill you. And you
can't get a single thing on Logan."

"Not a thing on him, eh?" Satan's green eyes sparkled
slightly. "But it's possible—just possible—that I might
kill Logan first."

And Satan moved quickly to the protection of a pole.
Over his shoulder he saw the shadow of the car; his sharp
ears had caught the sudden roar of the motor as a foot
pushes in the clutch and advances the gas.

IT HAPPENED. ABOVE the roaring motor were the sharp
staccato notes of a machine gun. He saw the black, belching nose of it from between curtains. He saw the white
face; the rat-like eyes and mouth below a peaked cap. Satan
fired once. Just a sudden quick movement of his right hand,
a single roar and a single spit of flame.

The machine gun came to sudden silence. The white face
seemed to be a shade whiter. Then red appeared over a thick
lower lip, and the face disappeared behind the curtain.

The clutch was released, the roar of the motor took on
life, and Satan stood on the sidewalk and emptied both his
guns into the rear of the fleeing car. He cursed softly. Then,
as the big car suddenly swerved, he smiled.

There was a crash as the juggernaut mounted the sidewalk, turned suddenly, just missing the stone balustrade of a brownstone front, careened across the sidewalk again, and striking a fire hydrant, jumped into the air and turned upon its side. Satan nodded as he watched it, and mechanically shoved fresh clips into his guns.

Logan was on the street now. A half dozen officers, hurriedly slipping into their coats—guns in their hands—were running by him, toward the overturned car. But Satan was kneeling beside Patrolman Shay, looking into his eyes. Satan had lived close to death and he knew. No coroner had to tell him. Shay was dead.

Satan straightened and half lifted his hat. A shadow came from behind him. He recognized Inspector Frank; saw him kneel beside Shay, lift Shay's hand and let it fall to the pavement again.

"Twenty-four, and dead," Inspector Frank said in a low voice. "What a bad break for the boy—what a bad break for his mother!"

Satan spoke half to himself, but Inspector Frank caught the words and puzzled over them for some time.

"What a good break for the boy—and what a fine break for his mother," was all that Satan said as he turned and walked toward the overturned car.

TWO MEN WERE dead. The man with the machine gun had been shot straight through the mouth. There was a bullet right through the back of the driver's head. Another gangster lay unconscious in the wreckage; a fourth had been thrown clear and was writhing on the sidewalk. Captain Logan was looking down at him, telling a sergeant he'd watch him.

Satan nodded down at the twisting gangster and said:

"Gunner Swartz. I wonder why he didn't work the type-writer." Then he turned and watched the cops drag the other man from the wreck.

"A good boy—Shay," he thought. "A good boy, swept up in the maelstrom of corruption by a single man."

Satan never posed as a super-detective. He admitted quite frankly that he wouldn't recognize a clew if he met it face to face. He didn't believe in hunches. If he wanted information he went straight to one of two dozen stool-pigeons and bought it. He believed in breaks and waited for them. Waited for them just so long, and then went out and stirred up his own. But he did believe in instinct. He didn't put it down to long association with the criminal. He put it down to instinct, and called it that. Living close to death, instinct warned him of danger. That is the only explanation of why he turned suddenly to face Logan—face Logan and Gunner Swartz, who lay upon the sidewalk. Gunner Swartz, whom Satan had distinctly heard Captain Logan tell a police sergeant he would watch.

And Logan was watching the gunner. Watching him with eager, unblinking little brown eyes. Watching him as Swartz steadied his shaking right hand with his left, and drew a bead about the middle of Satan's back with a jet black German Luger.

As Satan turned Swartz fired. That turn, saved Satan's life. Even in his condition, Gunner Swartz could not have missed such a perfect target as Satan's broad shoulders, not ten feet away from him. Gunner Swartz fired just once. The heavy caliber bullet tore through the sleeve of Satan's half raised arm, and leaving the tiniest red crevice across Satan's forehead passed on through his hat.

That was all of that. Gunner Swartz was chain lightning with a gun. But it is doubtful, even if he were on his feet and in the pink of condition, that he would have fired a second shot.

Satan's hand made a single sweep. There was a roar, and Gunner Swartz was dead, shot through the head.

"That's one for Clarey," Satan muttered, and he smiled.

For a moment Satan looked down at the dead body, the smoking gun still in his hand. Then he swung slowly on his heels and faced Captain Logan, those green eyes boring into the mean little brown ones.

Logan looked straight at that hard, pointed face; at the gun that those long strong fingers held—at a gun that was slowly rising; rising until the black snub nose had drawn a bead where an ordinary man would wear his heart.

Logan gasped once, tried to step back, and felt the stone balustrade against his shoulders. He opened his mouth to speak but no words came. He had seen death in a man's face before. He saw it now in the face of Satan. Saw it mostly in the hand that held that gun; in the long finger that caressed the trigger; in the nose of the automatic itself. Then, as the sweat rolled down his forehead, a voice spoke. A distant, far away voice that Logan did not recognize, then realized that the voice was his own.

"That—that," Logan's voice was saying, "will be murder."

And Satan grinned, and his green eyes shone, and the gun dropped to his side. The spell was broken. Inspector Frank had laid a hand upon his arm and was talking to him.

Satan nodded, and crossing the street with the inspector passed through the iron grating of the door of a speakeasy. They found seats in a dingy side booth.

3

THE HOLD OF THE PAST

INSPECTOR FRANK WAS a tall, loosely constructed man. He didn't believe in wasting words. He put his elbows on the table and said:

"Satan, what's the racket? Logan suspects that you're hunting up information for the investigation. I don't believe that. Logan would like to know where you stand. He wanted me to find out."

"He knows now." Satan moved his head as if it were on a wire. "He asked for the truth and got it."

Inspector Frank stiffened.

"I've done twenty-two years with the department. Logan's a good officer. We've all had temptations, and there are irregularities of course. It's part of the system. But he's an efficient officer. He has a record for cleaning up his district that stands out in the city. Logan has friends who'd stick to him in trouble," and very slowly—"who'd have to stick to him. Me, for instance. What do you think of me, Satan?"

"I don't think. I know. You're the straightest man on the Force."

"That's it." Frank nodded slowly. "The straightest man on the Force. I saw the possibilities in you years back, Satan, and dragged you off the pavement and put you in plain clothes. Now—" Inspector Frank leaned far over the table, "I'm not making a squawk; I'm not asking for favors. I'm simply stating facts. If you get Logan—you get me too."

"You!" Satan straightened. The thing seemed impossible.

"Yes. It goes back some years. But it's there just the same. It would break me the same as if it were yesterday." Inspector Frank laughed harshly. "Break Logan and you break me. You see, the past sometimes remains the present."

Satan's eyes became two slits.

"If Logan were dead," he said slowly, "he couldn't talk."

"That," said Frank, "would be murder. You're a killer, Satan, but you don't go in for murder. Besides—" and hunched shoulders shrugged, "Logan's a clever man. You've been at Rattigan's Park Avenue Casino; you've seen that safe. In the third drawer from the top, on the left, there's an envelope nicely labeled *Inspector Frank*. I saw it placed there and knew what it meant. Now—how big is it? Just what do you want Logan for?"

"I want him," said Satan slowly, "for the murder of Detective Cohen. For the murder of Cohen while Logan was having dinner with you."

Inspector Frank prided himself on his poker face. Emotion never showed there. But now that impenetrable countenance became readable. Fear, disgust, horror chased one another in quick succession across his face.

"I can't believe it," he said. And after a moment's pause, "I can't believe it."

"You've got to," said Satan. "Logan dined with you. Did he leave? Did he tell you you had to cover him on something—on murder?"

"Good God! No—not murder." Frank was on his feet, leaning on the table, breathing heavily. Satan cautioned him not to speak so loud. After a bit Frank said:

"Yes, Logan did leave me. But he's done that before. He was a careful man. He had to see Rattigan."

"He used you because your reputation for honesty and straight shooting is the best on the Force. And he didn't go to see Rattigan, but went straight to that alley—met Cohen and stabbed him to death."

"But why Cohen?"

"Because Cohen was working with me. Because Cohen had discovered that goods were being fenced through Jake Hearn. Because Cohen was to meet Mattie Hearn, Jake's daughter, and she was to talk—talk about Rattigan and Logan, though Cohen didn't suspect Logan then. That's why he died like he did—smiling. He still trusted his captain."

"But—Logan and—murder!"

"YES. LOGAN AND murder. Jake Hearn told Logan of the meeting of Cohen and Mattie. He didn't know that Mattie was going to talk; he simply thought Mattie would work Cohen into the racket. But Logan knew, and Logan killed him. Cohen told me he was to meet Mattie."

"Can you prove this?" Inspector Frank's hand clenched.

"Not a word of it," Satan said, truthfully enough. "I knew that Cohen was to hear something from Mattie—he told me that. She was to tell him the name of the big gun behind Rattigan. I knew it would be Logan, but Cohen didn't—else he'd have died with a gun in his hand. Cohen was quick."

"I can't believe it," Inspector Frank said dully. "Crooked, yes—but that Logan would go to murder, no."

"You know the racket. It always leads to murder. Logan had to kill, and he killed."

"Logan was gone half an hour—maybe, forty minutes." Inspector Frank was figuring mentally. "You prove that, Satan—and evidence against me or no evidence against me, I'll go on the stand and swear that Logan left me."

"No," Satan shook his head. "I'll do what I can for you, Frank—but Cohen was working for me. Clarey was working with me. We don't want others dragged into it. Just Logan and Rattigan. Why not take a vacation? In Mexico, maybe—until we see what breaks."

"No!" Frank's lips set tightly and his eyes knitted. "I've made my bed and I'll lie in it. I've never taken a run-out powder yet. I've been an honest cop for fifteen years." And thoughtfully, "There isn't any past in crime—just a present. I'll help you if it's true. How will you prove it?"

"By the evidence of an eyewitness to the murder."

"Someone saw it?"

"Yes. I found a glove in that alley, under a window. Mattie Hearn saw the murder. She's disappeared. Everyone in the underworld has orders from Rattigan to find her. But if I find her she'll talk. She loved Cohen. I've got to find her first."

"Yes, yes—that's right." Inspector Frank was talking with his head in his hands. "Logan asked me to put the dragnet out for Mattie Hearn. He—he— You think he wants to ship her out of the country?" But although those were Frank's words they were not his thoughts. Satan voiced his thoughts.

"They want to kill her," he said simply. "They wanted to kill me, and got Shay. Logan has to clean up the books, and only death will do it."

"God!" said Frank, "I could strangle him with my own hands. To think I covered him for murder—murder of one of my own boys!" And again, in a weak voice, "I don't believe it. I can't believe it. Logan says the Sicilian gang killed Cohen, and that Mattie Hearn will be found with a wire around her neck, strangled to death, like those other girls."

"That's right." Satan came to his feet and put a hand on the inspector's shoulder. "If Logan finds her, the wire will be there all right. I thought I'd let you see how it is. Take care of yourself."

Inspector Frank raised his hand and pressed the button as Satan left. Then he ordered a shot of rye and drank it neat.

"God!" he cried out inside himself, "if I'd only kept the record clean!" Inspector Frank was seeing the end of a glorious career. But he had no misgivings and no doubts as to his actions. He'd take the murderer of one of his boys down with him. The past, that he thought he had buried many years before, had crept up on him.

4

RATTIGAN GETS SLAPPED DOWN

SATAN WALKED DOWN to Sixth Avenue, hopped a taxi and ordered the driver straight to Jake Hearn's little pawnshop. He settled back in the seat and thought. He knew Jake fairly well, and his daughter, Mattie, slightly. And he felt that, like most of their race, Jake and Mattie in trouble would be drawn very tightly together. He felt certain that Jake would know Mattie's hideout—had even suggested it. Satan looked at his watch. It was exactly nine o'clock.

As he neared the shop Satan spoke to the driver.

"Stop here," he said. "I'll walk."

As he walked toward the shop Satan paused and stepped into a doorway. The back of the big black car before him attracted his attention. He peered at it closely through the drizzle. The license plates; the peculiar thickness of the glass; the straight, stiff back of the man behind the wheel. Then he nodded to himself, retraced his steps to the side street, passed down a few doors, entered an apartment, pressed a couple of bells at random, and when the latch clicked opened the door and stepped inside.

Satan moved fast, yet the measured steady tread of his feet never gave the impression of hurrying. Now he passed down the ill-smelling hallway, carefully avoided the rubbish in the back, found the rear door and entered the court beyond.

A couple of wooden fences gave little trouble to his long legs, and at length he found himself in the court behind Hearn's shop. He could have entered it directly from the alley but he didn't want to come that way. Someone might be guarding the rear entrance and he wanted his visit to be a complete surprise.

There was a light in the back room of the shop; a light that shone plainly through the worn pale shade with the many rents in it. The shade waved slightly too, where a pane of glass was broken in the musty window. Satan grinned. He knew that Jake was very rich; must be very rich, since he had been fencing furs by the van load. And he knew too, though he could not prove it, that Logan's protection had made Jake Hearn the most daring fence on the Avenue.

Voices came to Satan through the broken glass. No words exactly; just a mumbled drone. He drew close to the window and listened.

"Mattie's got to take a trip, Jake—free—all expenses paid and the highest class travel. We'll do things right for her. This dick, Satan, wants to make trouble."

"She's went, I tell you," a squeaky voice answered, which Satan recognized as that of the fence. "By boat she went out of the country."

Satan found a rent in the curtain and glued his eye to it as the first voice spoke again.

"What boat? To what country?"

"I don't know. Just her note. It said, 'I have left the country on a boat. Mattie.'"

"Where's the note?"

"I burned it, like you tell me to keep nothing."

JAKE HEARN WAS a hard man to pin down. But now that Satan had a fair view of the room he saw that Jake's questioner was a harder man to avoid.

He had a sharp, evil face, with a long nose that earlier in life had been battered slightly to one side. It gave his eyes a peculiar twist, as he had the habit of centering his gaze on the end of his nose. He was wearing a hundred dollar suit, a twelve dollar hat, and sported light yellow spats above brilliant tan shoes.

The man was Rattigan, the racketeer, and the stamp of the gutter was on his face, in his shifty eyes, and in the twist of his lips when he talked. Satan had been right. The big black car out front was Rattigan's. There were two hard looking men with Rattigan.

Rattigan came close to the trembling little fence, crouching in the big chair. Jake Hearn's eyes watched Rattigan and the two men who leaned against the door which led to the shop. He rubbed his hands together and made chuckling little noises back in his throat.

"She didn't leave by a boat. That's flat." Rattigan shot the words through his teeth. "She didn't leave at all." And twisting his lips and narrowing his eyes, "So you won't tell me where she is!"

"I tell you she's gone. She—"

"Stand up when you talk to me." Rattigan fairly bellowed the words, so that his companions glanced apprehensively toward the front of the shop.

Jake Hearn came to his feet. His shifty eyes sought escape, and one of the men moved to the side door.

"Now—" said Rattigan, "where is she?"

"I tell you she—"

RATTIGAN CLOSED A hamlike hand, let the fist fly forward and struck the fence flush on the mouth. It was a brutal blow. Jake Hearn was not expecting it, but even if he were it would have made little difference. Rattigan stood six feet tall; and weighed a hundred and ninety pounds, while the little pawnbroker was an old man, bent at the shoulders, his slender frame covered with parchment-like skin.

Jake fell back into the chair. The chair slid across the room, twisted slightly, balanced for a moment on its back legs, then crashed against the wall.

"Well—" Rattigan crossed the room and glared down at Hearn. "Where's Mattie?"

"No, no, no." All the fence's shrewdness was gone. He was frightened now, in a panic. "I can't tell you. You'll kill her. You'll murder her. She—"

"Stand up when you talk to me," Rattigan said again, and the two men laughed. "No—" and to the rougher looking of his friends, Rattigan said, "you, Joe—hold him up. I have an idea Mr. Jake Hearn is going to be glad to talk—if he can."

The man called Joe crossed the room, lifted the wizened little form out of the chair, held him on his feet as Rattigan closed his fist again. And there was an interruption.

The shade shot up with a snap, an arm came through the broken pane in the window—and Satan spoke, his gun moving slowly.

"I think that will be about all of that, Mr. Rattigan. Unlock the window and open it, Joe."

Three pairs of eyes sought that window at once. The little fence dropped back in the chair and buried his head in his hands. Three hands hesitated, half moving to armpits when Satan spoke again.

"I think you're making a mistake, boys. It's Satan talking. Now, Joe—open the window."

THERE WAS NO order of "hands up!" There was nothing melodramatic in Satan's words. Yet three pairs of hands shot into the air. Joe walked toward the window. The name of Satan had been enough. Rattigan and his bodyguard knew that Satan shot first and explained afterward.

"Keep a little to the side, Joe." Satan's voice was soft and low. "I like to look at your friends. You wouldn't want me to shoot a hole in you to look through. That's right!" as the lock clicked loose. "Now—my gun is only an inch or two further back. Fine!" And as the window creaked up on long unused pulleys Satan threw a foot over the sill and climbed into the room.

"Back against the wall!" Satan ordered Joe and the other thug as he faced Rattigan. He stood very close to the racketeer, his green eyes burning balls of fire.

"We're all armed, Rattigan," he said. "Three against one." And he shoved his automatic easily under his left armpit and let both hands fall to his sides. "All armed—all even." He spread his empty hands wide open. "Rattigan, the feared gunman—the big racketeer! Rattigan, the rat who hid behind an ashcan with Swartz and shot Clarey in the back. Three to one, Rattigan—all armed. Why don't you do your stuff?"

Rattigan's fingers twisted at his side. His tongue came out and he licked at his lips. He tried to cast furtive glances back at his two companions.

"Don't do it, boss," Joe warned from behind. "Don't you see? He's come to—to kill you."

Three to one. Three gangsters. Three gunmen. One the most feared gangster on the Avenue. All armed; all known to use a gun; all willing to shoot it out any time, any place— and Satan's hands were empty, both empty, both hanging loosely at his sides. These men who lived by the gun and expected to die by it. But they knew Satan. They knew his reputation. They remembered that Little Ricco had stood so, facing Satan. Little Ricco, the fastest drawing gunman the city had ever bred. And Ricco had smiled and reached for a gun, and died with it half drawn from its holster.

They remembered, too, the Ballast brothers. Quick, viciously cruel gangsters, who feared neither man nor devil. Satan had been walking from the room when they drew together. And they had died—both of them—on the floor of their own night club. Rattigan shuddered slightly. He had been there that night; he had seen the little round holes directly in the center of their foreheads. Almost as if Satan had taken a compass and drawn a circle, then placed the bullet right in the center of it.

So Rattigan never moved; only his fingers twisted at his side. His lips quivered, and his two men stretched their hands higher toward the ceiling.

"So you won't play, you dirty rat." Satan leaned closer to Rattigan, so that his hot breath was on his face. "You'd rather beat up old men. All right." And little Jake sat up in his chair and gasped. Satan was pulling the act he had become famous for in the underworld.

He simply raised his left hand and smacked Rattigan across the face with it. The blow did not seem a particularly

hard one and Satan's hand was open, but it rocked Rattigan. Then Satan raised his right hand and smacked him on
the other cheek. Just a moment's pause—and it happened.
Satan's closed right fist started some place below his knees,
flashed up and landed on the point of Rattigan's chin.

Without a word Rattigan folded up like a jackknife and
sank to the floor.

JAKE HEARN GASPED as he wiped the blood from his
lips. He knew Satan. He feared Satan. He had even seen
him perform his favorite trick of "slapping" desperadoes
down. But Jake Hearn had never expected to see the day
when Satan or anyone else would dare to so treat Rattigan.
Rattigan, whom the biggest men on the Avenue feared.
Rattigan, who could get a boy out of the Tombs almost
before the wagon had dumped him there. Rattigan, who—
But Satan was talking.

"Take him out, boys, and throw him in the car," Satan
said to the gaping gunmen. "Then on your way—unless,"
those green eyes slanted, "either of you object to the way I
treated the big boss."

"We don't intend to get mussy." Joe faltered the words.
"But we're armed. You—you know that." Joe had visions
of a bullet in the back when he left the shop. "You want—
our guns?"

"No." Satan shook his head. "I never interfere with the
law, and I know you both have licenses duly signed by a
magistrate, allowing you to carry them." And narrowing
his eyes, "If you want to use them on the way out, that's all
right with me."

Rattigan was coming to and cursing under his breath as

they helped him through the curtain and across the shop toward the front door.

"I'll get you for this, Satan. I'll kill you for this!" he said over and over as Satan stood by the little curtain and heard the front door click closed.

Then he stepped back into the little room behind the shop. Stood listening a moment, half expecting that a fusillade of shots might be fired into the shop. There was the roar of a motor, the hum of gears, and the black car shot from the curb.

Rattigan was worried. He trusted his two companions; had faith in them. But they were only human, and he knew that the story would get around. Also, that it would lose nothing in the telling.

"I'll get him for this—the lousy, yellow dick," Rattigan cursed. And his conversation all had to do with the sudden and violent death of Detective Satan Hall.

"Sure, boss sure!" His two friends agreed with him and patted him on the back, and explained how they saw Satan strike him when he turned his head. But over Rattigan's head they exchanged glances, and each had the same thought. Rattigan, the feared Rattigan, was slipping.

5

THE LAW OF THE GUN

BACK IN THE shop, Satan turned to Jake Hearn. Jake had recovered now and his shrewd little brain was working again. He had been saved from the brutality of Rattigan, the racketeer—but was he now in for a worse time? He watched Satan from the sides of shifty eyes and wondered if Logan would protect him. Then he wondered if Logan had sent Rattigan, and he wished he had been satisfied with the money he had saved and had returned to Poland.

Jake Hearn bathed his face carefully in the sink, and bemoaned the greed which had kept him in the city.

"Well," Satan questioned, "where's Mattie?"

"She took a boat and—"

"Yeah—" Satan nodded. "I heard that one and don't like it any better than Rattigan did. It's not my line to slap down old men, Jake. I'm not going to put the hooks into you. I'm just going to talk words—real words. You're in a tough spot. If you tell them where Mattie is they'll bump her off. If you don't they'll take you for a ride—a one way ride, Jake.

"They'll find Mattie anyway. The dragnet is out for her. You know the ropes, Jake. I don't have to tell you. A body in the park; a bit of wire around her neck—like those other girls. Black eyes—glassy, Jake. Young body—cold, Jake. Mattie—your kid. Your kid, whom you let be murdered. Your kid, who—"

"Don't—don't!" Jake cried over and over as he clutched at Satan's hand and held it tightly in his two parchment-like claws. "She's a good girl, Satan—a fine girl. All I've got since her mother died. You won't let them. You'll save her. You'll—"

"I can't." Satan held the old man half erect as he tried to fall on his knees at Satan's feet. "I can't unless I know where she is. Rattigan's through. Logan has the skids under him. If Mattie talks out, they won't bother you any more, Jake."

"But me—me!" Jake moaned. "If I take a jolt, what of Mattie then? There might be things I've done. Things—"

"I don't want you, Jake. I don't want Rattigan and Logan for stolen furs. I'm not interested in your racket. I want them for murder, Jake. Mattie saw Cohen killed. You won't be in it. I want her to put the finger on Logan." Satan clenched his hands. "I've got the evidence. I only need Mattie. They won't bother you any more. They won't be able to bother you any more. I'm going to fry them, Jake. Clarey was working with me. Cohen was my pal. They've got to fry, Jake—they've got to fry."

"Yeah—yeah." Jake had a faraway look in his eyes. "They gotta fry. Mattie's got to turn the trick. Mattie—" And suddenly, as his eyes widened with fear. "She didn't see it. She wasn't there. She—"

"Then why did she disappear—why did you hide her out? Why has Logan got the dragnet out for her? I tell you she was in the room by the alley. She was looking out the window. She saw Cohen killed. They'll find her, Jake.

They'll rake the city with a fine toothed comb. They'll watch your friends. They'll—"

SATAN PAUSED. THE old man was trembling. Satan wondered. "They'll watch your friends!" That was the line that got Jake. Those were the words that cut deep. Cut deep, because they were the truth. These Jews stuck together. They protected each other. The thing was logical, reasonable. Mattie was being hidden away by one of Jake's friends. Who were they? Which one? Satan should have thought of that before. Had Logan thought of it? Probably he had. Crook—murderer—yes. But Logan was an efficient worker. Jake's friends! That was it.

"Your friends—they'll find her, Jake. Will you talk?"

"I don't know. I don't know!" Jake moaned, and then suddenly, "I can't. They'll kill me."

Satan shrugged his shoulders and turned toward the door.

"All right, Jake. It's your funeral—not mine. Or maybe it's just Mattie's. You know, Jake. There's a slab—just a cold marble slab in the morgue waiting for Mattie."

Jake followed Satan out into the shop, clutched at his coat when his hand rested on the knob of the door.

"Suppose—suppose I want to talk, what then? Where can I find you? I might—might find out where Mattie is."

Satan looked down at the old man. He knew what was in his mind. Jake was going to put out a few strings—find out how close Logan or Rattigan were to finding Mattie. If the thing was hot—looked bad—Jake would talk to Satan. If it didn't look as if they'd find Mattie, Jake would chance it. Instinctively, Satan knew his man. Jake would not talk—not just then.

"Headquarters, Jake. Ask for O'Brien, nights. Sullivan, daytime."

"And the message? O'Brien don't know. He might talk to Logan. Logan has a way of—"

"Yeah." Satan nodded vigorously. "Just say, 'There's a guy who wants to talk.' I'll know, and give you a jingle here at the shop."

For a long moment Satan hesitated. Then he jerked his gray Stetson tightly down over his forehead, moved a gun from a shoulder holster to an overcoat pocket, and swinging open the shop door passed out into the night.

Dark, deserted streets; dark doorways. A dismal, rainswept night. Satan sniffed disdainfully as he kept close to the gutter. The slapping down of Rattigan would rankle in that gunman's chest. He would plan vengeance, but would he act on it? Would others of his kind—of his mob—care to act on it? Would they gang him there on the empty street?

"Rats—all rats," Satan muttered to himself as he walked. Yet his right hand caressed the butt of the heavy service automatic in his pocket. Rats were dangerous when cornered.

SATAN JUMPED A taxi and rode straight to police headquarters. He didn't waste time hunting up his information. Downstairs he leaned over the desk and spoke to the bent-shouldered, gray-haired Sergeant Oberheim.

"How long will it take to get me a list of Jake Hearn's friends? He's a pawnbroker over—"

Oberheim grinned.

"I know," he said. "It'll take me just as long as it'll take to open that cabinet over there and lift it out."

"Ready, huh?" Satan stroked his chin. "Fixed it up for Logan, eh?"

"Yeah. Captain Logan." Oberheim turned from the cabinet with three legal pages closely clamped together. "The names with the check marks are 'pretty close friends.' The lads with the X's—kisses—after them," Oberheim grinned, "are relatives. Them with the lines under them are known to be shady. Double lines are guys who have been in trouble with the cops."

"Quite complete." Satan glanced through the three pages.

"Too complete." Oberheim ran a finger down a card index. "Some of them probably just speaking acquaintances, but Logan wanted it that way. We've got a surprising lot of stuff about Jake Hearn, too. Amazing, considering he's never been in the lineup." And after a moment's hesitation, "Someone likes him a lot, I guess."

"I guess so." Satan nodded, shoved the list in his pocket. And he thought, as he left the room, that would be Logan's way. It would look okay if Mattie was found strangled some place in the city. It wouldn't be a bad story anyway, from Logan's point of view. Logan would have the same purpose in looking for Mattie that Satan did, as far as the law was concerned. Mattie was a witness to Cohen's murder. It would be natural for Logan to find her dead.

Satan's lips set grimly as he leaned against the corridor wall under a light and looked the names over. He had to find Mattie. Yes, he had to find Mattie—alive. If she was found dead, then what? The whole case would fall. Frank wouldn't talk unless he was sure it was murder on Logan's part. And if Mattie was found dead! Satan's sharp, white teeth bit into a thin lower lip. He wondered if he would kill Logan then, and if he did—would it be murder? Murder! Yes, in the eyes of the state. But what of the other law? The law that the criminal recognized; the law that Satan had even come to recognize. The only law the criminal knew. The only law the criminal feared. The law of the gun! The criminal's law. Satan's law.

6

LOGAN GOES TO KILL

SATAN TOLD O'BRIEN where to get in touch with him if a call came in; then he left the building, jumped a taxi and rode directly to Logan's precinct. It might be a good thing to keep an eye on Logan. It wouldn't take Logan long to cover that list; not with the mob he'd have working on it.

Satan didn't enter the precinct. A thin, emaciated, shabby little figure with a cap pulled down and a cigarette hanging from his lips stepped from the shadows and nudged Satan as he passed him.

Satan paid the driver, looked up and down the block, then followed the bent figure to the corner, around it, and entered the doorway of a tenement. The man spoke without removing his cigarette.

"Logan took a cab and went to Jake Hearn's. I spent my last four bits tailing him. He's there now. He was alone. I spent my—"

"Yeah—" Satan shoved a bill into the eager outstretched fingers and left the tenement. Ten minutes later he reached Jake's shop, found the door open and walked in.

A voice was speaking. It was Logan's. There was elation in it. Logan said, clear and loud:

"That's fine. That's great. I'll be right over and—and see to the removal."

As Satan parted the curtains and entered the little back room Logan laid down the phone. He frowned slightly as he saw Satan and let his cigar run across his mouth. Then he smiled.

"See what you can do with the old goat, Satan," he said easily and friendly. "I've got a feeling that Mattie could tell something about the murder of Cohen." Then he shook his head. "I've got a feeling, too, that we'll find her dead. That'd be too bad—just too bad for me. For you, too, I guess, Satan. Cohen was your friend."

Satan looked at Logan steadily.

"That's right," he said. "Cohen was my friend."

"Tough!" Logan straightened his coat and pulled it tightly about his neck. "But that's the way things happen." He grinned now and his cigar jarred up against his nose. "Be careful of yourself. Don't go and get yourself a shovelful of dirt."

"Not me." Satan chewed on his lower lip. He thought he knew Logan. But Logan in a facetious mood puzzled him.

"Well—I'll have to trot. Just got a buzz on a raid. Work on Jake, here. Mattie's an important witness for the state. There's nothing you can do about the murder without her?"

"No—" Satan said very slowly. "Nothing legal."

"Nothing legal, eh?" Logan caressed one of his chins. "So that's how it is." Brown, round balls grew smaller.

"That," said Satan, "is just how it is."

"The boys aren't over friendly to you, Satan. They don't understand you like I do." Logan buttoned his coat carefully. "But they're mighty proud of you—proud of your record. I wouldn't be surprised if they gave you an inspector's funeral." A moment's pause, then—"That is, of course, if you should get yourself killed."

"That," said Satan, "is a threat?"

"Hell, no!" Logan grinned. "You're working out of my precinct now. I always look after my boys. That's a warning; maybe a prophecy. Up town the neighbors think I'm psychic."

Satan simply nodded his head.

"I'm glad to know where I stand. I think Cohen would like it better just that way."

LOGAN PALED SUDDENLY and looked at Satan's hands—Satan's empty hands. Logan's right hand half crept toward his left armpit, then dropped quickly to his side again. He thought Satan would like it that way, too—just that way. Logan jerked back his shoulders. He didn't want to die now. Just when he was getting the break—just when he was sure that Mattie wasn't going to talk.

And he brushed by Satan, muttering:

"Got business. Bye!"

The front door closed behind him; the rain bit into his face. He breathed in the cool, damp air and felt better. A few minutes now—an hour at the most, and it would all be over. All over! Rattigan was a punk. Why didn't he do it himself? What did he want to get Logan in deeper for? And as he turned the corner Logan wondered—wondered if it would be any different, any harder to kill a woman.

Satan turned to Jake Hearn, who sat silent in the big chair. His hands were clasped before him, held tightly between his knees, and his eyes, wide and staring, settled upon the phone.

"Well—" Satan shook the little fence roughly by the shoulder, "you know now. You saw Logan. How did he act when he came in? Like that?"

"No—no." Jake picked out a spot in the corner of the room now to center his unseeing eyes upon. "He threatened. He wanted Mattie—and he told me to get my hat and coat and go with him. He was in a terrible rage. Then the phone call."

"Sure!" Again Satan shook him. "You're not just dumb, Jake. You know and I know just what that call meant. You've waited too long. They've found Mattie."

"No, no!" Jake was on his feet, clutching at the lapels of Satan's coat. "They haven't. They couldn't. You're just telling me that. You want to know where she is. You want her to tell about Logan. You want— Don't—don't look at me like that. It's not true. It's not true!"

"Just as true that an hour from now—two at the most—they'll give you a call to come to the morgue and identify the body. You know Rattigan and you know Logan, and you know Mattie loved Cohen. If Mattie lives, they die. If Mattie dies, they live."

"That's right—that's right." Jake jerked his head up and down. "But they can't know. They—"

"And Logan left you here. That's like Logan, with the hot seat staring him in the face! He left you because he didn't need you any more, Jake. They telephoned him where Mattie is. He's going now. On his way now! She had a pretty neck, Jake. A soft, white neck. The wire will cut and twist, and Mattie will make funny sounds. Then they'll cart her up to the park—a side street. And Logan will curse to the papers, and say that the man who got Cohen killed her. He'll be right, of course, but they won't know just how right he is." And as the old man clung to him and moaned and muttered in Yiddish, Satan pointed to the worn old alarm clock on the rough, homemade shelf above the shabby couch.

"There's time yet. Time for me to reach her before Logan; before Logan starts the job. Before the wire burns its—"

"I'll tell—I'll tell!" Jake Hearn fairly screamed the words. Satan placed a hand across his mouth and looked toward the door. But through Satan's slowly parting fingers that were across Jake's mouth he caught the words, gasped out now in husky whistling notes.

"She saw it. Mattie saw it," Jake said. "And she wanted to talk. I—I sent her to Aaron Rostan's." And as a dry tongue licked at drier lips, he rubbed the back of his hand across his mouth. "She's locked up in a room on the third floor. She's— God of my fathers! I had to do it. She's chained to the bed, and—"

"Chained to the bed!" Satan half drew back from the old man. "Chained there—fastened there for them to kill her. No chance. No— You fool—you brutal fool!" And grabbing Jake roughly and shaking him so the old man could hardly talk, "The address? Aaron Rostan's address?"

And Satan got it. Over on the east side. A private house; an old house that Aaron lived in alone.

HE DIDN'T LISTEN to the old man's prayers and entreaties to save his child. He didn't listen to the lamentations and the cries to Father Abraham to save his daughter. Satan only knew that the old man knelt upon the floor, his head in his hands, his hands upon the floor. A pitiful heap of old bones and skin. A father who loved his daughter. A father with the false idea he was protecting the last of his own flesh—his own flesh, who was chained to a bed. Chained there helpless to escape, while even now rats of the half world and a degenerate police officer who had broken faith with millions were on their way to find the girl.

Satan dashed from the room, through the curtain and out the front door. A cab was passing. The driver shook his head and jerked his thumb toward his fare in the back. But Satan was out in the street; had swung aboard the cab; was talking to the driver.

He brought the cab to a stop, swung open the door and ordered the fare from the cab.

"But I've got—" the indignant man started, and stopped.

The door swung wide and a hard voice spoke.

"Outside! Before I throw you out. Police business. Murder."

And the bewildered fare stood on the sidewalk, ran a hand through his hair, repeated once or twice the word "murder," and watched the taxi dash from the curb.

Twice they passed a red light and once a motorcycle cop started to force them to the curb. Satan didn't know the officer, nor had that particular officer met Satan. But he recognized Satan the moment he thrust his head from the cab. The glaring, green eyes; the pointed ears and chin; and now the pronounced sardonic twist to his thin lips.

"Jeez!" The motorcycle cop stopped by the curb and spoke to the patrolman who'd run up from the corner. "It's Satan Hall, and there's death for someone tonight."

7

BULLETS IN THE DARK

SATAN STOPPED THE cab just around the corner from Aaron Rostan's house.

"Wait here!" he told the driver. "Keep your engine running, don't leave your seat—and don't open your yap to anyone. There'll be more in it for you than just glory."

The driver grinned and said:

"That's all right by me. I ain't proud."

Satan walked quickly around the corner, and a lump caught in his throat. There was no big car before Aaron Rostan's door; there was no car even on the block. The car would be on the street behind. Satan knew the racket and understood what that meant. They'd take the girl—yes—the body of the dead girl out the back way.

And Satan's thoughts were sharp and clear, but unpleasant. Was Mattie dead yet? Had Rattigan found her or had one of his men? Was the murder committed before the telephone call; probably Rattigan's telephone call? Had he killed the girl and wanted Logan to turn the trick of planting the body some place up town? Did Logan go straight from Jake Hearn's to Aaron Rostan's?

There was no time to waste. Mattie would be murdered

as quickly as possible. Satan was running down the block toward the house.

There was no light showing in the front of Aaron's house. Satan reached the alley and turned into it. Caution was forgotten. His rubber soled shoes made no noise on the hard flagging.

Satan was a keen, clever hunter of men. He knew how to stalk his prey. He knew how to creep up on the man who must now be watching the rear of that house. But if the man was there there wasn't time to be clever. The man could only be waiting for the girl to be carried out. Satan would have to chance a surprise attack. So he didn't slow down as he reached the end of the alley which led to the court behind the house. He turned the corner on the run, a gun in either hand. This wasn't the time for caution. This was the time for action. And Satan liked action. He was going to blast his way into that house—a spitting gun in either hand.

He turned that corner. The man in the court, saw him, of course. He was there to watch that no one entered. But he was there to watch for skulking figures, or listen for the long, weird song of a police siren. He wasn't expecting a sprinting man to turn from the alley and hurtle toward him. What's more, the gunman recognized that running figure and stood so, his hands at his sides, a gun dangling in the right one. He didn't raise that gun and he didn't fire. It was the sudden paralysis of his muscles that saved his life. If his gun had raised the fraction of an inch Satan would have killed him where he stood. But the gunman didn't think of that. He only saw that devilish, sinister face and was frozen to the flags.

AS IT WAS, Satan fairly leaped across the few feet that divided him from the bewildered and thoroughly frightened man. He raised his right hand once, swung his gun viciously downward. There was a dull thud as steel hit bone, and the watcher dropped to the stones like a steer in the stockyard.

There was a flight of wooden steps, a locked door at the top and a window about waist high. Satan didn't think—didn't figure it out. It was time that he feared now more than anything else. Minutes—even seconds—counted. Maybe a split second would turn the trick.

He raised his gun, knocked a pane out of the window, heard it fall with a clink into a sink, and thrusting his hand through the hole slipped back the catch and hurled up the window.

If anyone was down stairs they would hear him, of course. But not in time to stop him, Satan thought, as he climbed over the sill, balanced for a moment on the wooden side of an old galvanized sink and dropped to the floor.

No footsteps there on the main floor. Just silence—and Satan's flash was out. He was through a swinging door, into a dining room, across it and in the front hall. At the foot of the stairs—thickly carpeted stairs.

And they did hear him. He was up that first flight on the second floor, turning toward the third when he heard the voices; heard, too, running feet—and then saw the light. It flashed up suddenly there on the third floor, just above the well of the staircase.

It was only a second, and then darkness but for the

semblance of light some place far back on the third floor. And a voice spoke. It was the voice of Rattigan.

"It's Satan. I saw him plainly over the banister."

Then three quick shots, but no spurts of orange blue flame.

Satan grinned evilly. Those shots came from someone shooting straight down into the well of the staircase, or from so far back in the hall that they must go above his head. They knew, then, his little trick of picking out those darts of flame and putting a bullet in the man behind them. Well—the shots could only be to slow him up, not to frighten him. Satan had a little too much pride in himself to believe anyone would try to frighten him.

But he was cautious now as he climbed those stairs. The gun in one hand went back into its shoulder holster and a flashlight crept into his left hand as a voice spoke above. It was a whisper, but a nervous stage whisper that carried clearly to Satan—and he thought he recognized the voice of Logan, but he could not be sure. The man was saying:

"She oughta be dead, but I don't think she's quite out. You didn't twist the wire tight enough."

And Rattigan answered—high pitched—fearful:

"Why take her out? Why not give her a load of lead and be—"

Then from the voice that Satan thought was Logan's:

"We've got to make it look like the Sicilian job and get her out and dump her. You fool, Joe. Satan's alone. What's the panic? You've only got to fire when you hear—"

DEAD SILENCE ABOVE. The stairs creaked loudly as Satan advanced a step. Then the roar of a gun; sharp spurts of orange blue flame as Satan threw himself flat on the steps. He didn't return the fire. He couldn't see the flashes from his position now. But he wasn't hit either—couldn't be hit unless he could see the spitting gun. He watched up the stairs, with his gun ready.

Five, ten, fifteen seconds passed. Mattie! Satan couldn't wait any longer. A door banged above. A man cursed and said:

"Maybe Joe got him. She's heavier than she looks. All right. Lead on."

Then steps above, right on the landing. And Satan chanced his flash—just one quick pencil of flame.

For a split second he looked straight into the wide, staring, watery blue eyes of Joe. And they fired together as the flash went out. Satan grinned. When the big moment came Joe didn't have the nerve for it. Satan was not hit. But above, there was the dull thud of a falling body. A moment of silence, then another thud—two in quick succession. And Satan gripped the banister for support. He knew. The body of Joe was hurtling down those stairs.

He braced himself there as the thudding thing came. He felt rather than saw it jump into the air. He twisted slowly as it struck his side. He drew his foot away as heavy shoes struck his shins. And it was gone, thudding, crashing down the stairs, to land with a sickening thump at the bottom.

"Now, Logan—" Satan gritted his teeth, "it's you and Rattigan. Drop your guns, and if the girl's alive I'll give you a chance to hire a good mouthpiece and beat the rap. But I want the girl."

Feet beat far back along the hall. Then Rattigan spoke from the top of the stairs.

"All right!" Rattigan fairly shouted as Satan pressed the flash button again. "Here's the girl—dead. Take her."

Satan held his fire.

Rattigan held the girl in his arms; held her so for a split second. Then with all his strength he hurled her from him, straight out and down at Satan. Plainly Satan saw the slender young body—even the flesh colored silk stockings, the blue skirt and the cream colored sweater above it. He saw too the whiteness of her face, the slender neck—the neck, and the wire about it. The lips too. Lips that were blue—maybe black.

Satan dropped his flash—dropped his gun—and extended both his hands, bracing himself there on the stairs. He was a big man—a strong man, but the force of that body was too much. His huge frame bent back, the breath was knocked from his body. Then he turned, tried to balance himself, held the girl in his arms, and half falling, half jumping, carried her down those stairs. But he was on his feet until he reached the bottom, and was able to so direct his fall that he and the girl crashed to the floor well over to the side of the hall and against the wall.

SATAN SMILED GRIMLY as his fingers tore at the wire about her throat. He had done well to throw himself and his burden clear of those stairs. There were four shots in quick succession. A moment's pause, as Rattigan must have drawn another gun, then six more shots, a half hysterical laugh and running feet. Then pounding feet. Satan nodded. Rattigan was following Logan down the uncarpeted back stairs. He didn't have the nerve to descend the front stairs and see if he had finished Satan.

One flight to go and Satan could head them off. He

couldn't fry Logan now for the murder of the dead Cohen. But if he could catch them there in the house—shoot them down there in the house, he could avenge Cohen; avenge the dead girl, who—who— And the wire came loose in his hand as he twisted it. And there was something else. A throbbing in the girl's throat—a convulsive gasp in her chest.

Somewhere far distant in the blackness a door closed with a bang. And Satan was on his feet. He groped for his flash on the stairs, found it, and retrieved his gun. Then he hunted up the bath room, found a glass. Water! The girl, Mattie, his witness—the star witness for the state was alive. He dared not leave her now.

She sucked in the water in great gulps. Her eyes had opened, misty and lifeless. The lids began to flicker. She saw things—saw Satan—stared at him—gasped once— clutched at her throat and screamed.

The scream was one of fear, horror, terror. It echoed through the musty old house. But Satan only smiled and held her head against his arm, ran a hand through her hair and said:

"You know me. You know Satan Hall. No one's going to hurt you. It's all right now, kid. The finger's on them. You want to tell, don't you? You want to tell who killed Cohen."

"Yes—I want to tell—want to tell who killed Cohen. I was at the window. I saw him with the knife." She gave one little convulsive gasp, and finished. "It was Captain Logan."

"Sure it was." Satan smiled. "Sure it was! Now, isn't that just fine?"

8

MORE DEATH TO COME

LOGAN WAS GONE. Rattigan was gone. Only Joe—the dead Joe—lay huddled in a corner, well back from the foot of the stairs.

It was with some difficulty that Satan got Mattie Hearn on her feet and had her bathe her head in fresh, cool water. But he kept her from seeing the dead gunman, yet had a look at Joe himself and clicked his teeth together in a certain satisfaction. It hadn't been bad shooting considering the circumstances, and Satan took a sort of pride in his work.

He led Mattie down the stairs, let her sit in the big chair in the hall while she told her story. There wasn't a great deal of it. Most of it Satan knew, or had guessed.

She loved Cohen, had planned to meet him and tell him about Logan. She only wanted her father protected. It was to be at a deserted place she knew of. She could sit there by the window and talk to Cohen, and he could move on and she could disappear in the darkness if anyone came by. But her father knew of the meeting; must have told Rattigan or Logan or someone. Anyway Logan came, and she drew back in the window. And Logan waited until Cohen turned and recognized him, and then he stabbed him in the chest.

"Three, four, five times—like that." Mattie made the motion with her hand. "Oh, he didn't see me, but he heard me. I screamed as I dashed back in the old warehouse, found an exit and ran all the way back to the shop. I told father and he was frightened. He got a car and he took me to Aaron's and told me I mustn't tell. When I insisted I would, they got the chain and ran it around the bedpost and locked me there. Father said I had to be quiet or they'd kill me and him both.

"Then they came tonight, and Aaron heard them and ran away. And they broke the chain and knocked me back on the bed." She pushed back her hair and showed a bruise on her forehead. "They spoke of killing me and"—she shuddered—"and of throwing my body out up in Van Cortlandt Park. They talked and acted as if I were already dead. Then Logan took the wire and Rattigan twisted it—and you came. In a way I knew what was going on."

"Did they say why"—Satan placed an arm gently around her—"why they were going to take you from here to the park? Was it a frame?"

"Yes—it was. Rattigan was against it, but Logan insisted. He said there had been two or three such murders and a Sicilian gang was suspected, and that Cohen had been working on the Sicilian case. And Logan said something about some message, and that Sicily George would be up by the park and they could pick him up and hang the job on him, and the papers would be satisfied."

Mattie got a little hysterical then, and when she quieted down and sat back in the chair Satan paced the room.

THERE WAS A phone in the corner. He only had to pick
up the receiver to have the hand of the law stretch out and
fall upon the shoulder of the man who had betrayed it.

"A police captain," Satan said to himself, "and murder.
The very stench of it will reflect back on every boy in
uniform—on me, too. It isn't right—it isn't just. I should
have given him the heat there in Jake Hearn's. Thousands
of men to suffer—thousands. And"—he stopped walking
and stroked his pointed chin—"and Frank—Inspector
Frank." He recalled the day that Frank had stretched forth
a hand and pulled him out of the line and taken him off
the pavement. Now he was going to repay him. He looked
at Mattie. If she didn't testify. If she didn't remember. If—

And Satan jerked himself erect. He was a cop—just a
cop. He was working for six million people—and Frank
was his friend. Well—you played the game on the level or
you were just a dirty crook, like Rattigan—like Logan—
like— He gulped. Like Inspector Frank.

It was tough. But the law was a machine. It couldn't cut
down here and miss there. Frank had picked him because
he was straight; because he was hard; because he was cruel;
because he was a hunter of men.

Satan went straight to the phone, and lifting the receiver
spoke a number into the mouthpiece.

"Inspector Frank," he said after a bit. "Make it snappy."
He waited a long minute, then sighed with relief.

"Frank—listen." He talked sharp, quick words. "I've got
Mattie, and she's going to talk. Logan fries. Now—does
Logan trust you yet? Will Rattigan listen to a message from
you, like it was gospel? Fine! I want you to call Rattigan's
place. Act natural. Say you're tipped off that the commis-

sioner is wise to the big safe; that he's getting Magistrate La Volley to sign a search warrant. That he'll be down there in two hours, with picked men, to open the safe—and he'd better get the stuff out. Yours especially. Act nervous. Tell him to take it to one of the night banks."

A minute Satan listened, and then:

"No 'buts.' I want it done now. No—they think they're sitting pretty. They think Mattie's dead. Don't give that away. Do as I tell you, and sit tight. If things break right I'll have good news for you. Fine!" And Satan smacked up the receiver.

"Come on, kid," Satan said to the girl. "We've got to go bye-bye."

Mattie came to her feet.

"I'm ready," she said. "You saved me. You were willing to die for me. I'll do what you want me to."

"Not for you, kid. For the law—for Cohen—for the people." Satan looked down at her. The black eyes were steady now. The head was raised high, and proud. The little hand that held his arm didn't tremble.

"You're a wonder, kid." Satan patted her hand. "You've got nerve." And after drawing his lower lip under his upper teeth, "How would you like to go and lay the finger on Rattigan—on Logan? You've been to Rattigan's place. You know how to get to him."

The girl felt of her throat and looked straight into those green eyes.

"I would like it very much," she said. "And I know how to get to him—his private office."

"THAT'S RIGHT. THAT'S right." Satan patted her arm as he led her from the house. And although he talked in a dreamy voice and seemed far away, his green eyes flashed up and down the block, into the areaways on either side of the stone steps, and his right hand caressed a gun.

"We've done the trick for old John Law." He spoke more to himself than to the girl. "Now we'll turn a trick for a friend. We'll turn a trick for Inspector Frank."

"Yes," said the girl. "Both of us."

"Both of us! When Rattigan gets a load of you it'll be better than bringing out the reserves. You won't keel over on me?"

The girl's face hardened, her lips set tightly and she clutched Satan's arm firmly. Then those black eyes filled with hatred.

"What do you think?" was all she said.

"Kid," said Satan, "if I'd known you I'd have come like I did—law or no law—Cohen or no Cohen."

And even though the name of his dead friend was on his lips, Satan laughed. The girl didn't know it, but she was the first person to ever hear him laugh. And the laugh made her shiver slightly. It was as if a heavy sleigh had been dragged across dry pavement.

The taxi was waiting, the motor running. They stopped at a drug store. The girl went in. Satan stood by the door. It was five minutes before Mattie came out. The rouge and powder and sharp, penciled eyebrows made a difference.

"That's right," Satan said. "I want you to look nice for Rattigan."

They got into the cab and drove straight to the Park Avenue Casino. Satan told Mattie what was on his chest and nodded when she spoke out.

"I've often brought him messages from father," she said.

"They always let me right up to his room. It ain't likely he'll tell them that he and Logan murdered me. The Casino is run separate from the fur racket. Only the man on his door will be close enough to know the truth. Harrigan will give him a buzz downstairs that a friend's coming up. He won't know. Do you think he'll be there?"

"Where else?" Satan was sure. "It's his standing alibi. They'll all swear to his being there all evening. He'll be covered well tonight. Maybe I shouldn't bring you, Mattie."

"You can't get up without me. You want to get in. It's the only way."

"That's right." Satan agreed with her. "I'd have to blast my way in, and he'd know and slip out. He won't be expecting you, Mattie. He won't even mention you to anyone. They should let you up. What about me?"

"You'll have to hang over the cloak room counter—at least until he's put the buzzer through. Rattigan's door is at the back of the hall. It's dark there. I often bring men from father, who want to buy stolen furs. Harrigan will be on the first door. You can slip through if he don't know you. If he does—" She shrugged her shoulders. "You can crowd him through the door and handle him, I guess."

"Sure! I can handle Harrigan. He won't give much trouble. Anyone else?"

The girl set her lips.

"Rattigan's careful. Big Jim Ralston will be by Rattigan's office door. Used to be a major in the army. Rattigan can trust him to the death. Rattigan has him because he's faithful. He can't be bought. But he don't know too much. Thinks it's all liquor business. Used to drink around the Casino before he was cashiered out of the army."

"It sounds bad." Satan shook his head and looked at the girl. "But I've got to take you, I guess. Frank's a fine guy; a good guy. Sure you'll see it through?"

The girl felt of her neck. Her black eyes blazed in the darkness of the taxi. She was thinking of Cohen—of the wire.

"I'll see it through," she said simply.

Satan looked at her and nodded. She wasn't more than twenty-five; probably not that. But she had seen life—seen death, too. And she knew the racket. But most of all, she had loved Cohen.

9

LOGAN GETS THE DROP

LOGAN SAT IN the luxuriously furnished room and chewed on an unlighted cigar while he talked. Rattigan was selecting papers from the big safe and stuffing them into a brief case. He went to the alcove and downed two glasses of water from the porcelain basin.

"As soon as you're ready," Logan said, "I'll cart them out the back way and over to the bank. If necessary, the night manager will swear I never came in. Frank seemed nervous and fidgety, didn't he?"

"Sure! Wouldn't you?" Rattigan pulled out an envelope and laid it on the desk. "That's Frank's," he said. "It's funny nothing happened yet. I wonder if Satan is dead, too."

"It doesn't matter," Logan said. "I told you he wouldn't squawk. He won't even peep. They all know he's out to get me. It's around that he slapped you down. Judge Quinlan P. Paulson and his secretary are in the private dining room. They'll swear we were with them all evening. You've got nothing to worry you. Look at me. Spending the evening with a notorious racketeer!"

"Hell!" said Rattigan, "I ain't so bad. No one has anything on me."

"I'll say you wanted to give me a tip. Sort of line of duty.

The judge wanted it that way. Tomorrow I'll raid Platz's place and pick up Ed Donahue. It'll look fine. A good cop has got to mix."

"I ain't so bad," Rattigan said again. "Some of them bullets must 'a' got Satan." And after a pause, "I don't like the silence. Satan's a killer. If he's alive he'll have to be smoked out. Why the hell don't someone bust into that house? I tell you, Logan, it might be days, if Satan's croaked."

"Not days. Aaron will be afraid of the police, but Jake Hearn loves that dame. He'll go there in time. He won't want to, but he'll go." And very low, "I'm afraid Jake will have to be taken care of."

"Cripes!" Rattigan swung on him. "Clarey and Cohen and Mattie and Satan—and now Jake. You can't go into it wholesale, Logan."

"Jake's a natural." Logan shrugged his shoulders. "You can get it done for a couple of grand. We'll throw a banquet that night." He looked thoughtfully toward the ceiling. "We'll throw it for Inspector Frank. Great guy, Frank. Straightest shooter on the Force. Yeah. That's it. We'll throw—"

Logan bit off his final words and sat straighter in the chair. Rattigan stopped halfway between the safe and the brief case on the table. There was a slight buzzing high up on the wall.

"It's a friend." Rattigan nodded.

"What a break!"

"Why didn't you say you weren't to be disturbed?" Logan demanded.

"I couldn't." Rattigan spread his hands far apart as he

pushed the safe door partly closed. "I always see the boys at this time. None of them know about Mattie. I wanted things to look natural. It won't take a minute."

"Yeah. But me!" Logan frowned. "It's all right with the judge and his secretary—but up here with you!"

"I ain't so bad," Rattigan said again. "Take the back stairs there." Rattigan went over and slid back a panel. Then, "Maybe you better listen in. It might be Jake Hearn."

"Maybe." Logan nodded. "Maybe we might find out who knows he came, and—"

"Not here!" Rattigan's narrow eyes snapped. "God! Logan, I can damn near smell blood on you."

LOGAN SHRUGGED HIS shoulders as he passed through the panel, but just before it closed behind him he looked at Rattigan with those unblinking little round, brown eyes.

"It's better than smelling burning flesh, Rattigan," he said. "Much better, if the flesh happens to be your own."

Rattigan watched the panel close. He shuddered once and shook his head. Logan gave him a pain. Yes, a physical disturbance far down in the pit of his stomach. Then he picked up the phone and spoke quickly.

"Sloppy and Finnigan and the Weasel and Grouse and Hogan." He rushed the words. "That's right. Round them all up and have them back at the cloak room." He had to do it. He couldn't get that damn house off his mind, with Joe and Satan and Mattie at the foot of the stairs. He'd send the pick of the gang there. He had to know about Satan.

He thought he heard sounds in the hall outside his door while he talked, but he couldn't be sure. Then there were two sharp raps, three slow ones, a moment's pause, and a single rap.

Rattigan grinned. Things were all right. That would be Ralston. Ralston was a white guy. Rattigan had put him on his feet. He'd die for Rattigan. There was something in this blue blood business after all.

Rattigan crossed the room, paused long enough to see the name Inspector John Frank upon the envelope he had laid on the desk. He turned if over. Then he went to the door and opened it. Ralston would be there.

And Ralston was there. But Rattigan didn't see him at first, for Ralston lay unconscious on the floor, at the feet of—of— And Rattigan drew back into the room. His mouth was open, his eyes were wide with horror. He was looking straight into the white face of Mattie Hearn. Mattie Hearn whose body he had hurled straight at Satan Hall upon those stairs. Mattie Hearn, whose neck Rattigan's hands had twisted the bit of sharp copper wire about. And it was there—the mark of the wire. The red, purplish welt about the whiteness of her neck.

For a moment only Rattigan had strange illusions running through his head. Then he drew in a deep breath, took another look at Mattie as she stepped into the room, and his hand started slowly toward his left armpit.

"I guess not, Rattigan." Satan stepped into the room, and closing the door behind him locked it. "You had your chance to kill Mattie." And as Rattigan's hand dropped to his side, empty, "I want to know about Clarey, Rattigan. I want to know now, or—" Satan's raised gun finished the sentence.

"I don't know. I don't know." Rattigan fairly gasped the words, his eyes glued on Mattie's throat. "Swartz did him in. It was Swartz who did him in."

"Laying it on the dead, eh? Well—it don't matter so much. Logan will squeal like a stuck pig before they roast him. He's built that way." Satan's quick green eyes brightened as they took in the open safe.

HE MOVED TO it now, covering Rattigan with his gun. Then he called to the girl.

"The third drawer from the top, to the left," he said. And a moment later, when she found nothing, "The brief case then. He's moving the things, according to plans. I wouldn't try for a gun, Rattigan. You're not much use with it, you know. Now—I want that envelope marked Inspector Frank." He walked toward Rattigan, his gun raising slowly, picking a spot just above and between his eyes. "Come across, Rattigan," he said.

"So—" A voice spoke behind Satan. A voice he knew well. It was a throaty, hoarse voice, but it was calm and hard. Logan was talking as he stepped into the room. "So Frank double crossed us. Got Rattigan to open the safe so you could cop off the evidence against him. No— Don't turn, Satan. And drop that gun."

Satan's gun lowered, then stopped almost in the center of Rattigan's stomach.

"You may kill me, Logan, but my finger's on the trigger. The shock of the bullet in my back will tighten it—and Rattigan will go out."

"That," said Logan, "will be too bad for Mr. Rattigan."

"Logan—" Rattigan wheezed the words in his throat, "don't. He's—"

And Satan dropped his gun to the floor. After all, Logan was right. Satan had played the Avenue long enough to know that the man with the gun talks and the other listens.

Also, things were pretty hot for Logan. He wouldn't miss Rattigan any. So far as Jake Hearn and Rattigan and Logan were concerned, that racket was over.

"Damn your hide, Logan," Rattigan said. "You'd have let him do it."

"Keep your shirt on, Rattigan. I know my business. I wouldn't let him dump you over. I just called his bluff."

"What now?" said Rattigan as Logan backed Satan against the wall and jerked his other gun from its shoulder holster; had him raise his hands high in the air while he frisked him.

"The room's sound proof, isn't it?" Logan said, and when Rattigan nodded, "well—we simply start over again where we left off. This time there'll be two of them. Sicily George will be up in the park. Things can go through as scheduled."

"Mattie!" Rattigan licked at his lips. "She's got to die—die twice?"

"She's got to die anyway," said Logan. And turning suddenly he raised his gun and fired.

Satan's face twisted in pain and his left hand fell to his side. Blood trickled from beneath his sleeve, ran along his fingers and fell to the floor.

"What are you doing?" said Rattigan. "By God, you'll roast us yet!"

Logan raised his arm again, and Rattigan cried out in anger.

"Cut it, Logan. Here, you fool. I'll snuff him out and be done with it."

"What the hell!" said Logan. "The room's sound proof."

"Practically." Rattigan swore. "But it ain't no shooting gallery."

Satan stood against the wall, his right hand still in the air. And there on the floor, between Logan and Rattigan, was his gun—his fully loaded gun that he had dropped there. His gun lying there while he was to be shot slowly down!

Satan didn't expect to live. He didn't expect to get his gun. But he didn't intend to be shot to ribbons either. For a split second Logan's eyes had switched to Rattigan's. And Satan acted.

10

SATAN SHOOTS LAST

SATAN THREW HIMSELF forward, straight toward that gun between those two men.

Both men twisted their guns quickly and fired. But Logan fired first. The bullet tore into Satan's shoulder; twisted him around; pitched him to the floor.

Then Rattigan fired—blindly, wildly at the hurtling figure of Satan. But Satan was not there. Already Logan's heavy caliber service gun had hurled him to the floor. And as he fell his right hand rested upon his gun—but his eyes rested on Logan.

Logan, who stood there straight and stiff, his eyes staring before him. And just above his right eye was a hole. A red hole that was widening. Then Logan opened his mouth, spun suddenly on his heels and crashed to the floor.

In a dazed way Satan knew that Logan was dead and that Rattigan had killed him—that the bullet meant for him had passed through Logan's head. Satan also knew that Mattie screamed and that Rattigan had fired again, and there was a sharp pain in his side. His head buzzed. He rolled over, jerked up his gun and looked for Rattigan.

And he saw him. Saw him struggling there with the girl. Saw him hurl the girl from him—saw the gun in his hand.

Saw three guns in his hand—saw three Rattigans—three pairs of ratlike eyes—three pairs of thick sensuous lips, that were curled and snarling like an animal's.

And as the stab in Satan's side came again he fired; fired at the middle one of those three Rattigans. Then he blinked his eyes and smiled. Three Rattigans were clutching at their stomachs. Three Rattigans were trying to raise three guns that hung limply in three hands. And then as the three guns came up, Satan fired again at the whiteness of a face. A single face—a single Rattigan now. Somehow his head had cleared.

"It ain't a bad way to go out," Satan muttered as with an effort he kept his eyes open long enough to see Rattigan—a single Rattigan now—give at the knees, sink slowly to the floor, then pitch forward on his face.

Mattie was bathing Satan's head, stuffing towels from the alcove beneath his shirt—against his side. There was his necktie bound tightly about his arm, and he was lying back in a big chair.

He swung his head slowly and looked around the room. Logan and Rattigan were there. But they were dead. They looked funny to Satan, and he grinned.

"A smoke, Mattie." Satan tried to move his right hand toward his pocket, but it lay still upon the arm of the chair.

Mattie put her hand in his pocket, pulled out a package of cigarettes and stuck one in his mouth. She held up an envelope before him.

"Inspector John Frank," he read.

"That's nice," he said, and suddenly his green eyes sparkled. "Light the butt with it, Mattie—that's the girl."

He pulled on his cigarette and watched the papers burn. Mattie pounded the ashes in the tray.

"**YOU GOT IT** bad, didn't you, Satan?" She ran a hand through his hair.

"Pretty bad." Satan nodded. "But I've had it worse before. It's a lot of lead, but one or two in the right place is better. Frank's a good guy, Mattie—a fine guy."

Mattie looked at him long and earnestly. Then she leaned down and kissed him.

"I've wanted to do that for a long time," she said very seriously. "I guess there aren't many girls who want to kiss you, Satan."

"No—" said Satan slowly, "not many. I guess you're the first."

"You're going to live, aren't you, Satan?" And suddenly, "You've got to live."

"Yes, I'm going to live all right. I—"

And Satan stiffened in his chair. Footsteps were in the hall without. Voices—loud. A curse, and the sound like a falling body.

"Mattie," Satan whispered, "there's the back door, there where Logan was. Take it. Remember listening at the door. Rattigan was telephoning. There'll be too many now. They'll gang me out. Beat it, kid."

"No, no!" said Mattie, and she grabbed up the phone. "Police headquarters!" she called into the receiver.

"Mattie—" Satan was moving the fingers of his right hand, finding that the arm had a little life again. "Mattie, stick that gun in my hand. Hurry!" With an effort Satan's fingers closed about his gun.

A body pounded against the door. A man called. There

were loud, threatening voices—clear enough perhaps, but jumbled words to Satan. More bodies against the door. A heavy pounding, as an axe against wood. Then a single crash and the door flew in. A single figure was framed in the doorway.

Mattie screamed and Satan's finger closed upon the trigger. Satan didn't know it then, but a bullet from his gun passed within an inch of Inspector Frank's head.

"Hell!" said Satan, when Frank stood looking at him. "I thought you'd be home in bed."

Frank came close and was whispering in Satan's ear as men in uniform tramped the room.

"Mattie told me. It's a good story and she'll stick to it. Logan and you came here to get Rattigan. He shot Logan. There's the bullet from his gun to prove it. Then you got Rattigan.

"You wanted him for the Cohen and Clarey killings. Why not, Satan? It's for the honor of the Force—the boys in uniform. For the six million people you're always talking about serving. Why the stench now? Logan's dead. It's for the system."

Satan closed his eyes.

"All right, Frank," he said, and his head fell back against the chair. "But, mind you—I won't go to his funeral."

"No—" thought Frank, as he watched Satan carried from the room, "he won't go to Logan's funeral—and I hope to God he won't go to his own."

Four days later Satan sat up in his bed in the hospital and looked into the black rimmed, sleepless eyes of Mattie.

"It's Inspector Frank," she said, as Frank came and stood by the end of the bed.

"It's over," Frank told Satan. "They buried Logan yesterday. Since you were working out of his precinct I put you down for ten bucks. It was a beautiful wreath, Satan."

Satan frowned, then his lips parted and he grinned.

"It seems hard," he said slowly. "Ten dollars to bury Logan! But I guess it was worth it."

SATAN'S KILL

Satan Hall Stalks the Denizens of the
Underworld to Rout Out the Two-legged
Jackals Who Prey on Human Lives

1

REGARDING MURDER

LIEUTENANT GILPATRIC STOOD in the entrance to the police station and told the swaying stranger where he got off in no uncertain terms.

"Come in here drunk, and tell me you were robbed of forty dollars in a Speak somewhere in the neighborhood, but don't know where! Look 'em over." He waved both hands, one up and the other down the street. "Half them brown stone fronts is Speaks."

The man on the steps grinned stupidly.

"The name of the place is 'Tony's,'" he said.

"Yeah—Tony's." Lieutenant Gilpatric sneered. "Most of them are 'Tony's.' Come—on your way!" He pushed the man down the steps, saw him totter; lose his balance. Tried unsuccessfully to reach him before he could fall, then saw him tumble into the arms of a tall broad shouldered man who turned suddenly up the steps.

"Easy does it, there!" said the new arrival, pulling the inebriated man erect, but still holding his arm. "What's the trouble?"

"I'll tell you, sir." The man started his story for the tenth time. "I was robbed in a speakeasy around here some-

where." He waved a hand aimlessly up and down the street. "They took a pen and pencil that—"

Lieutenant Gilpatric was down the last step and had sunk a hand into the lapels of the new arrival's coat.

"And what may be your interest in this lad? Friend of yours, eh?" There was sarcasm in the lieutenant's voice.

"I'm just one of the boys. A plainclothes man." The stranger knocked the lieutenant's hand from his coat with a violence that seemed entirely out of proportion to the offense. He jerked back his coat and flashed a badge.

The lieutenant picked out the letters on the shield in the semi-darkness. Then he tried to look into the detective's face. But the man's slouch hat was pulled well down over his forehead. Only slanting, piercing eyes were fastened on the lieutenant.

"So you're a Department detective, eh? I'm Lieutenant

"Nix on that stuff, Starro. This lad likes it that way.
Drop your hand, you fool. It's Satan Hall"

Gilpatric. At present, in charge of this precinct. Good
night!" He turned and started up the steps.

The drunk talked on.

"The pen cost eight dollars and the pencil matched
it." The detective was turning him toward the sidewalk
and the corner when he finished. "You see—the place was
called 'Tony's!'"

"Tony's!" The plain-clothes man paused, turned
suddenly with his swaying human burden and started up
the steps of the precinct. The lieutenant was now by the
door. He swung around, let his huge mouth hang open a
moment, and said:

"Now, what? You can't be bringing that—"

But the detective had already pushed his man against the

partly open doors and forced him through to the lighted room beyond. The irate lieutenant followed him quickly.

"A damned, ordinary dick running my precinct and telling me where I get off! A stool-pigeon of a Headquarters man out to find trouble in other lads' territories! But you're dealing with a lieutenant now, my man. I'll let you explain your actions to Inspector Jim Towsey. He's a brother-in-law of mine. You've run up against the wrong bozo this time."

"I'm not working from Headquarters," the detective said indifferently, as he leaned against the desk, his back turned to the angry lieutenant. "And I want a chance to douse this man with water, shake him into some sort of shape and talk to him. You've got a duty to—"

"Have I got a duty?" The lieutenant fairly bellowed the words as he saw Officer O'Reilly at the end of the desk making peculiar facial contortions, which he took as anything but complimentary. "Yeah—I've got a duty, and it's not to take back talk from any dick who thinks, once he quits flat-footin', that he owns the Department." He reached the detective now, grasped him by the shoulder and swung him viciously around.

"Well—take off your hat when you speak to me!" he continued.

With a swipe of his left hand Lieutenant Gilpatric tore the gray fedora from the plain-clothes man's head and threw it across the room. He heard Officer O'Reilly draw in a quick breath of surprise, but he didn't pay any attention to it.

"Give us a look at that face of yours. A dick who walks all over a superior officer and—and—"

LIEUTENANT GILPATRIC PAUSED, stopped dead and licked at his lips. For a good two minutes he looked straight into that face before him, and every line of it was stamped firmly in his mind. Even the green, slanting eyes—with eyebrows that tapered off as if they intended to reach those pointed ears. Pointed ears? Yes—and pointed chin. And a V-shaped cut to the hair, the point of which came well down on his forehead. Every feature was a point, with the exception of the mouth. Thin straight lips, there. Cruel, hard lips! Lieutenant Gilpatric drew back a step.

He had never seen this man before. Yet he knew him just as well as if he had met him every day of his life. Before him was the most feared, the most hated, and certainly the most relentless detective in the city's police department.

"My God!" said Lieutenant Gilpatric. "Satan! Detective Satan Hall."

Then Lieutenant Gilpatric did a thing he regretted for a long time afterward. Mechanically he crossed the room and picked up Satan's hat; mechanically he handed it to the first grade detective who stood before him.

Detective Satan Hall was speaking quietly.

"I'd like to talk to this man and you—in the back." He jerked a thumb toward the little rear room.

Gilpatric wasn't afraid of Satan Hall. Physically, he wasn't afraid of any man. Blustering was just his stock in trade. But things get around in the Department. He knew as well as any other officer knew, that Detective Satan Hall worked straight from the Commissioner of Police himself.

Detective Satan Hall had influence, and Gilpatric respected influence. Wasn't he about to wear the stripes of a captain? When he turned to Satan again he was no longer blustering. He was slightly sulky.

"Your being who you are," he addressed Satan, "don't give you any more rights to dictate to me than you had before I recognized you. But fair is fair. You can make a smell that won't help me any. Now—what do you want?"

Satan grinned.

"I want to save you your job," he said.

Lieutenant Gilpatric hesitated a moment; then said:

"Come inside. You can drag that 'stew' with you."

Detective Satan Hall placed the man in a chair and slapped water over his face and head. Then he turned to Gilpatric.

"Haven't you guessed why I'm up here? The commissioner hasn't liked those three murders in the last six months. Every one was a man of standing; every one from out of town; every one wealthy—and every one was said to carry a few thousand dollars in cash."

"I've heard that often enough. What's this lad to do with it?"

"This lad," said Satan, "may point out the very house in which these three men were murdered. Remember—the first man to die spoke before he cashed in. And he said, 'Tony's.' But let's get this man's story."

And they did get it.

His name was Malcolm Strause. He came from Yonkers. He transacted some business in the Paramort Hotel and later met a stranger in the lobby. They had a few drinks in a Speak on Forty-second Street. He didn't know how he got to the last speakeasy; picked up a taxi somewhere. The driver had said he'd take him to a nice little place—Tony's.

There was music, and a woman singing. He had gone down a dark hall, to a bar; had a drink or two. A door opened and someone spoke—and then he was on the street again, walking with two men. He was not sure if they took his money outside or inside the place—but it was gone. They walked him a block, or maybe five—he didn't know. He wanted his pen and pencil.

"Now listen to that," said Lieutenant Gilpatric. "Forty dollars, by men who— Those lads that were murdered carried thousands. Such guys wouldn't go in for a forty dollar steal!"

"That," said Satan, "is where this murder ring slipped up. Somehow they got the wrong man in Mr. Strause. No harm was done. He was just another drunk thrown out of a Speak."

"But why rob him and—"

"AH!" SATAN SMACKED his lips. "The answer to that is, 'greed.' Probably it was done by the two who took him from the Speak and lost him. But Mr. Strause found his way or was directed here, and has given us our first break."

"I don't see any 'break.'"

"I do," said Satan. "A living man, not a dying one, speaks of Tony's. Subconsciously Mr. Strause will remember points about the place he was in. He may be confused at first, but after he sees plenty of places he'll get a recollection. I have an idea whose place it will be—but it's evidence, not ideas, that convict men. We'll start now. Any recollection he has may go when he sobers. Also, perhaps, his desire to help the police."

"They're pretty tough spots." Gilpatric shook his head. "Some of them owned by big influential shots."

"Good! I'll want the toughest spots to start with," said Satan.

Gilpatric continued to shake his head, then noticed the glint in Satan's green eyes and remembered other officers who had crossed him.

One other fact Satan got from Malcolm Strause. The Speak was up stairs, not down. And Strause thought the stairs were narrow. That would simplify the search somewhat, and Satan thought he knew the place where that search would end. And the name of it would not be Tony's.

"I'll go with you of course," Gilpatric said. "I've covered most of the places since the second murder. How does my job fit into this?"

Satan told him.

"They like you around town, Gilpatric; think a lot of you in the commissioner's office. But you're only 'acting captain' here. Your stripes depend on your success in clearing up those murders. I've been detailed to the case. Independent, mind you. But give me a break, and I'll work with you. You'll get the credit."

"That's mighty decent of you." Gilpatric thought that now was the time to extend his hand.

Satan took the hand and grinned.

"I tell you," Gilpatric stuck a match in his mouth and chewed the end of it, "some of the boys in the Speaks are not bad—not bad at all. They expect a little courtesy from me, being tax payers—like. Understand?"

"Yes," said Satan, "I understand. It's part of the system— and a damn bad system. You don't need to come in with me. Just check off those Speaks up stairs."

"Hell!" said Gilpatric, "I don't play around those dumps

and I don't know the up stairs ones from the— Well—I
know a few of them, of course; look 'em over sort of irreg-
ularly. I don't stand for murder—and I want those stripes."

2

ABOVE THE NARROW STAIRS

WITH GILPATRIC, NOW in civilian clothes, the two officers, and the nearly sober Malcolm Strause started out.

Brown stone front after brown stone front Satan
checked off. When the way led up stairs Malcolm Strause
was called. Twice he thought it might be the place and
twice he shook his head.

Then they got a break. As they stopped before a house
far over on the other side of town, Malcolm Strause jerked
erect and spoke as Satan climbed from the car.

"There was a hydrant just like that, before the house.
I nearly stumbled over it. You go up steps like those, too.
Then inside, long narrow stairs to the floor above."

Satan turned to Gilpatric.

"Wait in the car. We won't bring you into it. At least,
not tonight."

"But what if it is the place? That doesn't prove anything."
Gilpatric seemed nervous. "He doesn't know if he was
robbed here or outside. He might even have lost the roll."

"I don't care where he was robbed. I don't even care if he
lost it." Satan's eyes flashed. "I only want to know where
he got the name 'Tony's.' Come on, Strause."

Gilpatric leaned forward in his seat.

"Go easy or get yourself a search warrant," he said. "Hickey Moran runs this—this Night Club. He's got friends. He's tough!"

Satan nodded.

"Somehow, Gilpatric, I thought it would be Hickey Moran's," he said. "We've been enemies a long time. He'll need friends if he gets tough with me." Then turning to Malcolm Strause, "Come on!"

They mounted the few steps to the stone balustraded porch. Satan pressed the little button beside the iron grating which served as an outer door. Almost at once the wooden door behind it opened. A sharp, peaked face with narrow, blinking eyes looked out at him.

"Open up!" said Satan, making sure that Strause was back in the shadows.

"Got a card?" the man asked, trying to peer at Satan in the pale light.

"Detective!" Satan flashed his badge. "Looking for a lad." Confidentially and with well simulated indifference, "Just perfunctory. Been going the rounds. Open up!"

"Sorry—" said the man at the door, still trying unsuccessfully to peer at the face beneath the gray slouch hat. "Can't let you in." And as Satan opened his mouth, "That's orders. There's no use beefing."

"Police business! And this is a public place. Better be nice."

"Got a warrant?" The man spoke through the side of his mouth now and his voice was no longer pleasant. "I know my rights. You can't get in here without a bit of legal paper. On your way, Flatfoot, or you'll get yourself a beat in the woods. This is a private club and you've got to have a card, or—"

The man at the door never saw Satan's hand move. He never even saw the gun until the nose of it was through the grating and almost touching his forehead.

"Is that good for a card?" And as the man's eyes bulged and his lower lip drooped, Satan added, "Open up! And if you press that button I'll shoot your head from between your ears."

The doorman was of the underworld and he knew the rule; the man with the gun talks and the one without, listens. The iron grating swung noisily open; the man's other hand dropped from the little bell to his side.

"All right!" Satan called Strause out of the darkness. The suddenly sobered man stood trembling in the hall. "Do these look like the stairs?" The stairs leading above were narrow, with a slight curve to them.

Strause swallowed the lump that came into his throat and said:

"Yes. It looks like them, but I can't be sure."

Mr. Malcolm Strause, of Yonkers, was beginning to wish he had gone straight home.

"Up the stairs, Strause." He pushed Strause ahead.

Satan swung suddenly, his gun raised in his hand.

Strause heard the words, and even his dulled senses caught the viciousness in Satan's voice.

"You would—would you?" was all that Satan said.

Then came a dull thud, a clatter like glass or steel against wood, and Malcolm Strause turned in time to see the suddenly limp body of the doorman sink slowly to the floor, move an arm grotesquely from beneath him and lie still. And he saw, too, the glittering blade of a knife that was close to the unconscious man's right hand.

MALCOLM STRAUSE'S HEAD whirled; he gripped the banister for support. In the pit of his stomach was a queer, strange feeling of nausea. He knew, too, that the iron-grated door swung noisily back and forth, with no one to guard it.

It was Satan who jarred him out of it.

"Get going! That lad," he jerked a thumb indifferently toward the crumpled mass to the right of the stairs, "didn't recognize me. Or at least, not in time." And as a door opened above and for a moment a flood of light shot down, Satan stepped quickly before Strause, with the low warning:

"Follow me. Hold my coat, so I'll know you're there. I get nervous alone." He smiled grimly.

The door above closed, and now only the light from a dull yellow globe guided Satan up the remaining steps of those narrow stairs. His broad shoulders hid Strause completely.

As a white face above a white bosomed shirt looked down at him from the landing, the orchestra started to play in the room beyond; a girl was singing. Satan liked music, and he shuddered. Other things beside music were murdered in this place, he thought.

"Just one?" The head waiter at the top of the stairs held a small pad and pencil in his hand as he backed toward the door and eyed Satan. "A stranger in town, sir? I don't remember your face."

"Well—you'll remember it now." Satan raised his head

and looked at the man. "And there are two of us." He dragged Strause under the light.

The swarthy face of the head waiter paled slightly, his lower lip quivered, and he half looked at the partly open door behind him. Then his right hand slid over to his left wrist, and Satan flashed his badge.

"The man down below fancied a knife," he said to the waiter softly, "not a blackjack. You do things quietly in this place, don't you? I want to see Hickey Moran."

The waiter gulped once.

"Mr. Moran isn't in. We're closing up."

Satan's left hand shot out suddenly, and long strong fingers bit into the man's shoulder as he backed toward the door.

"I saw Moran come in, and I want to speak to him— now." Satan lied easily.

"It would be worth my job," the waiter started, and stopped. Green eyes were boring into his. A gun, seemingly from nowhere, was jabbed into his stomach.

"It'll be worth your life if you don't. Now—move!"

"It's back of the dance hall—Mr. Moran's office," the head waiter stammered. "You can't march me through there with a rod in my back. And—and—you'll be sorry for this."

"Not half as sorry as you'll be if you lead me wrong. Turn around. Take us straight to Moran. There'll be a gun covering you, but the people in the dance hall won't know it—unless it goes off."

The man nodded his head, but did not speak. He turned and entered the main room, Satan close behind him, his left arm hooked through Strause's right.

The music blasted out its notes in an unsuccessful

attempt to drown out the yellow haired singer who walked back and forth across the floor. Three or four girls and perhaps a half dozen men were seated close together, near the door. They were not drinking, but were talking in low voices.

Hostess—was the official label attached to the woman. The men were simply gangsters. They needed no official title to designate them. It was just one of the many such dives of a great city.

Satan took all this in as he crossed the room; noted that probably no more than four or five tables were occupied by paying guests—and then he was back of the orchestra, through a doorway; into a narrow hall. He heard voices, there in the room to his right.

"Mr. Moran's in there." The head waiter raised his hand to tap at the door, when the detective grabbed his arm. Satan had noted with satisfaction that the door was not locked. Light came through a generous crack.

"I'll just walk in on him," he said. "Hickey and I are old friends. Back to your job! And close that door at the end of the corridor, near the music."

Detective Satan Hall stood for a full minute as the head waiter walked the length of that hall, passed into the main room and closed the door behind him. Then Satan acted quickly, for he knew that Hickey Moran would immediately be notified that all was not as it should be.

He pushed open that door, slid the now fearful Strause into the room and entered himself, kicking the door closed behind him.

3

ANOTHER BODY

TWO MEN WERE in that room. One sat behind a wide flat desk; the other sat upon it, one leg beating up and down against the expensive side. Both turned their heads slowly. The face of the man on the desk showed nothing more than a slight curiosity.

But the man behind the desk came to his feet, knocking his knees against the top of the desk and half stumbling as he thrust back his chair. The other man turned and looked at him. It was the first time he had ever seen emotion of any kind in Hickey Moran. Now—for a moment there was fear in Hickey's watery blue eyes.

The man on the desk understood that there was danger of some sort. And of course it came from the two men who had entered the room; from the single tall man who had thrust the door closed and stood there with his back against it, his hands empty.

Hands empty! The man on the desk repeated those words to himself several times, then seeing that the eyes of the big stranger were on Hickey Moran he let his right hand slip slowly across his chest, under his coat—and Hickey spoke.

"Nix on that stuff, Starro. This lad likes it that way. Drop your hand, you fool. It's Satan Hall."

"Oh—" said Starro. "Hall, eh? Satan Hall." But although he tried to make his words steady and his tone sarcastic, he dropped his right hand quickly from his left armpit.

Satan said nothing. Just stood there regarding the two men. Hickey Moran he knew well. Gangster; racketeer; night club owner—and, yes; murderer. His record was bad, but not as bad as the records of those courts which failed to convict him. Three times, at least, he had beaten the rap for murder.

The other man, Satan didn't know. He was willing to draw a rod in Hickey's Night Club, and maybe willing to use it. An out-of-town gunman. That was it! One who did things in Chi or Philly.

Hickey Moran was the first to speak.

"The commissioner doing a bit of personal raiding? All right; let me have the warrant and—"

"I haven't any warrant. This is just a personal visit, Hickey."

"And the punk with you?" Hickey grinned. He liked to see people afraid of him—and Malcolm Strause, now dead sober, was trembling visibly as he leaned against the wall. "How the devil did you get up here?"

The telephone on the desk rang. Hickey reached for it mechanically, then drew his hand away as he looked at Satan. He knew Satan—knew him well. He feared Satan as he feared no other cop. He feared him because he saw in him a gunman, like himself. A man who shot and killed. Now this man was here—in his club. Why?

Satan smiled and nodded toward the phone.

"It's your phone," he said, and his lips curled slightly. "Use it if you want."

Satan stood there, his back against the wall, his two arms hanging at his sides; both his hands plainly visible, and both empty.

Hickey Moran's swarthy face paled slightly as he picked up the receiver. When Hickey put down that phone, hell blazed in his watery blue eyes. He fairly shot the words at Satan.

"You've got nothing on me," he said. "You've got nothing on this place. You near caved in the head of my doorman. This place is a club—a licensed club. I'll break you for this."

"You're not interested in why I came, nor in who this man with me is?"

"No!" said Hickey Moran, and in the same breath, "Who is he?"

"Well—he lost forty dollars here, and a pen and pencil."

"My God!" There was relief in Hickey's voice now. "You're getting down to that? Forty dollars! What if he did? You don't think I've got it?"

"No," said Satan calmly, "I don't—and I don't even know that he lost it here. I want you to take me through the place. You see, he was very much attached to that pen and—"

"And you knock out my doorman for a lousy forty berries!" Hickey knitted his eyes. The thing didn't sound right and he was worried. He wished he knew just why Satan had come. Forty dollars! That was ridiculous!

"WHY NOT SHOW your friend over the place?" Starro cut in. "Maybe he isn't so bad. Maybe this guy did get hooked for forty berries. You can't be responsible for the guests he might have met here."

"All right!" said Hickey. "Come on, if you want to see around. I've got nothing to hide."

"Of course you haven't," said Satan. "Why should you? We'd like to see the bar first. The boy friend, here, could stand a shot." And he straightened Strause from his position against the wall.

Starro laughed. Then Hickey laughed. It all didn't, somehow, jibe.

"I guess we all could do for a little drink," was what Hickey said as he led them from the room. Damn it all! He would like to know what was on Satan's mind. But many men had wanted to know the same thing—and many men had died without knowing.

The six men who had been in the single party had separated and were now scattered about at different tables when Satan entered the main room. As Moran looked at them they glared back ferociously and even tapped their pockets suggestively. But when Satan's eyes found them, as his eyes did find each one, their eyes dropped suddenly and their threatening hands seemed to find something to do upon the table. Empty hands, that were in plain view.

One man, sitting straight and stiff in a corner of that room, brought a grin to Satan's face and a frown to the face of Hickey Moran. The man was Lieutenant Gilpatric. He was ill at ease, and the left hand that held the glass of white rock could not entirely hide the awkward bend of his right elbow, the hand of which was beneath the table. It was plain to Satan, as it was to Hickey Moran and his companion, that Lieutenant Gilpatric was concealing—at least, visibly—a heavy police automatic.

"Hello, Hickey." Gilpatric came awkwardly to his feet

and shoved the gun, that for the moment showed plainly, into his jacket pocket.

"Hello, Lieutenant." Hickey Moran sneered. "You're in on this racket too?"

"Well—not exactly." Gilpatric jerked down his vest. "The door was open, so I came up. Just a little adverse criticism which the commissioner doesn't fancy, and—" he shrugged his shoulders, "Satan'll make a fair report."

"Sure!' said Satan. "That's just the way it is, Hickey."

But Hickey Moran didn't like the way those green eyes watched him.

The entrance to the bar was at the head of the main room. Hickey kicked open the door; held it so, and they all five stepped in.

"This look like the place?" Satan asked Strause. And when that individual only eyed him blankly, maybe fearfully, "Well—does it? You've nothing to be afraid of."

"That's right." Hickey nodded and put his blue eyes on Strause.

"It's—I think it's the same place. Yes—there's the side door and—" Strause stopped. Those blue eyes had changed. Strause couldn't just explain it—but he knew what fear meant.

"That's right!" Satan walked to the side door, and finding it locked and the key in the lock, opened it and looked out into the hall. "Looks like this is the place."

"Yeah—maybe." Hickey walked over to the bar and spoke to the man behind it. "What do you say, Joe?" He addressed the bartender as he jerked a thumb toward Strause. "See this lad here tonight?"

"Cripes!" Joe wiped down the bar, but looked more at

Satan than at Strause. "We had a busy night, Boss. It's hard to tell."

Joe's mean face, with its crooked nose and pock-marked features, stuck far over the bar as he shook his head. **"AND THAT'S THAT."** Hickey Moran dug a hand into his pocket. "I didn't get the name, brother, and I don't admit any responsibility. But if you think you were shaken down here—why, I'll pay for it. Here!" He offered two yellow backs to Strause, who drew back—flat against the wall.

"Mind you—" Hickey Moran turned again to Satan, "I'm not admitting, even, that this man was here. It's just— Hickey Moran's way of doing business."

"I don't want it," Strause said in a husky, frightened voice. "It looks like the place and all that, but the—they called it Tony's, and—" He broke off suddenly. A sudden, quick flash set the dull blue of Hickey Moran's eyes into sharp points of hatred. Then Satan had stepped between Strause and Moran.

"Take the money," said Satan, as he took the bills and shoved them into Strause's trembling fingers. "You might change your mind, later, and Moran mightn't be here to offer it again."

"What do you mean—I mightn't be here?" Moran tried to keep his blue eyes on Satan's green ones, but they wandered to the face of Starro. There was a warning in Starro's eyes, and uncertainty, too, as his upper teeth drew in his lower lip.

Satan walked toward the little side door as he spoke.

"Nothing much. Fellows in your line of work don't live so long. And, again—" This time Satan stared at Hickey

Moran for several seconds, "you might be at Tony's, you know."

"My line of work suits me all right," was the best Moran could bluster as he avoided Starro's eyes and followed the three men down the stairs. Just one word was ringing in his ears; just one name. Tony! He had read the papers and remembered the single word the murdered man had spoken before he died. The single name, Tony. Hickey Moran's right hand crept toward his left armpit, then fell to his side again.

The iron grating at the foot of the stairs was locked again. The unconscious man had been removed and another doorman had taken his place. The three men passed into the night.

Malcolm Strause, with his forty dollars regained, was packed off in a taxi at the next corner—for Yonkers.

"There goes," said Satan to Gilpatric, "a man of destiny. Who'd think that a little man from Yonkers, with a drunken sentiment for a pen and pencil, would—"

He stopped and listened. Plainly he heard the screech of a police siren. Two minutes later, with Satan driving and Gilpatric in the seat beside him, they turned down a side street three blocks up town, in the wake of the police car. One minute later brakes screeched and they came to a stop directly behind the Department car.

But they didn't need the car, now, to tell them where the trouble was. Already a dozen or more people were gathered on the sidewalk. A cop in uniform was standing guard before the basement entrance to a four story dwelling. Satan reached the few steps to the basement almost before the men in the police car got there. Plainly he heard the short wave set in the car droning out its message of death in the dull monotone of an unimaginative announcer.

"Cars number 986 and 729. Go to No.— Body of a man lying in basement entrance. Ambulance on its way. Cars number 986 and—"

And behind Satan came the voice of Gilpatric.

"My God! Another one. That makes four."

Five minutes later Satan straightened above the body. Inspector Walsh was there. An ambulance had already drawn up to the curb. And Satan and Gilpatric faced each other on the sidewalk.

"Just about Strause's height and build," said Gilpatric. "And from the line across the bridge of his nose, he wore glasses. Gray suit too, but a light brown hat."

"Yes." Satan nodded grimly. "He could be taken for Strause—easy, if a lad had only an oral description of him."

"From Illinois, eh?"

"Yes." Satan stared off over the tops of the buildings. "Chicago. Stabbed through the back—three times in the back."

4

A MURDER IS ARRANGED

BACK IN THE so-called Night Club, Hickey Moran paced the floor of his office behind the deserted orchestra pit. Seated on the desk again was Johnny Starro.

"So that," he said slowly, "was the great detective, Satan Hall. The man who's got your city buffaloed. You call yourself a rod-man, Hickey. Why—out in Chi—blooey—like that anyone of a dozen of us would gun him out."

Hickey paused in his walk, took a cigarette from his pocket, and lighting it from the butt between his fingers, looked at Starro. Then he said:

"Satan's been to Chi—and came back." And after a pause, "Each time a man died. There was Ferdon and the Wop, Congalies. Don't tell me they were a couple of—"He broke off suddenly. "I'll cut the stomachs out of those two rats who shook down that punk. They must have done it when they took him out of here."

"Yeah." Johnny Starro smiled over at Moran. "I told you to let the kill ride tonight. If Satan had come in here ten; yes, five minutes earlier—what then?"

"Then," said Hickey very slowly, "I'd of had to shoot him to death. There'd of been no other way."

"That would be a good way now," Johnny Starro said.

"You don't believe that forty dollar racket, alone, brought Satan Hall here! And the 'Tony's!'"

Johnny Starro came off that desk and clutched Hickey roughly by the arm.

" 'Tony's,' eh? Was that punk given the name Tony's before he was steered here?"

"I think so. They were all given it when they came in, in case things went wrong. There are a hundred Tony's, and the cops never could be sure. After Stapleton chirped the name, every 'Tony's' was covered."

"That's it!" Starro cut in viciously. "Satan's been working on those murders. He remembered that Stapleton piped the name Tony's before he died. Stapleton—the first knock-over you bulled up, before I came on. Now—Satan found this little punk, with his damn forty dollar roll. By God! Satan may have guessed that the wrong man was brought in here tonight. Will he guess that the right one came later?"

"You've got the jitters." Hickey laughed mirthlessly. And suddenly, "It was a bad break. Who'd have thought they'd have traced him here? And they wouldn't have unless those two boys who took him out shook him down for his lousy forty bucks. I'm half sorry I didn't do for the punk."

"Well—" said Johnny Starro, "it can't be helped now. And I guess they can't prove anything, no matter how you look at it. Satan's suspicions ain't evidence."

"Yeah—yeah," said Hickey thoughtfully. "But Satan ain't a regular cop. He's got peculiar ideas."

"What do you mean by peculiar ideas?"

"I mean," said Hickey, "he ain't above killing. He ain't above downright murder. Does he go out to produce evidence and convict a guy before twelve men? He does not. He gets a guy in a jam and shoots him to death. It sounds funny to you, a stranger; but it's a fact. It's happened too many times to be just bad luck for some 'rod.'"

"It'll be tough on you, Hickey, if he works that way this time."

"If he works this racket out, it'll be through you. He's not a dumb dick. He saw you tonight. Tomorrow he'll have your record; know you come from Chicago. He'll beat it out there and— Well—he's the only copper who could run us down."

"Hickey," Johnny Starro grew very serious, "this bird, Satan, was here for a purpose tonight. He's investigating them dead men. Now—ours is a good racket; the best ever. Even if Satan doesn't find the truth he'll be watching you." Johnny Starro leaned forward and took Hickey Moran by both shoulders. "What'll you dig if I put Satan on the spot?"

"When?" Hickey Moran just breathed the word.

"Now—tonight—this morning."

"Ten grand."

"Twenty!"

"Twenty then."

"On the dot?"

"On the first pay-off."

"On the dot!" Starro was persistent.

"On the dot," said Hickey Moran, after a moment's thought.

THE TWO MEN shook hands; sat down at either side of the desk. Then Hickey Moran drew a rough plan of Detective Satan Hall's apartment. He knew the location well; had studied it. What Johnny Starro planned to do now—at once, Hickey Moran had planned to do for some time. But he just hadn't gotten around to it. At least, that was the way Hickey put it to himself.

"I don't know." Hickey Moran shook his head when Starro took out his gun, examined it carefully and thrust it back beneath his left armpit. "Maybe I should go myself. I'm faster on the draw than you are, and I've got a better eye for distance. I think I could give the works to the rotten rat."

"You had your chance tonight." Johnny Starro grinned. "He was standing there by the door, both his hands empty. Never made a move."

"That's it. That's what gets a guy. It's his reputation and his luck. Some day we'll pull together, then Mr. Satan will find out what's what. I tell you, Starro, I've stood enough."

"There won't be any 'some day.'" Johnny Starro laughed. "When I go after a guy I go after him. I ain't particular how it looks to the boys. I ain't out for glory. I just poke a gun against a guy's middle or stick a knife—"

"Yeah—I know." Hickey was thinking of the man who had died like that—by a knife—a few hours before. "But Satan ain't no bloke with his hands in the air, begging you not to kill him."

"That guy did squeal," Johnny Starro reminisced. He reached the door and put his hand on the knob. "Don't you worry, Hickey. Satan will be dead tired, and I'll come in like a cat. You guys in this burg went about it wrong. Lads asleep in bed can't depend much on being gun wizards, and I need that twenty grand."

Hickey followed Starro down the narrow hall, across the

dance floor and down to the foot of the stairs in the now darkened hall. But Starro didn't leave by the front door. He parted a curtain at the side, opened a small door back of a closet and went down a flight of wooden stairs to the basement. There Hickey Moran pulled out a flash and ran a circle of light along the cement floor.

"Not a mark—not a spot." He looked at the floor closely.

"There never is." Starro laughed. "I'm a clean workman."

Hickey Moran shuddered slightly. He was a killer; relentless. But he was a gunman. And a knife! Well—perhaps even murderers are temperamental. Anyway, Hickey Moran shuddered.

They walked across the cellar floor the full length of the house, opened a rear door and passed to the street behind.

"No bars on Satan's window—nothing?" Starro asked again, and his voice did not shake.

"No bars—nothing. He even sleeps with the window on the fire-escape open."

"Thanks!" said Johnny Starro as he went whistling down the street. There was murder in his heart and a tune on his lips. Hickey Moran watched him for a moment, then he smiled. There comes a time when every man must die—even Detective Satan Hall.

Then he went to see Lieutenant Gilpatric at the station house. It wouldn't be the first time he had dropped in at that time of the morning for a chat. And this morning—Well, after Gilpatric's visit to him, it would be a natural—and it would be an alibi. Hickey Moran was lighthearted, for he felt that he would be needing just such an alibi.

5

DEATH STRIKES

THE MORNING WAS cold for that time of the year. Johnny Starro pulled his jacket tighter about him after consulting his watch. It was a good hour. Experience had taught him that people sleep soundest before dawn.

Satan Hall! Johnny Starro smiled to himself. What did a name have to do with it? The best gun in Chicago had died by Johnny's hand. A bellyful of lead doesn't play any favorites.

Only two stories up. Hell! He'd be back in the alley before the nearest neighbor was out of bed. And the bed room had one window on the fire-escape. Satan must be a fool to leave that open nights.

Johnny spotted the fire-escape and nodded his approval. It was wedged in tightly between two houses. One quick look up and down the deserted street, and he was in the alley. He waited there a moment, listening. Then he was down that alley, running low and keeping close to the fence. Even to Johnny's straining ears came no sound of his own running feet. He was proud of those running feet. Nodding his satisfaction, he slunk along by the fence and crept like a shadow beneath the fire-escape.

He looked up at the iron grating and set his lips grimly.

It was too high for a jump. But that was to be expected. That might even be why Satan slept with his window open.

Johnny Starro tried the end of the alley, close to the court. There were many barrels. Galvanized iron, most of them. They'd make a noise even under his trained feet. But somewhere there would be— And there was. A wooden barrel! He lifted it carefully over the iron ones, carried it under one end of the fire-escape and set it down gently. Johnny was a careful workman. He didn't hurry; he wasn't nervous. He had killed men before. Who the hell was Satan, anyway? And Johnny smiled.

He climbed onto the barrel, stretched up his hands and turned up his head. Then he jumped. His fingers wound easily around the iron rails at the side of the balcony. Hand over hand he moved up the iron support, his feet hanging straight down below him. When he finally climbed onto that fire-escape he had only to raise his right knee slightly, force it between the rusty supports and come to his feet.

He stood so a minute; found that he was breathing easily and naturally. Then he swung onto the iron ladder that led to the floor above—the apartment above. Satan's apartment.

His hat was pulled far down now, his jacket collar turned high. If he had to run for it, someone might look from the apartment across the court. What if they did? A slouch hat, a dark coat, and a running figure. Satan had many enemies.

Johnny got a real break. Satan's window was open high enough to admit his body. He discovered this as soon as he reached the iron balcony and saw the window almost in the center of it. Then he heard the deep breathing inside that room. It was regular and even. Johnny grinned evilly.

Satan was sleeping hard, like a tired man. There could be no fake about that. He knew from experience. No man could fake sleep on him!

Just a shadow against the light, Johnny bent for a moment. Then, without a sound he dropped into the room beyond, moved silently from the dull light of the window and was merged with the blackness. The breathing went on, and Johnny didn't move. He waited for his eyes to become accustomed to the darkness. Minutes passed, and Johnny could see the bed plainly now; could make out Satan's face. He raised his gun and drew a bead right between those slanting eyebrows. Johnny laughed inwardly. A step forward; a gun against Satan's head; the flash on his face, and it would be over.

Then he thought of the many stories he had heard of Satan; of the talk of his green eyes. This resemblance to the devil; these stories that Satan was— But Johnny Starro wasn't superstitious. He'd give him the heat and get it over with. A rat of a rotten dick shouldn't be given a chance, and Johnny would like to see those green eyes when the light went out of them.

And Johnny acted.

He did three things almost at once. He stepped two paces forward; he pressed the button of the flash; he laid the nose of his heavy automatic almost against Satan's head. But he held the flash so that Satan would see the gun.

Green eyes opened and seemed to stare straight into Johnny's eyes, and there was nothing of fear in them. Just the same cold, cruel, sinister eyes that had looked at Johnny down at Hickey Moran's place. And for the first time in his life Johnny knew fear. The hand that held the gun trembled.

He thought only of firing that gun, killing Satan—blotting out those sinister, deadly eyes and getting away.

His right hand moved; his right index finger flexed, and there was the single roar of a gun. A roar that vibrated through that room. But there was no sudden dart of orange blue flame; no smell of burning powder. Just the roar of a heavy automatic. And a man died.

6

AN ALIBI FOR JOHNNY STARRO

BACK IN THE station house Hickey Moran paced up and down, and for the fifth time put the same question to Gilpatric.

"You and me have been friends," Hickey said again. "Now—I want to know how we stand."

"Hell!" said Gilpatric as he thumbed over papers without seeing them, "I've told you that. We stand as we always stood." And turning on him and letting the fifty cent cigar that Moran had given him race across his mouth, "What's on your chest?"

"I don't know." Hickey dropped into a chair. "I don't know what's on my chest—unless I know what's on yours. In plain words, if things were right and above board, you'd of tipped me off tonight that Satan was coming."

"Hell!" said Gilpatric again, "I tried to steer him away from your place. It was too late to squawk to you then."

"But you didn't have to sit there with a cannon in your mitt. That didn't look like any forty dollar pinch."

"You said, yourself, that Satan's been after you for a couple of years. I know that. You know that. Every cop on the force knows that. But I didn't know it was your place that the lad was shaken down in. When Satan went in—

well— I got thinking to myself about you and him having bad blood, so I just went up—in way of protection."

"Protection for him—or protection for me?" And when Gilpatric did not answer, "In case of a jam, how far can I count on you?"

"Just as far as you've always counted on me, and no farther." Gilpatric hesitated a moment, and then, "Why don't you talk out like a man?"

"Well—" Hickey Moran leaned forward until his face was very close to Lieutenant Gilpatric, "You've taken my money and you've taken my booze, and if I need you— you'll stick, or I'll talk. Is that talking like a man?"

"That," said Gilpatric, "is talking like a rat. I've done nothing crooked as I see crookedness."

"Others may look at it different."

"Others won't get a chance to look at it different. The money's spent and the booze is drunk—and you can't prove nothing. You know your business and I know mine. Why shouldn't I take it from you? The city tolerates your dirty dives, and it's my precinct and my gravy. Should I let a sergeant or a common flatfoot shake down my plums? Not me. I know my rights. I know what I'm entitled to when I get a precinct. You'll pay or you'll close. I've got a wife and kids that want things."

Hickey nodded. Gilpatric was right. He couldn't prove anything. He was just talking now, to kill time. Why the hell didn't the phone ring? Certainly someone would notify Gilpatric of Satan's death. It was after four. But Gilpatric was talking, and his words jarred Hickey Moran to his feet.

"Where's Johnny Starro tonight?" Gilpatric asked.

"Starro. Starro! He's around," Hickey said after a bit, and

then he laughed. Johnny would need an alibi, too. But he'd arrange that later.

Gilpatric looked at him shrewdly. There was a puzzle here and he couldn't exactly fit the pieces together, properly. Hickey Moran kept sticking around, and he wasn't good company. Not any too good, anyway, for a man who hoped to wear the stripes of a captain. Still— Damn it to hell! Was the dirty racketeer using him for an alibi; using him to cover—

And he drew the cigar out of his mouth and pointed it straight at Hickey Moran. But the words already forming on his lips were never spoken. The phone rang. Gilpatric jerked off the receiver, gave his precinct, and said:

"Lieutenant Gilpatric speaking."

A moment of silence while Hickey Moran strained his ears and despite his satisfaction, paled slightly. Word was coming in at last. It had been tough waiting. Now—he eased back in the chair as Gilpatric gasped:

"Tonight! Satan's apartment. Good God! His window open again."

Another moment of silence while Hickey Moran lighted a cigarette with fingers that no longer trembled. Good old Johnny Starro! And for a while he had doubted him.

And Gilpatric was saying in an awed voice:

"Right through the stomach, eh? Died without a word. I always knew that open window was a death trap."

Window—death trap. Sure! Hickey Moran couldn't help but nod in agreement. But any "gun" might have done it. It didn't take so much nerve to slip in on a sleeping man and dump lead into his belly. It didn't—

But Gilpatric was telling him something, and he was

trying to get the words. Trying to get them and missing some. He must be missing some! But, no. Gilpatric said them plain enough as he swung around after hanging up the receiver.

"Johnny Starro got himself killed tonight, up in Satan's apartment."

"But—but—" Hickey Moran's words choked in his throat. "You're fooling, Gil—you're fooling. You said the window was a death trap."

"Sure!" Gilpatric nodded indifferently. "Satan's death trap. He leaves it open for the damn fools he wants to come and get the lead. At least, that's the way I look at it. Don't take it so hard, Hickey. Johnny had it coming to him."

"Yeah—yeah. I suppose so." Hickey Moran ran a cold damp hand over a moist forehead as he came to his feet and gripped the back of his chair. What was he going to do? Oh, yes—he was to fix up that alibi. Alibi! An alibi for Johnny Starro!

Hickey Moran tried to keep his knees from sagging as he passed out of that room, by the long station house desk and to the front door. At the door he caught himself up quickly. Johnny Starro blasted out! Well—that was one less to split with when the gravy started rolling in. It didn't make any difference. They couldn't get anything on him—not on Hickey Moran. Satan might guess, but he couldn't prove anything. No, he couldn't prove anything. Then he thought of Johnny Starro again. Satan couldn't prove anything on Johnny either—but Johnny was dead.

7

BEHIND THE DOOR

THE POLICE COMMISSIONER was a small man whose physical development had been sacrificed to his mental development. He had a soft quick voice, and held his hands together so that the ends of his fingers could touch and part now and then as he talked. Now he looked over the flat mahogany desk at Satan, and said:

"After this you'll sleep with your window closed, eh?"

"No. I'd rather be killed quickly than be slowly suffocated. I like air."

The commissioner frowned.

"You've hated Hickey Moran for a long time, Satan. You know how I've tried to get him and what I've run up against. Now—I want Hickey, of course, but I want the murderer or murderers of these four men first."

"I think," said Satan very slowly, "that they were all murdered in Hickey Moran's Night Club and dumped into the street. I think, last night, if I'd played my hunch and gone straight to Hickey's Club, I might have prevented the fourth murder. There was the single name 'Tony's,' which was slipped to each man before he died, so that if things went wrong and the murder didn't go through, the victim would not be able to locate the place. Malcolm

Strause had the name Tony's, and he recognized Hickey Moran's club. All these men were stabbed except the first one—Lawrence Stapleton. He was shot, and lived for a while afterwards, long enough to pronounce the name Tony's, anyway. I got Chicago this morning and found out something about Johnny Starro. He was mighty handy with a knife."

"You're building up quite a case," the commissioner agreed, "but we must have a stronger motive for Hickey Moran. He'd go to murder, of course—but not unnecessarily. And not, I think, for the few thousand dollars those men carried."

"I don't believe," said Satan emphatically, "that those men were killed for a few thousand dollars apiece. I don't believe they even had a few thousand dollars on them."

"But that they had a large amount of money with them is already established."

"Established! By whom?"

"H-m." The commissioner looked toward the ceiling. "In the case of the first victim—Lawrence Stapleton—by his wife. In the case of James Ralston, by his brother. In the Quincey Martin death, by his business partner. This fourth— Well—we've sent out for information."

"And where," asked Satan, "did these men get this money?"

"I don't know. But I presume—the bank."

"They didn't!" Satan was emphatic. "None of the three cashed a check for over two hundred before they came here."

The commissioner looked long and earnestly at Satan.

"I suppose there is no use of my suggesting a safe deposit box."

"None at all, except in the case of Lawrence Stapleton. He did visit his safe deposit box. But that may be—mere coincidence."

"Or," said the commissioner with a smile, "he may have visited it to bring a ring to his daughter, who lives here in the city. A ring her dead mother owned. You see, I have been looking into things quietly also."

"I knew that he had a daughter, but not that she lived here in the city."

"Lawrence Stapleton, as you know, was a widower who married again," the commissioner continued. "His daughter left him shortly after his second marriage, came to the city and took her mother's maiden name."

"Yes, yes." Satan nodded indifferently. "Listen, Commissioner. I want to go to Chicago. I want to find out about Starro; about each of these relatives who gave out the information that so much money was carried." Satan paused and turned his eyes to the slightly open door which led to the little private library where the commissioner spent so much of his time.

The commissioner was saying:

"Of course you can go to Chicago. But this— What's the matter, Satan?"

"Commissioner," Satan said, "there's someone listening at the door to your private room."

THE DOOR TO that private room swung wide open. A girl stepped out. She was small and dark. She walked to the desk and stood erect, looking at Satan. Her eyes were bright and defiant, and her chin tilted slightly.

"So you're Detective Satan Hall," she said. "I was listening. I'm Elsa Stapleton. I want to know who killed my father."

Satan came slowly to his feet and looked at the girl.

"Yes, Miss Stapleton," he said quietly, "of course you do."

"I'm tired of hearing that the police are doing everything possible. I want justice, or I want—"

"Vengeance." Satan nodded very gravely. "You got some of that last night, I think."

"Yes!" said the commissioner, also rising. "You may be sure, Miss Stapleton, that no stone will be left unturned. The law seems to move slowly to those who suffer, and—"

"Suffer!" the girl cried out. "My father came to see me the afternoon before he died. All our differences were made up. He was going to change his will. He was going to divorce my stepmother. Don't you understand? She killed him."

"There, there." The commissioner placed a hand on her shoulder, but she shook it off.

"Don't—don't!" she cried. "Don't treat me like a child. I hated my stepmother, that's true. I told you that. And she hated me. She married dad for his money She killed him for his money. She had him killed. She—"

"And these others! Three other men died the same way. All were robbed, Miss Stapleton. Surely you don't think your stepmother—"

"I don't care about the others. It's my father. She wanted him dead, and he is dead. She wanted his money, and she got it. All right"—she pointed a finger first at the commissioner and then at Satan—"if you don't care, and you don't care, and the law don't care—I care. You won't listen to me.

You won't believe me." She had turned back toward the door when Satan spoke.

"I would like very much to listen to you, Miss Stapleton," Satan said very slowly as she passed into the private room, slamming the door.

The commissioner spread his arms far apart and said:

"There you are. Her mother died and her father married again, and the girl took her mother's name and came to the city here. She's studying music, or art—or something like that. Poor kid! She's possessed with the idea that her stepmother killed her father, or had him killed. The Stapletons were rather prominent socially, out their way. I could not imagine Mrs. Stapleton killing her husband."

"Couldn't you?" Satan let those green eyes settle on the commissioner's face. "I could!"

"Oh, come now!" The commissioner was trying to draw Satan out. "That won't account for the others."

"Won't it?" Satan said grimly. "With your permission, Commissioner, I'll talk with the girl alone."

The commissioner hesitated a moment, then walked to the door of his private office and threw it open.

"Miss Stapleton," he said softly, "Detective Hall would—" Then quickly turning to Satan, "The girl's gone!"

And she was gone. The door leading to the corridor was unlocked. One look the commissioner took, up and down the hall. Then he crossed quickly to his desk, reached toward the telephone and drew his hand away again.

"After all," he said, "she's an impulsive girl, and better out of it. Her story was pretty wild."

"Pretty wild!" Satan pulled a timetable from his pocket and consulted it. "Pretty wild, eh? But I'll bet you it's not half as wild as the thing that's running through my head. See you in a week, Commissioner."

8

THINGS HAPPEN IN CHICAGO

BUT IT WAS close to three weeks before the commissioner saw Satan again.

"Where's the Stapleton girl—Lawrence Stapleton's daughter?" Satan asked bluntly.

"I don't know." The commissioner shook his head. "I tried to get in touch with her—just perfunctory, but she had changed her address or left the city."

Satan took a small notebook from his pocket and ran through the pages.

"The girl's stepmother inherited, through the death of Stapleton, over seven hundred thousand dollars. Stapleton had an appointment with his lawyer, Gordon Lackey, on the very afternoon he left Chicago for the city here. He intended to change his will in favor of his daughter." Satan looked up from his little book. "That lawyer, Gordon Lackey, never kept the appointment. So Stapleton came on here and was murdered before he could change that will."

Satan paused so long that the commissioner said:

"Come, come, Satan. Let me have it all now. You've got something."

"Have I!" Green eyes were thin slits of brilliance. "Mrs. Stapleton, alone, benefitted by the death of Stapleton.

Mrs. Stapleton, alone, gave testimony that he was carrying a large sum of money. There is no evidence to prove that he was—much to prove that he wasn't. So much for the first victim.

"The second victim, James Ralston, was also a wealthy man, and a bachelor. His brother inherits the estate, there being no will. This brother was a two time loser from Joliet. This brother also gave out the information that James Ralston was carrying several thousand dollars in his pocket.

"Quincey Martin was the third victim. He was a widower, without children, and had a half interest in a chemical factory. The surviving partner inherited that half interest. And the surviving partner lost heavily in the stock market and needed that half interest to save his own share. Also, this partner gave out the information that Martin was carrying several thousand dollars with him. Like the others, there was no evidence to substantiate this statement, and much to disprove it.

"The fourth victim was Thomas R. Ward. That was three weeks ago. I've seen his will. He drew it while angry with relatives, and left everything to a nurse who took care of him in an illness. He was becoming friendly with his relatives again and his affection for the nurse was growing cold. I guess that was why he had to die quickly. And it was the nurse who gave the information that Mr. Ward had shown her a large roll of money before leaving for the city here. Again we have the talk of much money, but every fact points out that Mr. Ward did not carry it.

"So—to sum it up. The only evidence that these four men carried large amounts of money upon them when they were murdered comes from the single individual who benefited by each one's murder. In plain words, commissioner, there is no evidence to show that any one of them obtained a large sum of money, except the unsupported testimony of the most interested party."

"It does seem like a great many coincidences," said the commissioner. "You checked up thoroughly on the money end, of course?"

"Checking accounts; safe deposit vault records of visits; saving accounts; and brokerage houses. None of the four men dealt with large sums of cash. None gambled for large stakes."

"And the reason for these people lying about the money, I presume, is to make each murder appear solely for robbery."

"Yes."

"And your conclusion?" The commissioner was drumming on the desk now.

"THIS LAWYER OF Mrs. Stapleton's, Gordon Lackey, made a trip to the city here shortly before Stapleton's murder. My guess is, that he met Hickey Moran and arranged for Stapleton's death. Hickey took on the job, shot Stapleton and dumped his body in an alley. Then Hickey conceived the idea of making a business out of removing wealthy relatives for a consideration. I think Gordon Lackey suggested the victims and the clients, and I think Starro interviewed them. It was probably approached very subtly at first. Remember—there was almost three months between the first and second murders. Hickey engineered the kill, with Starro doing the actual knifing, after that first shooting, when Stapleton lived long enough to speak that single word 'Tony's.'"

"You're not just guessing?"

"No—" said Satan. "I'm stating facts. Only guessing how those facts should be put together. Do you believe it?"

"Yes, I do." The commissioner came to his feet and paced the room. "Funny, too. Elsa Stapleton hated her stepmother and accused her of murdering her father. You hated Hickey Moran and accused him of murdering her father. The long arm of coincidence there."

"No. We just had something to work on. She had the feeling that her stepmother would go to murder, and I— the knowledge that Hickey Moran would." And very low, "And I had the name Tony's, and the man from Yonkers who wanted to recover a pen and pencil, which he never—"

"We've got to have a complete case." The tips of the commissioner's fingers were in action. "You've done good work—fine work. I know that. You know that. But we have to make twelve men know it. I got your telegram and I've given Hickey plenty of rope; no one shadowing him. I've heard, though, that he's running around with a new moll. One of his entertainers, or something like that, what do you suggest now?"

Satan stroked his chin.

"If Hickey engineered these murders he'll get plenty. No doubt he was promised a rake off in the estates. Probably a hundred grand. I've got a hunch that Gordon Lackey will be leaving Chicago soon with the money for Hickey. I'll get word from Chicago as soon as this Gordon Lackey leaves. I want to be present when that cash is slipped to Hickey. I think the weakest link in the chain is Gordon Lackey. I think, if I catch him red-handed, he'll squawk to high heaven."

"But it takes time to execute a will and—"

"Mrs. Stapleton is anxious to pay Hickey, or Hickey is pressing her for the money. Anyway, I found out in the bank that she's raising money on her inheritance. Going to buy a place in the south of France is her story."

"You'll need help. You're not thinking of breaking into their meeting alone?"

"I am thinking of just that, commissioner. I don't want anyone with me. I don't want anyone in on the know. Too many leaks in the Department!" And when the commissioner reddened slightly, "You know that. That's why I work alone, and for you."

"But how'll you get in? You can't—"

"I can," said Satan slowly. "Bodies came out of that Night Club of Hickey Moran's without being seen on the street. I can get in as those bodies came out." Satan yawned. "All I want now is—"

"Anything you want is yours," the commissioner cut in quickly.

"Good!" Satan came to his feet. "I want some sleep. Nothing else."

The commissioner shook his head as Satan departed. Hunting men was Satan's life. The commissioner sighed. Would it be his death? Hickey Moran was one of the most dangerous criminals in the city.

9

THE PAY-OFF

HICKEY MORAN PACED his room and waited for the telephone call which would tell him that Gordon Lackey was on his way up from the Pennsylvania Station. Things had been quiet lately. Hickey hadn't entirely given up the idea of going on with his murder racket. And if he went on with it, Gordon Lackey was indispensable. He knew the inside of family life out in Chi; he knew who could be approached; where the gravy lay—the victims and the clients. Well—he'd see. If he could only tie Gordon Lackey up a bit tighter; push him to actual murder!

Hickey Moran shook his head. He had hard work in getting Lackey to come on with that jack. And the phone rang. Hickey answered it and nodded his satisfaction. Gordon Lackey was on his way up town. He laid down the phone—and turned quickly. Someone had knocked on the door. He smacked his lips, and opening the door smiled at the girl who stood there.

"Come in, kid—come in." He put an arm around the girl and kissed her. She pulled away from him, but he followed her, lifted her up and sat her on the desk. "I got a chance to buy out the swellest apartment; furniture, lease and all, today."

The girl slid off the desk and looked straight into his foggy blue eyes.

"Hickey," she said very softly, "take me to see this apartment—now."

"Kid—" Hickey made as if to grab her, then let his hands drop to his sides. This girl was class; something different than Hickey was in the habit of meeting. Driven into the hostess racket by the depression, he thought. She was beginning to look at him different. Hickey was glad he had controlled the temptation to slap her down that first week. She was coming around all right. And Hickey thought of Gordon Lackey's visit.

"I can't, kid—not tonight," he said. And when she drew away from him, "It's business. It's big money."

"It's a girl!" she said, as she fastened black eyes on him.

"Ah, now—kid." Hickey liked her that way. "Jealous, eh?" He knew she'd come around. "There couldn't be any other woman, kid—not if you were right, like you're going to be. You beat it along home now."

"I won't go home!" She stamped her foot. "You just want to get me out of here. It's a woman."

"Nix, kid—nix." Hickey Moran straightened his tie and jerked down his vest. He sure had a way of getting the dames—even when it came to real class—thoroughbreds! "I tell you, kid. Take a seat in the corner; spot the guy that comes in—then beat it. I'll give you a buzz in the morning, and we'll look over this swell apartment."

She put up her face as she stood by the door and he kissed her full upon the lips.

"That's the stuff, baby!" Hickey said before closing the door. "I knew you couldn't hold out long. Let Tommy take you home. He knows better than to get messing around my woman."

The door closed, so Hickey couldn't see the girl rub madly at her lips with a tiny handkerchief. Nor could he see the shudder that went through her body.

Ten minutes later the buzzer beneath the flat desk rang. Gordon Lackey had arrived.

Gordon Lackey was tall and muscular, and immaculate of dress. He had a habit of rubbing his right hand through his straight black hair, when he was nervous. He was doing that now. His left hand held a small overnight bag, which Hickey looked at with greed-filled eyes.

This was the first time they had met since before the Stapleton murder. Johnny Starro had attended to everything since then. Now Hickey grinned. Gordon Lackey's hand was cold and moist when he grasped it, and the fingers trembled when he dropped them to his side. Hickey nodded to himself. This guy couldn't stand the gaff.

"So you're visiting the big city, eh?" Hickey wasn't trying to put Lackey at his ease. He was just showing him what a big guy Hickey Moran was; that nothing phased him. That murder was just an every-day business, and the collecting of a hundred grand nothing to be excited about.

"How did you like the girls outside? Not so hot, eh? Well—they're not meant to be. I don't want a big clientele. This is just"—and he slapped Lackey on the back—"just a private club—a murder club, eh? Did you bring the jack?" GORDON LACKEY SAID nothing as he threw the bag on the desk and watched Hickey open it and run practiced fingers through the tightly packed bills. Then Gordon Lackey spoke for the first time.

"You asked me," Gordon Lackey cleared his throat and looked back over his shoulder, "what I thought of the girls out front. I was interested in one of them. The dark-haired, dark-eyed girl, who sat in a booth by herself."

Hickey laughed.

"Well—mister," he sat on the desk and leaned far back, holding his left knee between his two hands, "you've picked the wrong girl to have an interest in. That's my girl—my woman, and the word on the avenue is—hands off."

"I see." Gordon Lackey seemed relieved—and then, "I wasn't interested in her in just that way. How long have you known her?"

"About three weeks, and—Hickey came erect on the desk. "What's it to you?"

"Nothing, I hope. You see—I didn't see her very well, but I thought I recognized her."

"Yeah—yeah?" Hickey looked at him. "Maybe you did. She's class, and the depression has thrown some pretty fine work over the line. They ain't—"

"You don't understand." Gordon Lackey's tongue came out and licked at his dry lips. "She looked to me like Stapleton's daughter, Elsa Stapleton."

10

WHERE OTHERS DIED

THE COLOR DRAINED suddenly from Hickey's face. He opened his mouth to speak, but no words came. Then the first sudden thought. Gordon Lackey must be mistaken.

Then other thoughts; quick flashes. The girl had been singing in restaurants. Three weeks before, she had asked him for a job. Her story was that she had had to leave on account of the bosses; the head waiters; the hangers on. She was class, and it sounded reasonable. Then—racing around with him. In that very room when he had called Chicago! And tonight— She accused him of meeting a woman. Woman! Hell! She just wanted an excuse to stay and see who came. Damn it! She'd be gone by now.

Hickey grabbed at the phone. He was talking to the head waiter who watched the door above the stairs; giving quick orders. No one was to come in or go out. And, had anyone left the club?

"No one—within the last few minutes. Miss Elsie Regan is just going down the stairs, but—"

Elsie! Elsa! Hickey Moran snapped into action.

"Don't let her out!" He choked out the words. "Tell her I want to see her in the hall outside my room—at once, and see that she comes."

He jammed the receiver on the hook as Gordon Lackey said:

"It may not be the girl at all. Just a side view I had, and—"

"You'd know her if you saw her—faced her?"

"Certainly. I attended to her father's law business from the day he married again."

"And she'd know you, of course?"

"Yes—if she saw me. But I don't think she did. She was—"

"If she's the Stapleton girl, she saw you." Hickey Moran nodded vigorously. "If she's the Stapleton girl, she was here to see you. But no harm's done yet. She didn't get out. Why the hell didn't you tell me he had a daughter?"

"Why, it was in all the papers."

"So it was—so it was." Hickey crossed the room and jerked open the door. "Wait here," he said. "I'll give you a look at her."

"But if she didn't see me, and—"

"Wait here!" The door closed and Hickey Moran stood in the narrow hall behind the orchestra pit. The girl was coming down the hall. The head waiter had her by the arm.

"She didn't want to come—and I brought her, Boss."

"That's right." Hickey Moran looked at the white face of the girl, took her by the arm and held it tightly. "Okay, Frank!" he said to the head waiter. "Don't let anyone else in. Clear the bar—close it. See that there ain't a soul in it. Afterwards open it up again, as usual."

"Another one—now!" The head waiter's eyes grew wide.

"Yes." Hickey Moran nodded grimly. "Another one."

"What's the matter?" the girl started, and stopped.

Hickey Moran threw open the door to his private room and thrust the girl roughly in. He was beginning to understand things; beginning to check up in his mind what he'd said and done since he met her.

"Know this girl?" He almost pushed her against Gordon Lackey as he rasped the question.

"Yes." Gordon Lackey had difficulty in speaking. "It's Stapleton's daughter, Elsa Stapleton."

"And I know you, too," the girl said suddenly, raising her head. "It was you and my stepmother and this murderer here, who killed my father. And you'll pay for it—all of you." She swung on Hickey Moran. "I came here to find out the truth."

"Satan Hall planted you here—that's it." Hickey Moran's fingers bit into the small arm.

"No—no," she cried out. "I did it myself. The police have failed, but I haven't. You and Gordon Lackey together—and there it is!" She broke loose suddenly and turned over the bag of money. "There's your pay for murdering a man. I'll stand up in court and—"

"How did you happen to come here?" Hickey had a hold of her by the arm again; his face was very close to hers.

"I was in the commissioner's room and heard them talking, and the name Hickey Moran was connected with the murder. And I knew that they couldn't—wouldn't do anything, and—"

"SO YOU'RE WORKING alone—and you want to find out how your father died! You dirty little rat; you dirty little stoolie. Well—you'll find out. You can't doublecross Hickey Moran. You're going to die, just like your father died."

"You can't—you can't." The girl raised her voice now.

"Let me go!" She jerked herself free again and backed toward the door, Hickey following her. "Don't touch me. Let me go! I'll scream. There are some honest people in that room out there. Some who—"

One piercing shriek the girl started, and Hickey stepped forward and swung his right fist. There was a dull thud; the girl's head jarred back. Then she sank slowly to the floor.

"What—what are you going to do with her?" Gordon Lackey gasped.

"What do you think?" Hickey was picking up the money; tossing it into a drawer; spinning the key in the lock. "Do you want her to stand up in court and put the finger on us—on me? I'm going to kill her, of course."

"A woman—a girl. A—"

"A witness of death."

"And I— I'd better—get away."

"Not tonight, Mr. Gordon Lackey." And Hickey's grin was not pleasant. "I'm going to need you."

Gordon Lackey drew away from the man. He looked down at the slender form on the floor. Then he shook his head, much as a dog might who had just come out of the water. It was true. He was there with Hickey Moran. The money! The accusations the girl had screamed at them! That they had killed her father. It was terrible, horrible, but it was true. She had to die.

The girl was moving now; trying to drag her head and shoulders from the floor.

"You rotten, two-timing little tart." Hickey Moran kicked her viciously in the side. And then to Gordon Lackey, "Here—watch her a minute, and kick her in the face if she opens her yap."

Hickey went to the door, opened it and peered into the narrow hall. No one was there. The orchestra had hit up a lively tune. It was very loud. Hickey cursed. Was Frank a fool, or did Frank think he was one? People might notice the blast of music. What the hell did Frank think—that he'd carry the girl screaming down that little back hall and through the bar? Regular music was enough. By God! people he put on the spot didn't run screaming all over the building before he did for them.

Back to the room, and Hickey lifted up the half-unconscious girl.

"Come on!" He jerked his head for Gordon Lackey to pass out the open door. Then, in the hall he thrust the girl into Lackey's arms. "Here, you cart her. There are some doors and some keys. I'll need my hands."

Mechanically Gordon Lackey obeyed. He knew that they went in the opposite direction from the music, turned a corridor, passed through a small door and doubled back, going along a hall beside the orchestra—on the other side of the dance floor.

He knew that they passed into a bar room, through another door and out on a landing above narrow stairs; the very stairs he had come up. Then they were on them—going down them, to the heavy wooden door that hid the iron grated one through which Gordon Lackey had entered. My God! They weren't going out on the street—with the girl like that.

And they weren't. Hickey turned to the left. A little coat closet, Lackey thought—then a door at the back of it, and a light flashed. Wooden steps. Hard, cold cement below it.

Although the girl was light and Gordon Lackey was a

strong man, he staggered slightly down those cellar steps. The words of Hickey rang clearly in his ears now.

"This is where her father died—where they all died. Come on—through here!"

The light, shining dimly, threw the place into queer shadows. Something seemed to move along the wall by a huge boiler. Gordon Lackey drew back; his voice whistled in his throat as he tried to speak. A rat scurried across the floor. Hickey Moran laughed.

"Don't like it, eh? Well—you'll get used to it, just like I got used to it. Hell! Let her down. No one will hear her if she screams her head off."

Gordon Lackey let his arms down; the girl slipped from them to the hard cement floor. She lay there, a pitiful little heap, her back against the wall. Black eyes, wondering at first, then frightened, bulged in horror as things shaped themselves clearly in her mind—too clearly.

She struggled to her feet and ran blindly across the floor. Hickey laughed and followed her; struck her once with his open palm, knocking her to the hard cement.

"WELL—YOU ASKED FOR it." There was a glare in those blue eyes now. A glare of hatred, that hid the fog completely. A hate born of hurt pride. This girl had played with him—made a sucker out of him. Made a sucker out of Hickey Moran! And it took a sap from Chicago—a punk mouthpiece—to come and put him wise to it. He stretched down now and took her by the throat; felt his fingers sink into the soft white flesh that he had hoped to touch in a different way. Then he swung suddenly. Gordon Lackey had grabbed him by the shoulder.

"You can't—can't do it. Not like that!" Gordon Lackey's

brown eyes were wide—popping. Saliva hung on his lips. He was breathing heavily. He had planned murders; was to collect money for them, and—and— He ran a finger beneath his collar. He wanted air. He had never pictured the thing he did—had done. Never pictured it like this!

Hickey regarded the man for a moment through thin slits.

"Yellow, eh? Just as I thought! No nerve when the show-down comes. Big talk! Big mouth! Big money! But, always, someone else to do the job. Well—" and in sudden thought, "You—you, Gordon Lackey—you give it to her, since you don't like the way I work."

"No, no!" Gordon Lackey threw an arm across his face. "Go on—go on. But get it over with. I can't— Why must I—" And to himself, but aloud, "It has to be done—it has to be done."

"Yes," said Hickey. "It has to be done—and you have to do it." What the hell! That was what Hickey wanted; to sew Gordon Lackey up tight in the thing. No turning yellow then. Lackey would understand that he'd have to stick, once he had killed the girl.

"Go on." Hickey took a gun from his pocket and tried to stick it into Lackey's hand. "Go on!" he said. "Go on and give it to her—let her have it. In the stomach. The dirty rat."

"No, no!" Gordon Lackey pushed the gun away. "You do it. I can't. I can't! I'm going—going." He turned and staggered blindly across the cement floor—toward the stairs.

"Come back here, you fool!" Hickey started after him, looked at the girl—and stopped. She was coming to her feet. "Don't move, Lackey!" He cried out his warning as the man reached the steps. "Stop!"

But Gordon Lackey didn't stop. He started up those wooden steps, clutching at the hand rail. He mumbled something, but Hickey did not get it. Then Lackey was at the top, reaching for the iron bar across the door; reaching—

And Hickey Moran fired.

Gordon Lackey straightened slightly and made a funny sound deep back in his throat—and his hand was on that bar. Hickey cursed and fired again. Lackey stood suddenly erect and still, upon the stairs. Then he spun quickly and tumbled down the steps.

"Hell!" said Hickey. "He would have it that way." Then he shrugged his shoulders. There was no one to talk now. No one but—

Hickey Moran turned suddenly and grabbed the girl as she would have run wildly by him. "It's your turn now, and—" His left hand sunk into her throat as she screamed. He dragged her toward the old boiler; felt her go limp as his fingers bit deep into her throat. Then he swung quickly, the girl close to him—before him—protecting him. A voice had spoken out of the blackness. A grim, ominous voice that Hickey knew well.

11

SATAN TAKES A HAND

HICKEY DREW THE girl closer to him with his left arm. His right hand held his gun, half against the girl's side, ready to slip from behind her frail body if a gun flashed there in the blackness. For Satan's voice had come out of the darkness, beyond the furnace.

"If you fire," Hickey's words were thick, "I'll croak the girl—give it to her right through the back. See?"

"You'll die then." Satan spoke, and Hickey tried to get the voice and train his gun on it.

And all the time Hickey was sliding back—crouching low, his face behind the girl's shoulder; his foggy blue eyes trying to peer beneath her swinging arms.

"Don't go back any further," Satan warned. "If you drop your gun, let the girl go, and raise your hands—you'll get a chance; a chance to beat the rap."

"You can't get me without getting the girl." Hickey was nearer the boiler now—nearer the heavy wooden support in the darkness beside it; the heavy wooden support that had an electric buzzer, that would ring above and bring help. Frank; the boys in the main room. Guns! Guns that would come to his rescue. He smacked his lips. Satan worked alone! He listened. No sound. No feet. Satan was alone tonight then.

"I tell you," Hickey sparred for time, "I've got a gun against her now. One shot from you and she goes out. I'll make a deal with you. You can have the girl—alive, for one hour's start; a half hour even." Hickey Moran thought of the money in the desk upstairs. But he thought mostly of Satan and the girl. If either of them lived, the game was up. It was his life or theirs.

Satan made an odd noise that might have been a laugh, and Hickey didn't like it. He was half in the shadows now; just a foot or two more and he'd be in the protection of the old boiler. Satan would have to come into the light then. Just a foot more, but Hickey did not move that foot.

"One step further—just one move of your body, and you get it," Satan warned.

And Hickey, stayed where he was—frozen to the spot. There was death in Satan's voice.

"What of the girl?" Hickey said—and he crouched low, the girl covering his head and the most vital parts of his body.

"I'm the law," Satan answered.

"Just another inch back, and—"

Satan added something, but Hickey did not hear it. His right hand was in the darkness; out of Satan's vision, he thought. Anyway, he'd have to chance it. There was the upright. Just a stretch of his hand, a press of the button— and he'd have help.

"I might as well die here as roast." Hickey tried to make his voice plaintive, and found little difficulty in doing so.

His hand was on the rough, wooden brace; along the insulated wire to the button. And he pressed it!

A few minutes now, and the boys would be coming—coming down those stairs. And Hickey cursed softly. Why had he dropped the iron bar across that door? They'd have to break it down. But as soon as they found it bolted they'd go around the back; come in as Satan must have come in. They'd gun him out, too, there in the darkness; hunt him like a rat. Frank and a dozen others. Satan couldn't get him—kill him anyway, unless he shot straight through the girl's body. Satan might get him in the shoulder or the leg; Hickey was a big man and the girl was small, but the threat of Hickey's killing the girl should prevent that.

CROUCHED IN THE darkness, Satan watched the slender form of the girl. Bulging out, on the left side of her small body, was Hickey's left shoulder—a part of his hip even—his entire left leg from the knee down.

And the girl! Elsa Stapleton, for Satan recognized her easily in the dim light! Her head was forward on her chest, but she was still alive. Plainly Satan could see that head rise and fall with her labored breathing.

Twice Satan raised his gun, drawing a bead just along where the right arm of the girl hung. He wondered—if he put a bullet through that right arm would he catch Hickey Moran in the head? Maybe—but he didn't know. But he knew one thing. Hickey would kill the girl before he gave up; kill her before he died.

He looked from the limp form of the girl, with the huge left hand of Hickey's plainly visible upon her chest, to the man who lay by the stairs. He could guess who the dead man was. Dead man! And Satan didn't know. It seemed as if the man's hand moved slightly. And Satan straightened and listened. Someone was at the door above. Someone was pushing against it; then beating on it.

"How do you like that, Mr. Satan Hall?" Hickey's voice was triumphant. "That's the boys above. They'll be beating down that door; coming from the rear, the same as you did. Now what?"

And Satan knew. Somehow Hickey had sent word of his danger to the gangsters above. A half dozen of them; maybe a dozen. Even now Satan heard stealthy steps far back in the cellar, the same way he had come.

He had meant to trap Hickey and now he himself was trapped. Steps were far back in that cellar; steps that he heard plainly between the heavy pounding on the wooden, barred door. Pounding that was getting louder; pounding that— And Satan looked up at that door. It splintered; metal flashed through the wood. They were hammering it down with an axe.

Satan set his lips tightly. His green eyes narrowed. He'd have to die sometime. But he'd give a good account of himself there in the cellar; there behind that boiler, close to which Hickey crouched, using the girl as a shield. But he would take Hickey with him. He'd— And Satan did it. He stepped forward quickly, gun drawn—straight into the edge of light.

Hickey fired once. There was the sudden sharp sting, as if a hot iron had been drawn quickly across Satan's cheek. But Satan wasn't thinking of that. Hickey had fired from under the girl's right arm, and as his head bent his right ear was visible—just visible, beyond the dark of the girl's blue jacket.

Satan closed his finger on the trigger and nicked that ear. Hickey felt the pain of it, jerked his head to the left, and for a split second his face was in full view of Satan. For a split second blue eyes stared at green ones. Then two guns spoke as one. Hickey fired blindly—wildly, from behind the girl. But Satan shot to kill.

Satan nodded as a tiny red hole appeared in Hickey's forehead; as foggy eyes became glassy and lifeless. It was easy, placing that bullet that crashed straight into the center of Hickey Moran's forehead. It was hard, shooting to nick that ear to cause Hickey to jerk his head to the other side—and himself into eternity.

But Satan wasn't interested in the cause. He was only interested in the effect.

Someone fired out of the darkness. Satan turned and put two shots where the yellow flame had splashed against the blackness. Then he ran quickly to the girl, thrust her back against the boiler and crouched there before her.

"It's all right now." He lied to her. She was young, to die like that—very young. And he wondered if they'd use a Tommy gun—and if they did, if it mightn't be better for the girl.

The door above the stairs crashed in. Satan raised his gun. They wouldn't come that way on him. That much was certain. His finger half tightened on the trigger, then loosened again. A heavy set figure stood at the top of those stairs. It was Lieutenant Gilpatric.

"The police!" Satan gasped.

"Yes." The girl spoke for the first time. "I telephoned them from the dressing room when I saw Gordon Lackey come in."

THERE WAS LOUD talk, and shouts of command. But at the sight of uniformed men crowding those stairs, the gangsters scattered from the back of the cellar.

After that—a lull, while the girl clung hysterically to Satan. Then the commissioner came, and Gilpatric was explaining things.

"You see," Gilpatric was loud and important now, "the girl, Miss Stapleton, telephoned the precinct, Satan. She was in a hurry and a bit wild and incoherent, and I got hold of the commissioner. He told me to tear the joint apart— that if Miss Stapleton was here and Gordon Lackey was here, you were here somewhere. How did you get into the cellar?"

"I made a mistake there." Satan shook his head slowly. "Though perhaps it was an error that saved the girl's life. I knew those bodies didn't come out the front way, and I found out that the house behind this was vacant. My mistake was—that I thought Hickey Moran would arrange to meet Gordon Lackey in the basement."

"He'll live to roast, though he thinks he's dying and is making a confession. You were right. It was a murder racket," the commissioner said.

Satan nodded and rubbed a hand across his cheek. It was only a scratch.

The commissioner winked at Satan and drew him aside.

"If you want anything, I'm in a good humor. Now's the time to ask. Gilpatric is trying to steal the show."

"The credit," said Satan slowly, "belongs to the little man who had a public duty and a sentimental attachment for—for—" He stretched out a hand to the commissioner.

"There's one thing I'd like, commissioner. I'd like to have

you help me pick out the finest pen and pencil in town, for
Mr. Malcolm Strause, of Yonkers."

The laugh died on the commissioner's lips and he
nodded. For he suddenly realized that Detective Satan
Hall was not joking.

SATAN'S CREED

*Satan Hall Believed That Those Who Killed
by Lead Should Die by Lead, So He Set Out to
Find the Kidnapers of Little Constance Colby*

1

MURDER

JACKSON COLBY WAS president of the Colby Investment House, Inc., and his personal holdings were of such a conservative nature that the government of the country itself must tumble before his selected securities. Occasionally he spoke his mind on important public problems. He abhorred graft and was strong against brutality in the police department. He looked on crime as a great social disease and on prisons as the institutions which must cure it.

At present he was engrossed in writing a book on Japanese Prints, the publication of which would be strictly a private matter.

It was after one o'clock in the morning, yet Colby worked on. Twice he was tempted to put away the prints and go to work on the letter he was preparing for *The Times*. It was an ironic rebuke to the police department in general, but a scathing denunciation of one detective in particular. He laid down his pen and looked across his desk at the triple chinned, hard visage of his grandfather upon the wall.

And the stern face of that individual gave him the name for the article against this detective.

The Man Nobody Liked. Peculiarly, that title would fit

his grandfather as well
as this detective, Satan
Hall.

Jackson Colby
turned over some
newspaper clippings
on his desk and stud-
ied the face of Detec-
tive Satan Hall. Hard,
cruel, yet there was
something fine about it. Character, of course. That was it.
Colby admired character. But there was character for bad
as well as for good. With a tiny grimace of satisfaction he
jotted that down on a piece of paper and drew a line under
it for emphasis.

Satan Hall. His name had been in the papers frequently.
A man who, under the protection of a police badge,
committed legal murder. Not that the city wasn't better
off for the deaths he caused. The men he had killed were
notorious. But they died without a fair trial by a jury of
their peers. They died in "resisting arrest" or in the perpe-
tration of a crime." At least, so the official report read. No,
this was not the kind of liberty for which Colby's forefa-
thers fought. This was not justice as he saw justice. This was
vengeance. The vengeance of the State.

Jackson Colby put aside his Japanese prints, leaned
back in his chair and frowned. He felt it a public duty to
encourage the investigation of this detective. Crime must
be stamped out, not blasted out through the muzzle of a
gun held in the hand of a legal murderer. The man was a

Then Colby saw the other figure. The silent man who stood beside the body

menace to the supremacy of that great American institution—the courts.

Colby sat suddenly erect, straightened the papers upon his desk, and coming slowly to his feet left the room and passed quietly into the hall.

He tip-toed to the landing, for he must pass his daughter's door. The child had not been well and slept lightly. Carefully he descended the stairs, took his hat and stick from the hall rack, and opening his front door stood for a moment upon the top of the broad stone steps that led to the Avenue and the park across the street. It was his habit to walk along the sidewalk close to the park wall and think. Great writers often did that at night, and found inspiration. The comparison was not odious.

The night was clear. The moon shone brightly. The park was like some dark tropical forest that lured him. And he went, swinging his cane jauntily in his right hand; stepping briskly along the smooth grass by the side of the road, wondering why the city didn't provide a footpath.

But Jackson Colby had lived too long in the city not to

realize that even the quiet of the early morning did not permit of a leisurely stroll along the road itself. It was a dangerous spot. At any minute a car might swing from a bend and a careless or even drunken driver bear down on him.

The man nobody liked. That was true. His own words at lunch only the other day, to a newspaper publisher, had borne fruit in an editorial along that line. He shook his head emphatically. You can not meet crime with crime. Two wrongs can never make a right. A detective must not elect to shoot it out with a criminal, like any common gunman.

Jackson Colby stopped dead. Clearly in the silence of the night there came a shot. A breathless moment, while he tried to tell himself it was the backfire of a car; then two more shots in quick succession. And those shots came from around the sharp turn in the road just beyond the thick clump of green, in avoiding which he was about to step into the road.

Standing there close to the bush that blocked his view Colby heard now the soft purr of a motor. He pushed forward, parted the bushes carefully, stepped into them and saw the light. Saw clearly the road beyond the turn.

A big car was parked at the side of the road. Its head-lights picked out vividly a crumpled blotch of black; the dark figure of a man stretched motionless at the side of the road. His right hand was thrown up over his head, as if to hide the whiteness of his face; the whiteness of a face that Colby, with a little sickening sensation in his stomach, knew was partly red.

Then he saw the other figure. The silent man who stood

beside the body. He was close to the car, so that all but his shoulders and head were hidden by it. The figure turned, and for a moment his face was clearly visible in the glare of those lights. Colby took in every feature of that coarse, evil face. The mean, slit eyes; the sharp, slightly crooked nose, and the thick sensuous lips. Then the man moved, his broad shoulders swinging as he passed out of the light. But before he disappeared from view Colby saw clearly the black thing against the whiteness of his hand, and he recognized that black thing. It was a snub-nosed automatic.

Colby never moved; never cried out. He just watched in fearful silence the shadow of the killer climb into that car. Heard the engine purr a bit louder, saw the car back slowly, then without haste move carefully forward, turn well out in the road, and missing the body of the man by inches, pass almost silently into the blackness of the night.

For perhaps a full minute Jackson Colby remained motionless in those bushes. Then he moved from them, trying to make out more clearly the outline of the thing on the road; the dark, indistinguishable blotch—the dead body of a man.

He turned suddenly, and half running, half stumbling sought the entrance to the park. It was Jackson Colby's first experience with sudden and violent death. And for the few minutes it took him to reach the stone wall and the park entrance he was as other men; just a frightened, uncertain citizen seeking the aid of the police.

2

AT THE CLUB OSTEND

THE CLUB OSTEND had been very exclusive. It was an odd, dismal looking restaurant three steps down from a broad alley that gave off one of the main streets in the financial district. It had an iron door, guarded by a smiling attendant who for years had not had to look at the cards of the members. He knew them all by sight. But things had changed now. Even new members were urged to introduce their friends.

Jackson Colby still had his particular booth against the left wall, close to the rear of the room. The food, perhaps, was not what it was a year or two ago, but the Napoleon brandy which Colby took after each noonday meal was still of an excellence that he demanded.

Colby waved away the attempts of his guest to force the conversation into the channel that it had taken preceding the meal. But now that the lunch was over, the coffee upon the table, the pony of Napoleon brandy before him, he leaned back in the booth and looked across at the younger man.

"I handled," he said very slowly, "your father's investments for years. I have taken care of yours and your aunt's. Now—I am prepared to give you the time that courtesy demands this most unpleasant subject. But I have told you that my mind is closed. When the time comes, I will go upon the stand and perform my public duty. I can not possibly be mistaken. I will point out the murderer and accuse him before the court. But I won't have policemen following me around and standing before my house."

"And everybody admires and respects you for it." The young assistant district attorney leaned forward eagerly. "I don't wish to alarm you, but you're the star witness for the State and must be protected. Don't smile, Mr. Colby. Your life is in danger."

"I have been threatened before." Colby continued to smile. "A man in the financial world, no matter how conservative his house, is subject to such cranks."

"But these men are not cranks. The man you saw commit this murder; the man who will go to the electric chair in Sing Sing by your testimony alone, is the right hand man of August Saprillo. Saprillo isn't a crank. He's the biggest menace in the city today."

Jackson Colby straightened slightly.

"You're influenced by your position, Sawyer; your constant association with crime and criminals. It's all right for these men to assassinate each other, intimidate crooked officials, and perhaps at times frighten average citizens. But I think I can say without immodesty that a Colby is a step beyond the threats of hoodlums."

Charles Sawyer turned his head to smile, but he swung back almost at once and was deadly serious.

"I have come to you straight from the commissioner of police himself, Mr. Colby." Charles Sawyer stuck to the subject of an armed guard. "He understands how you feel.

Doesn't wish to make you conspicuous, and has suggested that you allow a single man to accompany you from your house to the office. He'll keep well in the background."

Colby smiled broadly.

"I am afraid the police are looking to their own glory, Sawyer. You talk of one, August Saprillo, a master racketeer, who has only to speak to strike death. You paint a melodramatic picture of roaring machine guns, and then expect one man to prevent all this. He must be a very remarkable man. The commissioner must have great faith in him."

"He has. You may have heard of him. He's Detective Hall. Satan Hall, they call him. He's fast with a gun, deadly with his aim and— What's the matter, Mr. Colby?"

The smile had gone from the banker's face; a frown had replaced it.

"He's a common gunman," he said stiffly. "A disgrace to the force. Only today I had a lady from the Woman's Citizen's Union urging me to head a movement for an investigation that is contemplated. If— What do you want? This is a private table."

Jackson Colby stopped dead. His eyes opened wide. His face blanched slightly.

A shadow paused for a moment by the end of the table. Then a man slid along the high backed bench beside the assistant district attorney. For the single moment before he entered that booth his hat was in his hand. Now, as the two men looked at him, the hat was on his head; pulled well down over his forehead. His eyes were hidden by dark glasses, his coat collar turned up. The little mustache on his lip was plainly unreal; there had been little attempt to have it pass as a natural growth—at least, at close range.

He spoke far back in his throat and it was hard to tell if the accent was real or assumed.

"Quiet, gents," he said. "Hands as they are; on the table. My business is only with Colby, here. The guy what's been asking for a bellyful of lead."

Plainly Charles Sawyer saw the napkin that covered the man's hand; the hand that moved across the table toward Colby, threateningly, menacingly. Plainly, too, he saw the outline of a gun beneath it.

"You can't get away with this." Sawyer spoke through trembling lips. "You won't take five steps from the table before a half dozen men in the dining room will be—"

"Yeah?" The metallic voice cut in. "Maybe I'll see that you're not one of the half dozen." And with a sudden jab of something hard against Sawyer's ribs beneath the table, "You're not in on this show, Buddy. Sit tight, and remember I've got two hands."

JACKSON COLBY WATCHED the outline of that gun, fascinated. He didn't know whether or not he was frightened. But many things flashed through his mind. His wife, who would have finished lunch and would now be in the park with Connie. Connie, who only last night he had sent to bed; ordered from his knees, not because the hour was late, but because he wanted to read his evening papers. Now, what was he thinking as that white bit of linen, with its peculiar contours, came nearer him; what was his dominating thought then? Just a single thought. He wished he hadn't sent Connie to bed.

The man was talking.

"You'd put the finger on Duffy, would you? You shot your face off all over police headquarters, and now you expect to stand up in court and do the loud mouth act. Well—you asked for it and you're going to get it."

Although Jackson Colby felt deadly cold, beads of perspiration broke out on his forehead. He opened his mouth once and tried to speak, but no words came. He was looking straight into evil, black eyes. And though he had never seen it in a man's eyes before, he recognized it at once. It was the lust to kill.

Upright in that seat; frozen with terror, Colby's eyes fell to the hand that held the gun; the moving hand beneath the napkin. It was coming nearer to him; curving upward from the whiteness of the cloth. He was going to die, and he couldn't move. Couldn't shout even; couldn't— And suddenly he could.

His right hand jarred alive and swept with a speed and strength he did not know he possessed toward the napkin with the gun beneath it. The gun roared. There was a burnt, black hole in the whiteness of the napkin; the gray nose of a snub-nosed automatic showing through; then a dull burn along his wrist, on his arm. A numbness as that gun shot up and pounded against his chest, straight over his wildly beating heart.

He must have raised his eyes then, for he was looking straight into those evil, rat-like ones of the killer. Burning, glaring orbs, with a certain elation in them. Just a second he would see that; just a split second—then swift death.

The shot came. It didn't seem as loud as the first one. Duller, more distant, and there was no pain. It wasn't hard to die like that, then; not hard in a physical sense, anyway. But he couldn't be dead. The man would fire again. The man would empty that black, steel—

Jackson Colby sucked in a great gulp of air. He was still looking into the eyes of the gunman. The glaring— And they weren't glaring. They were dull, filmy and lifeless now; with no sparkle of elation. Colby gasped. The truth dawned on him before he heard the thud of that gun as it pounded to the table. He was looking into the unseeing eyes of a dead man.

The gunman's head sank slightly, until his chin was on his chest. The head hung so a moment, then the killer dropped across the table.

Charles Sawyer was talking and climbing along the seat of the booth, behind the man. People were shouting in the dining room. A tall figure was standing beside that booth, looking down at Jackson Colby. Colby stared at the man a long time before he made out his features. Then his impression was simply that they were all points. The slant of the eyes, the tips of the ears; even the chin was pointed. And the hair! It was shaped on his forehead like a great letter V.

The man was tearing off Colby's coat; jerking up his shirt sleeve; tying a napkin about the arm.

"Just a scratch, Mr. Colby," he was saying. "The bullet didn't do any damage to speak of, but we'll have a doctor look at it as a precaution. There, drink that." He held a glass against the banker's lips. Fiery liquid burnt far back in Colby's throat. "It's a shock, of course, when you're not used to drinking it."

"The man— He's—he's dead?"

"Don't worry about him." There was a peculiar rattle in the newcomer's throat, which might have been a laugh; a cruel, sinister laugh. "He's deader than hell."

Colby looked long and steadily at the man who had

somehow saved his life. Then it suddenly came to him where he had seen that face before.

"It's you. You—" He could think words, but couldn't make them form coherent sentences.

"That's right. It's me. Detective Frank Hall."

"Hall—Satan Hall." Jackson Colby gasped out the name and collapsed upon the table.

3

BEHIND THE DOOR

THE POLICE COMMISSIONER shoved his small body tightly in the chair behind the broad desk, put the tips of his fingers together, looked at Detective Satan Hall along the end of his sharp nose and said, in his soft, quick voice:

"I'm the only one who understands you, Satan—or, at least, thinks he understands you. You had to kill the gunman, eh?"

"No." Satan shook his head as he put hard, green eyes on the commissioner. "I could have let him kill Colby. I just got in when the first shot came. There was only time to shoot from the hip; the gun was against Colby's heart. A bullet in the killer's shoulder would have meant Colby's death."

"I know, I know." The commissioner nodded. "It was pretty shooting. Almost directly through the eardrum and into the brain. I tell you, Satan, you're the only man for this job."

"But if Colby doesn't want me—"

"Sawyer has talked him around. He's taking you, of course, because he has to. He's got a sense of obligation, you know. You're to live with him, sleep with him, eat with him until the trial comes up Friday."

"He's going through with it then, after this?"

"Yes, he's going through with it. More determined than ever, and just about as pompous and cocky—at least, outwardly. He's a peculiar man, but he's built up an idol and worships it. Almost a fetish with him. He calls it 'public duty' and makes long-winded speeches about it."

"He doesn't like me."

"Of course he doesn't. But then, nobody likes you, Satan, and you've always been a little proud of it. But you're not working for Colby. You're not working to save his life, but to take the life of Duffy, August Saprillo's right-hand man." And, leaning far across the desk, "And maybe the life of Saprillo, Satan. The man the Department has always wanted; the man you have always wanted."

Satan's green eyes flashed.

"You're sure of a conviction against Duffy?"

"Absolutely. I was talking to the district attorney today. Perjured witness; good alibi; high priced lawyer. All good in an ordinary murder case, but it won't work this time. Jackson Colby has standing in the community. The jury will take his word absolutely. When he stands up there in the court and points at Duffy and says, 'That is the man,' why—" The commissioner's hands came far apart.

"All right." Satan came to his feet. "I'm to work alone."

"As far as you are concerned."

"That means there will be others on the case?"

"In a way. Not to give you orders, Satan. Not even to play along with you. Just to keep an eye on the house nights; sort of patrol the office building. It's a big thing, Satan."

"And I work my own way?"

"Absolutely. But be a little tactful. He's a big man in his

way; has friends in and out of the Department. He's a man who can help you."

Satan's lips set hard. He said:

"No man can help me. Influence won't silence the roar of a machine gun. I've got all the influence I'll ever need under my arm here." And Satan shot his right hand to his left armpit.

"Fine!" The commissioner walked to the door of the private office with the detective. "Colby will be expecting you tonight. They're to make up a bed for you downstairs. You have just the single duty of seeing that Colby shows up at the trial on Friday."

"He'll be there," said Satan, "or I won't." The door closed.

Satan frowned as he approached the big gray stone house across from the park. Two uniformed police officers covered the block, carefully avoiding looking at the Colby house when they passed it. Their studied indifference took the frown from Satan's face, and he grinned. Across the street he saw the man in civilian clothes who, leaning against the park wall, looked toward the moonlit sky with the theatrical intensity of a stage astronomer.

YET, WHY NOT? No one knew better than Satan the danger that surrounded Jackson Colby. The very foundation of August Saprillo's rule in the underworld depended on the banker's death. At least, on the fact that he did not testify, which amounted to the same thing. But Satan didn't think that Saprillo would strike at night. That wouldn't be his way. Saprillo's enemies were taken for a ride or blasted out by machine gun fire on the public street. Since it would be impossible to take Colby for a ride, then the answer seemed to lie in the staccato notes of a machine gun.

The policemen, passing the house, nodded abruptly at Satan. The plainclothes man across the street jerked his head and went on staring at the sky. Satan had few friends on the Force, or off it for that matter. He worked straight from the commissioner himself; had nothing in common with the great police system of the city, and was considered by many as the commissioner's spy; by other, older members of the Force as the commissioner's pet. A man with special privileges, which they resented. Certainly the title, The Man Nobody Liked, fitted him perfectly. Only the commissioner himself stood between him and complete ostracism.

The butler who admitted him was gray, slightly bent, and long in the service of the Colbys. He took Satan up the wide old-fashioned stairs and led him down a long hall into the little library, where Jackson Colby spent most of his time.

"I'm Hamilton, sir. Mr. Colby is engaged for a few moments with some documents. If you wish anything, ring for me." He indicated the bell and departed.

The room was not very large. It was more a den than a library, but many technical books on Japanese prints filled the few shelves along the walls. There was a single closet, and another door, which might lead to Mr. Colby's bedroom. Satan did not know. He would not familiarize himself with the house until he met Colby. How long would he be left there to cool his heels?

Satan walked to the flat desk, lifted the cover of a humidor, closed it again when he saw the cigars and lighted a cigarette. Then he went to the single window at the end of the room, raised it and looked down at the stone court of the rear yard below. Turning from the window, he threw himself into an easy chair and blew great clouds of smoke toward the ceiling.

Lazily he let his eyes drift again about that room. To the window; the books on Japanese prints; the closet door; the door which he thought led to the bedroom, and— His eyes came back to that bedroom door. It was open a crack, and he was positive that when he looked at it before it was closed tight. Now—the crack materially diminished in size as he looked at it. There was that instinctive feeling that eyes were watching him; eyes that, hidden by darkness, looked into the light.

4

A SURPRISING DISCOVERY

SATAN CAME SLOWLY to his feet and walked to the book-
cases, examining the books with apparent interest. He
stepped to the window and peered into the night. Then
he eased his way from the window toward that bedroom
door, slipping close to the wall where he could not be seen.

His right hand was close to his left armpit when his
left hand shot suddenly out, grasped that door knob and
jerked the door open. There was a gasp of breath; a body
stumbled into the room and dropped to the floor on hands
and knees. Satan reached down and placed a hand roughly
upon a shoulder.

A white face with wondering brown eyes looked up at
him. Satan's tightening fingers loosened. He leaned down
and lifted the small form erect. He was looking into a
childish face. There was surprise in his own hard, green
eyes as he took in the pajama clad figure in the bright
green bathrobe.

There was no fear in the girl's face; just an uncertain
quivering of lips and the sparkle of eyes, then an uncon-
trolled little laugh.

"You sure surprised me." The little girl spoke. "Just like

the detective in books. So you're the man they call The Devil?"

"Am I?" Satan still held her by the shoulders, looking down at her. The situation was new to him. But he finally said, "Who are you? What are you doing here?"

"I'm Constance Colby. You're Detective Hall, aren't you?"

When Satan nodded, she said, "Well— I wanted to see what you looked like and why nobody liked you." And after a moment's pause, "You don't look so much like the devil. Why don't anybody like you?"

"I don't know, Constance. Did your father tell you all about me?" Satan sat down.

"He didn't tell me, but he's been writing things. And there are a lot of newspaper cut-outs on his desk. I read them and I think you're awful brave. And—and I do like you, so you can't be The Man Nobody Likes any more."

"You like me?" Satan was slightly incredulous. "Why?"

"Well—" she put a finger close to her lips. "First, because nobody likes you, I guess. I know how that feels. Sometimes I think that nobody likes me. Oh, I don't mean father and mother and Lucille—she's my governess, but she's away now. I mean the other children. You see, I can't play with children I want to play with. Father's afraid they might not be nice children; have nice fathers and mothers." Her eyes filled slightly. "But I don't want to play with their fathers and mothers, and even though I like them they call me stuck up when I play in the park. Maybe that's why people don't like you, because you can go with people you like. I'm going to let you call me Connie."

"Are you?"

"Yes." She climbed on his knee. "Mother is the only one

who calls me Connie. Father doesn't like it. It makes him make a face. But once in a while he does, like after he was shot." And after a minute's pause, "You like me, too? That's because I like you a lot. You got'a like people who like you a lot, don't you?"

"Yes, yes. I guess so."

"Then I'm going to let you kiss me good night."

Startled, Satan sat erect, almost jarring the child from his knee. Then he said gruffly:

"No, no, I don't think so." And at the hurt look in her eyes, "I'm not much of a hand at kissing."

"But I'm not afraid of germs from you. Nice people don't have germs, and you're a nice person. If you weren't nice I wouldn't like you, would I?"

"No, I suppose not." Satan set her down on the floor. "You run along to bed now. What will your father say at your entertaining a stranger at this time of night?"

"But you're not a stranger. I've known you for a long, long time—in the papers. There!" She jumped suddenly onto his knee again, and throwing her little arms about his neck kissed him.

Then she was gone, dashing across the room. She paused at the door. "Don't tell father I was here. And I don't think you look like the devil at all. I think you look awful nice."

For some time Satan sat motionless. Then he ran the back of his hand across his thin, sinister lips. It came away slightly moist. He shook his head and grinned. It was the first time a child had ever kissed him.

Five minutes later Jackson Colby walked into the room. His attire was as perfect and as somber as ever, but his right arm hung in a sling across his chest. He was plainly ill at ease as he addressed Satan.

"**I AM SURE**," he said very slowly, choosing his words, but making no effort to shake hands, "that the commissioner of police has repeated to you my thanks and deepest gratitude for saving my life." And somewhat querulously as he looked down at his arm, "It was not, as you stated, 'simply a scratch.' One of the bones suffered a fracture."

"I'm not a doctor," Satan said abruptly. "I came here on police duty and not to receive gratitude. What I did was simply police duty."

Jackson Colby looked slightly surprised. He removed his glasses and slowly studied Satan Hall. A strange man, certainly. A cold, cruel, relentless face.

"I see," said Colby. "Most people would not consider the saving of my life as a simple departmental duty. At the same time, there is no dodging the fact that you put me in a most embarrassing position. For I deplored your—your activities." And suddenly he came out with what was bothering him. "Was there no other way but to kill that man?"

"That would depend on the value you place upon your life." Those thin lips parted, and Colby wondered if the man was smiling. It seemed as if his lips were. But his eyes were hard, green globes.

Colby had come up, determined to treat the man fairly. To wipe out his past antagonism toward him. To try and remember, that Satan Hall had saved him for his wife and Constance But now he only said:

"You are very sure of yourself, Mr. Hall."

"Absolutely," said Satan. "Now I shall want to see the whole house. The room that you sleep in; every room."

"Very well. Hamilton will show you about downstairs, and also the servants' quarters. This," he led the way to the room through which the child had come, "is my bedroom. The door, across, leads to the hall."

Satan was surprised when he met Mrs. Colby. She was the opposite of her husband. A quiet, unassuming woman, with a natural dignity. There was nothing stilted or forced about her gratitude. She didn't try to put it into words. It was in the grip of those two hands she placed about one of Satan's; the mist that formed in her eyes when she spoke to him. In her whole attitude of sincere pleasure in meeting the man who had saved her husband's life.

"This is Constance's room." Colby stopped by the door. "She's a nervous child and sleeps lightly. It isn't necessary to go in there, is it?"

"Every room." Satan stood his ground until Colby turned, opened the door softly and entered the room. He lit a single, shaded lamp. After examining the room, Satan stood looking down at the sleeping child. For a moment his green eyes seemed to soften; the hard lines of his face gave slightly as his lips parted. Then Colby called softly to him from the door.

Satan hesitated, and then for a single moment looked down at the child again. This time his slanting eyebrows raised. Connie had opened her eyes, gazed at him a moment, then her left eye closed and opened again.

Satan slowly followed Colby from that room. The child had winked at him. The thing was surprising, of course, but the most surprising thing, to Satan, was that he had winked back.

Satan was a methodical man. Before searching every

corner of that house he saw each of the three servants. The butler; the cook; and the maid, Nora. The butler had been twenty-seven years in the Colby household; the cook, twelve; and the maid, close to four years. Lucille, the governess, was away, taking care of a sick aunt in Boston.

Alone in the big library downstairs, with its several thousand books, Satan looked at the bed made up for him. He could sleep there peacefully enough. The slightest noise would find him awake, with every sense alert. It was his habit to sleep in the shadow of death.

Satan removed his coat and shoes, and throwing his tie and his shoulder holster over a chair lay down on the big comfortable couch. The heavy police automatic he placed under his pillow. He didn't drop off to sleep immediately, as was his habit. Peculiarly, his thoughts were not on the magnitude of his responsibility; nor were they on August Saprillo. He smiled as he finally dozed off. Big brown eyes were smiling back at him; one of them closed and opened—and Satan slept.

5

FOOTSTEPS ON THE STAIRS

IT WAS JUST about two o'clock when footsteps came down those front stairs, turned along the hall and entered the dining room. They had hardly passed the library door before Satan was fully awake and on his feet. They were light, careful steps.

Satan's shoeless feet noiselessly left the library and crossed the hall. He was in the dining room before the door which led through the butler's pantry to the kitchen had stopped swinging. The light from the kitchen flashed back and forth. Who would have business in the kitchen this time of night?

Satan's gun dangled in his hand as he opened that door and peered into the long narrow pantry. It was empty. He passed quickly from one swinging door to the other and entered the kitchen. A cold draft of air came from the open door which led to the electric ice box.

And he saw her. It was Connie. She was coming up the two steps, staggering slightly under a heavy platter.

"It was to be a surprise," she told him without fright or embarrassment. "I thought I'd get things ready and we'd have a feast together."

"But, Connie, you should be in bed."

"No, I shouldn't." She shook her head. "You see, they make me go to bed at eight and then want me to sleep late in the morning."

Satan took the platter with the roast chicken and placed it on the table.

"You go right back to bed," he tried to say sternly, but somehow there was a catch in his voice. It was not hard and cold. He had never had any trouble before in getting his sternness over.

Connie pursed her lips.

"I'd just lie there and not sleep. Then I'd get lonesome and I'd cry. It's not nice to cry all alone; and it's not nice to make mother come in when I cry." And when Satan tried to stare at her, "Look here. You want me to be big and strong, don't you?"

"Of course I do." He heard the words and knew that they were his. He recognized, too, that they were very emphatic.

"Father says I don't eat enough; that's why I'm under weight." She came close to him and took one of his hands and looked up at him. "You let me stay and I'll eat something with you. Please. I'll even take a glass of milk."

"I suppose so," Satan half stammered, and then it was too late to draw back. She was getting bread from the bread box, setting the table, talking and laughing, yet cautioning Satan to be quiet.

They sat down together, the child keeping up a continuous chatter.

"There." She finished her milk. "I told you I would, and I hate milk. Funny—it tasted nice tonight. Just think of you and me sitting here eating so late. I never ate in a kitchen before. Did you ever eat in a kitchen?" And without waiting for an answer, "It's fun, isn't it?"

She spoke of Nora, the maid, who looked after her while Lucille was away.

"She's more fun than Lucille. She talks to me more like I was grown up, and I like her lots. She never had a fellow because, she says, she's so homely. But she isn't a bit homely; only different looking. Now she's got a beau. They're going to be married."

This time, when she finally did go off to bed, Satan leaned down to let her kiss him good night. And when he went back to the couch and to sleep, his last waking thoughts were of the newspaper editorial—The Man Nobody Liked. He smiled slightly as he fell asleep.

Three days passed and August Saprillo made no attempt on the life of Jackson Colby, the star witness for the State. That is, no direct attempt on his life.

But Saprillo was not lying down on the job. A sawed off shotgun had been found behind the park wall, ten feet from where the plain-clothes man on night duty usually stood; and in a down town store almost directly opposite Colby's office, only rented the day before, were found two Thompson machine guns and a large quantity of ammunition. The tenant had disappeared.

Satan was worried. It was not like Saprillo to so bungle a job, leaving evidence of his intention to save the life of his lieutenant, Duffy. Unless, the commissioner argued— and with some logic—that it was done to impress upon his followers that failure had been the result of all his efforts.

But Satan shook his head. Saprillo was not a man to give up without a real attempt upon the life of Colby.

Of course, August Saprillo would desert his best friend in time of need if he could do so and save his own face. But Duffy, with the assurance that he would beat the rap, would be a different Duffy than the crouching frightened rat in the shadow of the hot seat at Sing Sing prison. To save his life he might point the accusing finger at Saprillo. Satan nodded. And what an accusing finger that would be, coming from August Saprillo's right hand man! It would be enough to fry Saprillo a dozen times over.

There was only one thing for August Saprillo to do. He must save the life of Duffy in order to be assured of his own life.

Each of those three nights spent at the house of Jackson Colby was a happy one for Satan. Not that he had ever exactly been unhappy before. Maybe he had; maybe he hadn't. He had never thought on the subject. But each night he found himself wide awake, waiting for the midnight visit of Connie. Connie had brought something into his life, of which he had never suspected himself capable. Deep affection for a child.

Then that fourth night—Wednesday, the blow struck.

Connie drank her milk and laughed when she told Satan about Nora.

"She's got a really, truly beau and it makes her act silly. I'm not silly about you; am I, Satan?"

Satan said that he didn't think so. He was beginning to notice that her little nose turned up and that she had freckles, and that there was a tooth missing on the right side of her mouth when she laughed.

"After this is over and father's done his public duty and you've killed all the bad men that don't want him to, then you and me'll go off in the park and have a picnic. We won't tell father." And, after a minute of thought, "We'll tell mother though. She likes you, Satan."

"That's fine, Connie, and—" Satan stopped suddenly and came to his feet. Jackson Colby stood in the doorway.

His eyes flashed, but his voice was steady.

"Go to your room, Constance." Jackson Colby held open the swinging door. "I'll attend to you later."

The child came slowly to her feet. She looked directly at her father. Her face was very white. The little hand upon the kitchen table trembled.

"To your room, Constance!" Colby said again.

The child hesitated, looking from her father to Satan. Her voice was very weak, very low, when she finally spoke to her father.

"You're not going to be mad at him, father, because I came down?" And as his stern face never relaxed, "Look"— her eyes brightened slightly and her lips parted—"I drank a whole glass of milk. He made me, or he wouldn't let me stay. I ate—"

"Go—to—your—room." Colby's voice was no louder, but it was sterner, and each word was pronounced as though it were a sentence in itself.

The child swayed slightly, straightened, and walked quickly across the room, reached the door to the pantry, pushed it open; then suddenly said, a little defiantly:

"I'll always like you, Satan."

She dashed from the kitchen. There was the soft patter of feet across the pantry, the swish of a swinging door, and she was gone.

Turning to Satan, Jackson Colby said stiffly:

"I will leave you now and not interfere with your arrangements for my protection."

Satan shrugged his shoulders when the man was gone. Imagine having a clothes horse like that for a father. No wonder the kid wanted company. He supposed they'd keep her locked in her room at night now. Well—that was their business. He had liked the kid a lot, too. But he didn't fully realize, then, just how much he really did like her.

It was the next morning after Satan had eaten his breakfast that Hamilton told him he was wanted on the phone. It was the commissioner, and his voice was crisp.

"You've gone and rubbed the old boy's hair the wrong way. You're off the case, and that's that. Mr. Colby is getting ready to blow the whole police department. He can't see one good reason for your remaining in the house, and has a dozen or more why you shouldn't. He's willing to have a police parade to get you out. Take a walk through the park, cool off, and come down to my office."

Colby looked up from his desk in the little upstairs den where he had requested Satan's presence.

"I have decided," Colby laid his glasses against the palm of his hand, "to accept the police escort which the commissioner thinks necessary. I have come to this conclusion after careful deliberation. It is a duty I owe my family." He coughed once and held a slip of paper out to Satan. "I am not unmindful of my obligation to you. You may take this check as payment; as appreciation for saving my life. You won't be further needed here."

Satan looked at the check that was placed in his hand. It was made out to the order of Frank Hall. It was for ten thousand dollars.

"Just what do you expect in return for this?" His lips set tightly. "You are not, I suppose, ashamed of your reason for dismissing me from the case? The commissioner did not make himself clear."

Jackson Colby hesitated. But he was a man who did not dodge issues.

"I have," he said, "as you surmised, requested your withdrawal from the case. It is in no way a criticism upon your ability as a policeman. It is simply a matter of family duty. Constance is an impressionable child. She has become unduly attached to you; an attachment, in my opinion—which, of course, is not conclusive—that is detrimental to the child's best interests. I am sorry, Mr. Hall, if my words must give offense to one who saved my life. But I am putting aside personal feelings of gratitude for the best interests of my only child, as I see it. I have written letters denouncing you as a common gunman. That you did me such a service does not change your character. In plain words, you are not the type of man I would choose as a companion for my daughter."

Satan's hands clenched; his slanting eyes narrowed. He sucked in a deep breath. Red flashed in his checks; angry words rushed into his mouth. Words that were never spoken. With an effort he choked them in his throat. He looked at Colby, holding the check in his outstretched hand. He wondered if the man was right. Satan Hall—The Man Nobody Liked! There was blood on his hands. He had killed many men. It was his code. Those not fit to live should die. He had killed men that other men might live. He had killed one so that this very man who condemned him as not fit company for his child might live. He didn't know if Connie was the worse for those few hours of association with him, but he did know—with a queer lump far back in his throat—that he was the better for them. He didn't speak. He couldn't speak.

"That is all." Jackson Colby's words were final.

"No," Satan finally spoke, "that is not quite all." Very slowly he tore up the check, resisted the temptation to hurl it in Colby's face, and, laying it on the table, said, "You value your life too highly, Mr. Colby." Then he turned quickly and left the house.

6

ALIBI

AUGUST SAPRILLO WALKED into his sumptuously furnished room behind the bar of the Golden Grotto. He eyed the two men who awaited him, sitting stiffly on the ends of their chairs. Arnold Chester, high in city politics, was one. The other was Platt, a racketeer in charge of Saprillo's downtown business. Saprillo saw them both out of the sides of sharp black eyes. It was characteristic of the man that he half turned as he passed them, and backed into his seat behind the flat desk. He didn't like turning his back on men. Even his friends. A friend had once turned his back on Saprillo.

Platt was the first to speak. He didn't mince words.

"The boys are raising a stink down town. Duffy's getting irritable, and there's nothing doing. Duffy's making threats."

"He is, eh?" Saprillo stuck a match in his mouth, bit off the end of it and shot it across the room. "I have a good mind to spring that guy and blow his head off."

"You'd better spring him first," said Platt, and there was a half sneer on his lips.

"Duffy's temperamental." Chester pulled his chair forward, removed his cigar and spoke in a conciliatory

voice. "He's restless and impatient. It's no more than natural. He has great faith and confidence in you, Augie, as we
all have." And as his beady little pink eyes snapped, "How
are things going, Augie?"

"They ain't going," Platt cut in. "A couple of bums picked
up for loitering; an arsenal left in a store; a shot gun behind
a wall. Plans! Ugh!"

"They are plans—yes." Saprillo looked at Platt; kept
looking at him until the man avoided his eyes, and said:

"If you'd of let me work it, I'd open up and blast him out
smack on the street, cops or no cops."

"What street?" Saprillo demanded quickly.

"Any street. Whatever street he takes on his way to his
office, or home at night."

"He takes a different street every time he moves. This
morning he traveled with a car full of dicks, another car
behind him. Cops are as thick as flies in front of his home
and his office. You couldn't plant a single gunner any place.
That's flat."

"But you tried it in the empty store across from the
office. The cops have doubled their guard since then. Why
didn't the owner of that 'typewriter' make use of it when
he had the chance?"

"He didn't have a chance." Saprillo was very impatient.
"The gun was planted there by a kid. Just dropped there for
the Flat-feet to mull over; make them double their guard
on Colby."

Platt came suddenly to his feet.

"So as to make the boys think the knock-over was
impossible. To wise up the cops. To save your face on the
job. To—" Platt stopped. His face turned slightly pale as he

looked into those deadly black eyes of Saprillo's. Saprillo didn't speak. He didn't need to. The man hesitated, stuttered, and finally blurted out, "Cripes! Boss. That's what the boys are saying, not what I'm thinking."

"And just what are you thinking?"

"Nothing. Nothing much. Just thinking that you've got me wrong."

"So you think you know what I'm thinking, Platt? And you're right. Exactly right. I was thinking you talk more than is good for you, and certainly more than is good for me." There was a long silence, in which Platt's tongue came out and licked at dry lips. Then, "I'm marking you, Platt; I'm marking you."

Platt sank back in his chair, sucked in his lower lip, and said over and over:

"Cripes, Boss. Cripes! You ain't got me at all."

Saprillo kept his eyes on him a moment, then turned to Arnold Chester.

"You've followed my instructions? The judge will be in his room from ten to twelve. That'll give me plenty of time. You're sure he won't wilt?"

"He won't dare." The politician nodded vigorously. "I'll be there with him. I've gone over the conversation. We—" He jerked his head toward Platt.

"That'll be all, Platt." Saprillo came to his feet. "Tell the boys not to worry. I'm handling things. And tell them not to watch for Colby's death. He's made a statement before the grand jury that wouldn't help Duffy none if the old boy kicked out. Tell the boys that Colby is going on the stand and swear he made a mistake about Duffy. That the police talked him into an identification and that he now finds out that he was mistaken; that the man he saw in the park didn't look at all like Duffy."

"**CRIPES! BOSS, YOU'RE** great." Platt stood by the door, his face chalky; his attempted smile of appreciation a ghastly affair. "I'll tell the boys how you take care of your own. I—" He hesitated and held out his hand. "You know how it is, Augie. I just wanted to warn you that the boys were—were nervous like."

August Saprillo looked at the frightened man for a full minute. Then he smiled, and there was nothing of whiteness in his face nor anything forced about his smile. He took Platt's hand and shook it enthusiastically, even patted him on the back.

"Sure, Platt," he said whole heartedly. "I know how you feel. You get excited in my interest. Forget it!"

"Thanks, Boss—thanks." Platt laughed. A slightly hysterical rattle in his throat. Then he left.

August Saprillo turned to the big shot.

"Platt isn't satisfied with being the jack in the deck," he said. "You know what happens to guys who get ambitious, Chester? They either become the leader, like I did; or they get rubbed out, like Platt will."

"You're not thinking of—"

"We won't discuss it further," Saprillo cut in abruptly. "His number is up. Now to business! I've got to be sure, because I'm working this racket alone."

"Alone!"

"Sure. Colby is worth a cool million. It's a mean job and the boys wouldn't have much stomach for it. A million's a lot of jack; enough to sell your soul for. What's the matter with one of them selling my soul for it? No—it's a lone job."

"But I thought you had this punk, Delanto, in it with you; you said—"

"Yeah." Saprillo grabbed his hat from the costumer in the corner. "He's in it and out of it. He ain't going to sell his soul, or mine either." Saprillo laughed harshly. "He ain't going to have any soul to sell."

"No—no. I suppose not." Chester's face turned from a dull white to a pasty yellow.

" 'No,' is right. On your way. I'll give you five minutes' start, then I'll be at the judge's room. Well—beat it along."

Chester coughed.

"Say, aren't you forgetting something?"

Saprillo frowned, then laughed.

"Cash on the nail, eh?" He went to his desk, flipped open a drawer and carelessly drew out a big roll of bills. "There'll be five grand more when I come back to the judge's." And as Chester looked slightly disturbed, "Hell! he'll have to do the business that way. He's in the racket now. It's a lot of jack; a lot of risk, for a guy like Duffy. The judge don't suspect the reason for the alibi?"

"No. He doesn't care as long as he's paid. He's just vouching for a two hour alibi. With me and him, it should look good."

"You!" Saprillo laughed. "You're just a prop to see that things break right. The judge has a standing for honesty in the community—the crooked bum. Get going, Chester. I'll follow directly."

Almost at ten o'clock to the minute, August Saprillo appeared outside the judge's door. He nodded to the attendant on duty. An honest, fearless, gray haired man who had been on the force many years.

"You needn't make a face, Rafferty," he said. "I've got business with the judge. Information he'll be glad to get, if he gives me a break."

Two minutes later the door closed behind Saprillo and he faced Judge Beaty and Chester.

"Chester's told you the trick?" Saprillo didn't waste words. He ignored the judge's gesture of greeting and came right to business. "I haven't got much time. I want to be here when those birds come to take you to lunch. There'll be another five grand in my hand when I get back, before twelve.

"Don't get nervous, judge. You always get your jack. Rafferty will swear I was here all the time. You and Chester will back it up. If it comes to a show-down, which I don't think it will, we even have our conversation. I came to tip you off to the Braddock racket, in return for your influence in taking a second degree plea for Duffy. You couldn't stomach it, of course, but you threatened and argued with me. Set?"

The judge nodded.

"Nothing that will embarrass me, August, I hope."

"You're getting ten grand, and you'll never figure for what reason if you don't want to know. Everything ready, Chester?"

"You'd better move quickly." Chester eased his fat body out of the chair, and walking to the door opened it just a crack. "Ready?" he asked.

Saprillo nodded, walked quickly toward the door, but before reaching it said to the judge:

"What Chester tells you about Braddock is hot stuff. Use it if you want. It'll put a feather in your cap, and Braddock's been muscling in on me."

AND AS CHESTER swung the door quickly, Saprillo slipped out. With his back flat against the marble wall he slid like a shadow down and spotted Rafferty, with his back turned, talking to a man. As Saprillo disappeared from view Rafferty turned to the closed door of the judge's room.

For close to two hours the judge and Chester waited. After the first hour they were silent. Three or four times Chester had opened the door and had told Rafferty that the judge didn't want to be disturbed. Twice Rafferty listened to the judge addressing Saprillo by name, and once even heard him say that Saprillo couldn't bargain with justice.

At ten minutes of twelve the phone rang. Chester picked up the receiver.

"All right," was all that he said, and hung up. Then taking out his watch and laying it before him, he said, "He's back."

For three minutes Chester looked at the watch, then called a number.

"Thirty seconds, Joe." He barely whispered the words over the phone. "Just ask Rafferty for the key to the wash room."

Two minutes later Saprillo slunk through that doorway. He was breathing heavily, and though his face was chalky white his black eyes shone in triumph.

"All right?" Chester breathed the words as he led the super-racketeer into a far corner of the room. "It came off all right?"

"Yeah." Saprillo stuck a match into his mouth and bit off the end of it. "I don't think the Colbys will spill it to the cops. I rang up and said I'd cut her to ribbons if they squawked. There may be some jack in this later; it may pay me more than just the Duffy spring."

"Money to return her, eh?" Chester rubbed his hands together. There might be a real piece of change in it for him. "Where did you take her?"

"A safe enough place." Saprillo was evasive.

"What's the matter, Augie? You're as white as a sheet."

"Well"—Saprillo looked straight into Chester's beady eyes—"I got a sort of a bad break; at least, the kid got a bad break. I thought she was out. But she pulled off my cap and got a good look at my face. Of course—" he shrugged his shoulders. "Well— you know what that means."

"You—you did for her?" Chester did not like the word, murder—especially when the association was so close.

"No, not yet." Saprillo shook his head. "I'll wait until Duffy's sprung. After that— Well, I can't have a kid standing up in court and frying me."

"Then there can't be any money. You can't return her."

"Her old man don't know that." Saprillo laughed hoarsely. "You don't think I'm going to tell him she saw my face! I might as well go the whole way, and get some jack. Then I'll return her if he wants her that way."

"Your hand's shaking," said Chester. And again, "You're very white, Augie."

"I'm superstitious, I guess. What do you think that brat was bawling out when I left her? She was calling for Satan Hall to save her. Satan, mind you. But—hell! He can't know anything about it!"

"She was?" Chester stroked his hanging jowls. "She was,

eh? If I were you, Augie, I'd tell Colby particularly not to let Satan know about the kid. He's bad. He's a killer."

"Yeah. You're telling me!" August Saprillo sneered. "I—" and as three sharp raps came on the door, "That'll be the men to lunch with the judge, and part of my alibi." He bit at another match and spat it viciously across the room.

7

THINGS HAPPEN AT COLBY'S

THE POLICE COMMISSIONER kept Satan waiting for some time. When he finally did enter the room his eyes were narrow and his forehead wrinkled. He said at once:

"Just had word from Detective Lacey that Jackson Colby left his office in a hurry and went straight home. Made trouble for the boys, but a couple of them squeezed into the car with him. I don't know what the trouble was, but it bothers me. Do you know, Satan, I'm afraid of August Saprillo. More afraid of him than of any other public enemy the city has bred."

"I'm not." Satan fairly snapped the words.

"No, I suppose not. You're a human bloodhound, Satan. You've made an art of a sordid business. Damn it! I believe you like to hunt men. If Colby were just an ordinary man I'd put him in jail and post two of the best officers on the force outside his cell day and night. Now"—he shrugged his shoulders—"Colby told me he was going to give you a check. I suppose you tore it up and threw it in his face?"

"I didn't throw it in his face," Satan answered.

"I wanted you in that house nights, Satan. Duffy will break if he gets the chair, and Colby is the kind of a witness to give it to him. If I know that, it's a certainty that Saprillo also knows it. Duffy will talk before he burns. Saprillo hasn't been long enough in the game to grow soft, pack his bag and flee the country. Not him. Outwardly he's a power in the underworld. But inwardly he's the same gangster and killer he always was."

The desk phone rang. The commissioner swung and lifted the receiver.

"Put him on, of course," he said, and a moment later, "All right, Lacey, let me have it." There were several minutes of silence and then, "Anything else? Where are you now?" And finally, "Well—stick to the Colby house. I'll be right up."

The receiver jammed onto the hook. The commissioner called his secretary in the outer office.

"Have the car ready. I'm going uptown. Get Inspector Rankin." The commissioner came to his feet, took his hat, top coat and stick, and ignoring Satan entirely walked to the door. Satan took him by the arm.

"What happened at Colby's?" he asked.

"I don't know." The commissioner was impatient. "Lacey says he thinks something happened, but Colby has denied it and ordered them from the house. He says Colby's a mess, and Nora, one of the servants, is crying that the child has been stolen."

"Inspector Rankin is out," the secretary said from the room beyond. "But Walsh is on duty. Will I get him?"

"Tell him to—" the commissioner started, and stopped. Satan stood between him and his secretary.

"I'm going in with you, Commissioner," he said.

"I'd like to have you, Satan, but Colby doesn't want you."

Suddenly he realized that Satan had not asked permission to accompany him. His words had been a statement of fact. He looked straight at Satan. Green eyes were burning, sunken balls of fire; thin lips were a single gash of red. The commissioner half nodded to himself and killed the hasty words of reprimand on his lips. He understood perfectly, now, why they called him Satan. Certainly, at the moment the name was not a misnomer. But he only said:

"All right, come along. But keep away from Colby if he's fussy about it!" And to the secretary, "I won't need Walsh. If I'm wanted badly, call me at Jackson Colby's residence—but don't say where I've gone."

As they mounted the steps of the Colby house and Detective Lacey threw open the front door the commissioner spoke.

"Where's Mr. Colby?" he asked Lacey.

Lacey pulled a long face.

"He's in the library. It's a cinch something terrible has happened. I'm pretty sure the child's been kidnaped. No, no—he denies it, but I'd have had it out of him if his lawyer hadn't showed up."

"His lawyer!"

"Right. Theodore Milliard. I couldn't give him any lip, Commissioner. He knows his way around. He let me wait until you came. He's in there now. The story's twisted somewhat again. They say, now, that the kid's with her aunt, but don't say where."

"You wait here." The commissioner thrust Satan back in the hall, and walking to the library door pushed it open without knocking. There was a broken, gasping sort of a voice, then a quiet steady one, and the door closed behind the commissioner. Lacey turned to Satan. He was excited. He wanted to make conversation.

"COLBY'S CRAZY, AND that mouthpiece is worse. It's dollars to doughnuts the kid was snatched up in the park. Right out in the open. Can you imagine them trying to keep the police out of it? The maid, Nora, turned the waterworks on all over the place."

"Where is she now?"

"In her room, raising hell. She'd talk the roof off the place if you squeezed her."

Satan rubbed a hand over his thin lips, then he said:

"If you're asked, say I stepped out, Lacey. I'm going above."

Lacey started to speak, then changed his mind. He watched Satan taking those stairs two at a time and wondered that he did not hear the fall of his feet.

Satan reached Nora's room and turned the knob. The door was unlocked. Nora lay on the bed. Occasionally she sobbed hysterically and beat her feet up and down. She did not know Satan was in the room until he took her roughly by both shoulders and jerked her to a sitting position on the bed.

"What happened to Connie?" he asked.

"I don't know. I don't know," the girl cried. "Ask Mr. Colby. She went to her aunt's."

"That's a lie." Long hard fingers bit into the girl's shoulders. "Come on—tell me." He shook the hysterical girl until her sobs stopped.

"They took the child, didn't they?" He glared down at her now as he held her face close to his. "How much did they pay you? What did they promise you?"

The girl's mild blue eyes opened wide. She gasped out the words without thinking.

"Do you think I'd do a thing like that? Do you think I'd take money for that? I never knew. I just turned away, and—" She tried to clap a hand over her mouth, but Satan knocked it away roughly.

"And they took her, eh? Come, Nora, who are you protecting? I know you helped the kidnapers."

Blue eyes grew wide with fright.

"I didn't. I couldn't." She looked wildly about the room, but always her eyes came back to those green, burning ones before her. "She screamed once, and was gone. I tried to save her."

Satan nodded.

"And where were you, Nora, when it happened?"

"My handkerchief blew into the bushes. Miss Constance was on the grass. I went after it, and before I could get back she was gone."

"You went into some bushes, Nora, looking for your handkerchief. Connie screamed and you ran out. You didn't see anyone carry her to a car—or see a car? How far were you from the road?"

"Just the other side of the bush. Maybe I was frightened and didn't come at once. I—I was stunned. I was afraid."

"You were afraid of Connie's screaming?"

"Yes— No. I don't know why I was afraid."

"You're lying, Nora." Hard, gripping, vise-like fingers were slipping along her shoulders, towards her throat. "You're lying, Nora. Who was the man with you?"

"There wasn't any man."

"Who are you trying to protect, Nora? I know that there

was a man there. That he's been there every day. He's your
sweetheart, Nora. The man you're going to marry. Who
was that man?"

"There wasn't any— Stop, you're choking me. You're—" The
blue eyes flashed over Satan's shoulder. The door behind him
closed with a click. Satan turned his head quickly.

8

NORA SPEAKS

MRS. COLBY STOOD by that door. Her face was very pale and her eyes were very red from weeping. But her voice didn't break when she spoke.

"I don't think Connie would like you to do that, Mr. Hall; abuse a woman."

"Woman!" Satan glared at Nora for a moment. "Man or woman, what does it matter? She sold the child for a few kisses and some promises. Now—she's got to talk."

"Let me make her talk." Mrs. Colby walked to the bed and took hold of Satan's arms. "If Nora did wrong, she didn't mean to, and will do everything now to right it." She pulled Satan's hand from the girl's throat and looked up at him. She had Connie's brown eyes.

"It's the first time I ever laid hands on a woman." Satan knew that the words were his, but didn't know why he spoke them.

Mrs. Colby looked at him a long time.

"Connie was very fond of you," she said. "This morning, after you—you left, she told me all about it and cried a great deal. She thinks you are a very wonderful man. I want her to continue thinking so. I want to think so myself. You won't abuse Nora again, if they should arrest her?"

Satan drew in his lower lip and his teeth clamped down hard on it.

He said:

"If she's got the information that will save that kid, I'll strangle her with my own two hands to get it." Somehow Mrs. Colby, whose life had been free of the hate of men who hunted and killed in the night, knew that he meant it.

"You are very fond of Connie, aren't you? May I talk to you as a man—a friend of Connie's, and not as a policeman?"

Satan nodded as she led him across the room to a window.

"Connie has been kidnaped. The man who took her telephoned and warned us not to say a word to the police, or—" She hesitated as her voice broke a little. "The price of Connie's life is Mr. Colby's repudiation of his sworn statement that he recognized the murderer in the park as Duffy."

"And you are going to keep the police out of it? Let this man terrorize you; cause Mr. Colby to perjure himself; force the State to let a murderer go free because—because—"

"Because another—another murder is threatened." She swayed slightly, and Satan caught her in his arms. For a minute she gave way to her tears, then straightened suddenly. "I mustn't. I mustn't." Her hands clenched and she bit her lip. "Connie needs me more now than she ever did." And raising her head, "You know more than I do of such things—such people. Would this man make good his threat?"

Satan's green eyes stared straight into brown ones. He was the law; the hunter of men. He showed no mercy to the underworld; he made no deals with them. He recognized but one duty. To bring the criminal to justice. Now—just one thought. "Would this man make good his threat?" And he knew the answer to that question. He would.

"I want you to advise me, Mr. Hall. I know that you will think of Connie first, and the law afterwards. I have terrible memories of newspaper accounts of other children; memories that fill me with fear. What are we to do?"

"Mrs. Colby," Satan finally said, "perhaps it is better not to have this all over the front pages of the papers. It might endanger Connie's safety. But you must do something to protect her against the possible bad faith of these people. I suggest that you let me work my own way. Do everything you can to help me, and—and—" a few hours before, Satan would have thought it impossible that such a statement could come from him, "and leave the police out of it."

Mrs. Colby didn't speak. She just took Satan's hand, held it a moment, then turned quickly and went back to the bed and to Nora. Satan stood by and listened to Mrs. Colby talk to the girl.

"You loved Connie, just as we all loved her, Nora. She loved you very much, too. Now you are going to help us by telling us the truth about who was there. There was a man, wasn't there?"

"Yes," Nora gasped through her tears, "there was a man. He— We were going to be married."

Word by word, sentence by sentence, Mrs. Colby drew the whole story from her.

The man's name was Frank Smith. He had been a chauffeur, but had just inherited some money and was planning to open a garage. As soon as he found the place, they were to be married. She stammered a little when she admitted she had known him only a short time. He had asked her a lot of questions about the house, but had seemed to lose interest in it lately.

No, she had never left "Miss Constance" alone like that before. But that morning he said he had found the garage and brought her the ring, and just wanted to "give me one kiss when he put it on, ma'am."

From then on it was a little more difficult to get the truth, but finally it came. Constance had cried and Nora had started to her when her lover grabbed her. He had placed a hand over her mouth when she would have screamed, and held her so.

"He said," she went on between outbursts of tears, "that he could see a man with a gun looking in at us and he was afraid I would be killed. Afterwards, when Miss Constance was gone and we looked for her, he told me not to say he was there. He told me to say about the handkerchief blowing in. Oh, it's not his fault; you won't do anything to him! It's my fault."

"You needn't worry about him, Nora," Satan said. "If you've told the truth you'll never see him again."

"He was sent there then—sent to trap this poor girl!" Mrs. Colby put an arm about Nora.

"He was sent there." Satan nodded vigorously.

As they left the room Satan told Mrs. Colby that he would like to have Nora look over the pictures in the Rogues' Gallery.

"I'LL SEE THAT she gets there this afternoon." Mrs. Colby was fighting hard for composure as she stood at the door to her room. "You won't speak of our talk to Mr. Colby. He's a broken man today. I'm trying to be brave. But I do—do so want my baby."

She turned quickly and left him. But Satan heard the choking sobs that came from behind the closed door.

Satan reached the ground floor as the commissioner and Theodore Milliard, the lawyer, stepped from the library. Milliard was playing with the black bit of cord that hung from his glasses while he talked.

"I shall be able to handle, without police aid, Mr. Colby's business." Then knitting his eyes slightly, "If we should need the police I presume that you will be ready."

"You're going to stand there and tell me that the child has not been kidnaped? Why—look at the man!" The commissioner jerked his head toward Mr. Colby, in the library.

Satan looked into the room. Jackson Colby sat slumped in a big chair. His face was pasty and yellow; his chin sunk upon his chest. He was staring vacantly at the floor.

"Mr. Colby has had a shock certainly," the lawyer said. "I doubt that he could stand the ordeal of going on the stand tomorrow. Besides, I don't think his testimony would be to the best interests of the State. The shock, you see, my dear commissioner, was caused by his sudden doubt—perhaps even certainty, that he very nearly sent the wrong man to the chair. He feels that he was mistaken about the man in the park." Mr. Milliard went back into the library and closed the door softly.

As they rode down town Satan said to the commissioner:

"You've been advising me to take a vacation for years. I want a few days' leave now."

"Now!" The commissioner looked at him closely. "Why—you never would take a vacation before. Even if we can't take any official action in this case, we can—" He stopped suddenly, "All right, Satan, you're free to—to do what you please. But don't let anything happen to that child."

That afternoon Satan spent with Nora, looking at photographs of criminals. He was slightly disappointed, for he expected immediate results by carefully choosing those men he had known to be associated with Saprillo from time to time. But he stuck to it, having her study carefully the face of every man between the ages of twenty-one and thirty. He was surprised when Nora at last made a positive identification.

The man she picked was Frank Delanto, a petty sneak thief and drug addict, whom he would have thought the last choice of Saprillo in an undertaking of such danger. He wondered, after all, if Saprillo did have a hand in this kidnaping. Was it possible that Duffy had grown impatient and made overtures to other friends—enemies, perhaps, of Saprillo?

But one thing was certain. Someone had made a terrible mistake in choosing Frank Delanto to win the affections of Nora. Not that he wasn't handsome. Frank Delanto was known as a dandy, but he was also known as a weak sister. One who would talk if squeezed; one whom the big shots of the half world steered clear of. Perhaps whoever had used him had counted on Nora's silence. Certainly Delanto had never pulled that job himself. Satan smiled grimly. He knew a way to make men talk. Delanto! He could get everything out of him in five minutes.

A half hour later Satan had all the information he wanted about Delanto. He was not, at present, wanted by the police. But they knew his favorite hangouts and where he lived.

Before hunting up Delanto, Satan dropped into the commissioner's office.

The commissioner smiled half-heartedly and said:

"Not started on your vacation yet!"

"But I have." And Satan told him of Nora's identification of the man in the park. "That doesn't look like Saprillo's work, does it?"

"No," said the commissioner. "It doesn't. Listen to this, Satan. It's not known in the underworld that the child was taken. Generally such word spreads quickly. They seem to be just as worried about Duffy's conviction as they ever were. As a matter of fact, there's the feeling that Saprillo isn't going to make good."

"Could Saprillo possibly be out of this?"

"Personally, he is. The child disappeared between a quarter to eleven and eleven o'clock. That's the closest we can time it. From ten until twelve o'clock Saprillo was in conference with Judge Beaty and Arnold Chester. They both swear to that."

"Chester's crooked," Satan stated flatly.

"But Judge Beaty has a reputation for honesty. Look at his record of convictions."

"He's been making money lately. I don't like lads who make money in these times."

The commissioner shrugged his shoulders.

"Rafferty was on the door and swears Saprillo was there for two hours. Rafferty isn't making money."

"There's just one thing," said Satan, "that keeps me from going up to the Golden Grotto and scraping the nose of my gun down the front of Saprillo's face and making him talk."

"His alibi?"

"No. Frank Delanto. No one but a fool would use Delanto. Saprillo's not a fool. Yet, it's got to be Saprillo."

Until eleven that night Satan hunted for Delanto without success. He had not been at his boarding house. The landlady said he often stayed away all night. Then Satan Hall telephoned Mrs. Colby. Her voice broke over the phone.

"Come at once. Something— I heard from them again. They warned me against you, Satan—said it would mean Connie's death. I was not going to see you again. I was going to ask you to stop hunting for her. Now—something has happened. Come at once!"

9

"SHE'S GOT TO DIE"

SATAN REACHED THE Colby residence at eleven twenty-two. He slipped carefully into the alley and sought the rear door. Mrs. Colby heard him and let him in at once. She clutched him by both wrists. Her hands were melting ice. The words stuck in her throat.

"I was going to let you go, Satan. Now—I don't know. I can't. Read this. It came in the late mail. I've been trying to get you. Mr. Colby read it. He's been sitting in the big chair in the library ever since. He won't go to bed. He doesn't talk. I—I can't stand it much longer."

Satan read the note. It was written in pencil short and terse.

Mr. Colby:

   Your child pulled off the man's hat and saw his face. You know what that means. I'll tell you who he is for ten thousand dollars, and protection. I can't see murder done to a child. If you'll pay and protect me, burn a light in the room on the south end of the third floor at twelve o'clock. I'll see it and come in. Don't try anything foolish with the cops. Remember—she's seen his face and she's got to die unless I tip you off where she is. He's a bad guy who's got your kid. Have the light burning at twelve tonight and I'll come.

A FRIEND.

"A friend." Satan repeated the last words with a snarl. That would be Frank Delanto, of course. He had helped pull the kidnaping and was turning yellow. He nodded his head and folded up the note.

"We'll receive him when he comes, Mrs. Colby."

"But if you're here he may not talk."

"He'll talk," said Satan. "I'm pretty sure I know who wrote that note."

"I've left the light burning," Mrs. Colby said. "I shall pay the money and I shall give him protection. I haven't the money here, of course, but I'll convince him that he will receive it. I wanted you here, Satan, to help me; then to save Connie." It didn't strike Satan odd at the time that Mrs. Colby used the name "Satan" naturally and easily.

Mrs. Colby spent the time talking of Constance. Half a dozen times she asked Satan the same question.

"If we know where she is, can we save her?"

And each time Satan answered:

"Once I know where she is nothing can prevent me from saving her."

Once or twice Satan left the little sitting room, and going into the dining room peered into the night. Mr. Colby was sitting in the library, his head in his hands.

Satan shook his head. Jackson Colby was a great man to give it. But Mrs. Colby was the one to take it. Just once Mr. Colby came as far as the sitting room.

"It's all my fault," he said. "My fault. I should not have

interfered in the ways of a world I do not know or understand. I—I—"

And Mrs. Colby was across the room to him, putting her
arm about his shoulder, urging him to go to bed. When he
just shook his head, she led him back to the library again.

The clock struck twelve. Mrs. Colby jarred erect.
Twelve-fifteen; twelve-thirty; one o'clock came. Satan
paced that room. Tried to give Mrs. Colby the assurance
that the man who wrote the note would telephone; that he
had lost his nerve in approaching the house.

But she only looked at him with great, frightened eyes
and said:

"She has seen his face and she must die."

The phone rang. Satan started toward it and stopped. It
wouldn't do for him to answer. He turned to Mrs. Colby.
She came unsteadily to her feet; her teeth bit into her lower
lip; her hands were clenched at her sides. Then she walked
steadily to the phone. Satan thought of Jackson Colby
slumped in the big library chair. It was the woman, the
mother, who was carrying on. Yet—she must be suffering
ten times as much agony.

Satan followed her to the phone; leaned down beside
her; tried to listen. And she turned to him.

"It's the police commissioner," she said listlessly.

Satan clapped the receiver to his ear.

"Been looking for you all night. Trot down here at once.
I've found the man you want." The commissioner gave
Satan an address. It was an old warehouse.

Satan didn't ask questions. He didn't need to. There was
confidence in his voice when he spoke to Mrs. Colby.

"You needn't worry any longer about the writer of that

note. I know why he didn't come. He's been detained. There, there," he stopped her quick anxious words. "I'll see that he gets protection, his liberty, and the promise of money for his information. I won't take the least chance."

"You'll call me back? You'll call me back?" She held onto his arm.

"I'll call you back," he promised. "And I'll have Connie home before dawn."

"You will. I know you will."

She stood at the door and watched him leave. Her face was white, her brown eyes sunken—haunted.

THERE WAS A harness bull and a quiet clothes man standing by the entrance to the deserted warehouse when Satan reached it. He nodded to the patrolman and followed his directing thumb inside.

A detective stood before a door to the right. He opened it at once and Satan passed into a small damp room. The medical examiner was there, a fingerprint expert from Headquarters, and a camera man. The commissioner nodded to Satan.

"Where's Frank Delanto?" Satan said, and hardly recognized his own voice.

The commissioner nodded toward the corner of the room. Satan turned his head slowly. A white sheet caught his eye. He walked quickly to it, leaned down and jerked it back. Glassy eyes stared up at him. A white face that was twisted in agony. It was Frank Delanto, and he was dead.

The commissioner led Satan into the hall.

"I wanted you to see him before we took him away. Someone stuck a knife in his chest and turned it around. What do you think?"

"What do I think, Commissioner?" Satan's eyes blazed. "I don't think now. I know. I couldn't believe, with all the high class criminal talent at Saprillo's disposal, he would use a punk like Delanto. Now— Well, Saprillo used him and silenced him."

"But Saprillo has a perfect alibi."

"Where is he now?"

"He's gone duck hunting with a party of friends. That's not unusual. He always does, this time of year. I don't know who he went with. No one seems to know."

"But he'll turn up later with another alibi. A good one. Big people! Honest people! People who'll perjure their souls to keep that reputation for honesty. Like Judge Beaty."

"If Saprillo did this—well, Judge Beaty wouldn't know it."

"And Chester?"

"Oh— Chester's crooked, I'll admit. But he plays only 'honest graft.' " The commissioner tried to smile. "He wouldn't go to kidnaping."

Satan shook his head.

"You can't play the racket half way," he said. "Many think so in the beginning, but I've seen too many swept into murder who only intended to make a few easy, crooked dollars. The chain is tightly linked, Commissioner. If Colby puts the finger on Duffy; Duffy talks and Saprillo takes the rap. If Saprillo talks, Chester gets it. Chester mightn't like it, but he'll have to stick. It's a murder rap now, unless—" And Satan told the commissioner about the note. " 'She's seen his face and she's got to die.' " He repeated the words.

"You think I'd better throw caution to the winds and put out the dragnet for Saprillo?"

"No—" said Satan. "He'd kill the child at once."

"But it's Friday morning now. Duffy goes to trial at ten o'clock today."

Satan shook his head.

"If you found Saprillo and not the child—and she wasn't dead, she'd starve where he's hidden her. Don't you see? He's working it alone, unless—unless—"

"Unless—" the commissioner encouraged.

But Satan shook his head.

"I'm not working for the Department now. I'm working alone. I have leave of absence. I'm not responsible to you. You're not responsible for me."

The commissioner looked into that drawn face. He knew Satan well; better than any man, and he was startled by the transformation. There was more than just a physical likeness to the accepted pictures of the devil now. The likeness came from inside the man. Mostly from those blazing green eyes; eyes that were cruel; eyes that were evil. The deadly, hateful eyes of a killer.

"What are you thinking of, Satan?" the commissioner asked as he placed both hands upon the man's shoulders.

And Satan laughed. At least, the commissioner thought it was meant for a laugh. Then roughly shaking the commissioner's hands from his shoulders he spun quickly around and went to the open door and the street.

Two steps the commissioner took after him, and stopped.

"The Man Nobody Likes!" he said half aloud, and then:

"God help the kidnaper or murderer who crosses his path tonight."

10

THE SHADOW OF THE CHAIR

LATE AS WAS the hour, Arnold Chester was still up. Although the house was warm, he had a fire going in the grate in his library. For the first time in his life the straight and narrow path of honesty seemed the most desirable. He had gone too far. It wasn't his conscience that bothered him exactly. It was his stomach. When he thought of the child who must die, he thought also of Arnold Chester, who would be as guilty in the eyes of the law as the man who twisted the knife, or—or—

Chester looked at the note again, and looked at the fire. He should burn the note, of course. Or should he? It might help him to prove his claim that he knew nothing about the child.

He read the note again. It was in Saprillo's cramped hand.

> Don't try to rent any of your vacant property. Frank
> Delanto died tonight with a knife in his chest.

There was no signature of course. There didn't need to be. The first sentence could only mean one thing. Saprillo had hidden the child away on Chester's property. His property! Just at present he had but one vacant house. It was on Seventy-Fourth Street.

If things went wrong and they found the child there— Chester shuddered and went closer to the fire. He had better burn the note.

He started to toss it into the fire, then hesitated and looked toward the open safe. That note might prove he hadn't known about the kidnaping. Else, why would Saprillo write him not to rent his vacant property? A skillful lawyer would twist that around to his advantage at the trial.

At the trial! Arnold Chester straightened quickly from the fire. What was he thinking of? Damn Saprillo! Why had he taken the kid to his house? And he knew why. That was the reason he was alive and Frank Delanto dead. Saprillo had use for him. He was sewing him up in this kidnaping and murder.

Murder! The thing struck Chester far down in the pit of his stomach. The wanton killing of a child. He wouldn't have that on his conscience, he told himself. But he meant, he wouldn't have it on his stomach. What bothered Chester was that when the thing was over—the child was found dead, the man-hunt would be on. Who would they look for but Saprillo? Then—

Arnold Chester made up his mind. He'd go and see Saprillo now. He'd insist that the child be returned to her parents after the trial. They would swear not to tell. At the worst, Saprillo could skip the country for a while. Then Chester wouldn't have murder on his conscience for the rest of his life; the electric chair stamped on his brain; yes, the odor of burning flesh forever in his nostrils.

Arnold Chester placed Saprillo's note in the safe, carefully spun the dial, and putting on his hat and coat started toward the door. Then he thought of the last line in that note. "Frank Delanto died tonight with a knife in his chest." But Frank Delanto was yellow; Frank Delanto was a quitter. He, Arnold Chester, was not yellow; was not— But that was his own opinion. What would Saprillo's opinion be now?

He went back to the library, took a pen and wrote rapidly for several minutes. Then he opened the safe and placed the statement in it. He didn't like to think of it as a confession. He guessed, if it were necessary, he could threaten Saprillo with that statement and save himself from being found with a knife in his chest. It would explode that alibi of Saprillo's.

Indecision was uppermost with Arnold Chester. He hesitated as the clock in the big living room struck the hour of two.

He wouldn't go out the front way. It was just possible that a detective might be watching out front. He'd go through the back, to the street behind.

VERY CAREFULLY CHESTER let himself out the basement door and very carefully he locked it behind him. For a moment he thought that he heard a noise there by the ash barrels in the alley and he was frozen to those steps with terror. But the noise was not repeated. Besides, he had heard many noises during the night, or at least imagined he had.

He wasn't as young as he used to be and had trouble mounting the fence between his rear court and that of the house behind. Although he was winded when he reached the other street he dismissed the idea of going over to Broadway and hunting up a taxi. He'd leave no trail that might pop up later to fry him. He shuddered slightly.

As he walked briskly uptown now, he felt almost like a public benefactor. He was on an errand of mercy. He was about to save the life of a little child. And he thought that he would first plead, then insist, and finally threaten.

As he approached the house on Seventy-Fourth Street his steps lagged. He did not feel so sure of himself. Would Saprillo be there? But of course he would. Would he be watching from the window? And if he wasn't, would he hear him enter? He'd be very careful of that entrance. He'd use the knock he so often used on Saprillo's private door in the Golden Grotto.

One quick look up and down the street and Arnold Chester ran up the front steps with a speed that was surprising in one of his bulk. His keys were in his hand. Quickly he unlocked the outside front door and as quickly stepped into the vestibule beyond. A wooden door with a dirty glass pane in the top confronted him.

It was with an effort that he closed the heavy outside door behind him—not physical, but mental effort. It was as if he shut himself off from the outside world.

He listened; feet moved inside. He didn't hesitate now. He rapped gently upon that glass. Three quick ones, two slow ones; then he counted three and rapped just once.

The door opened almost at once. Chester thought that he made out the face of Saprillo in the darkness. But he was sure he recognized his voice.

"You're a fool, Chester, to come like this," Saprillo was

saying. "It's lucky I saw you from the window, or—" White hands moved far apart in the darkness.

"I had to come," said Chester as he stepped inside. He tried to be calm when he heard Saprillo bolt the door behind him.

"I know that." Saprillo spoke easily. "It must have been something very important to bring you here. Let me have it."

"It's the kid," said Chester quickly. "You can't kill her." He grabbed Saprillo by both arms. "I tell you, Augie, you can't do it."

"No?" Saprillo was very calm. "I'm to let her fry me because you're—you're like the others—the others I wouldn't take into it. You're yellow, like Frank Delanto."

"I'm not, I'm not." Arnold Chester tried to keep from becoming panicky. "I'm here to save you, that's all. After the trial, return her. Get the Colbys' promise of silence. Maybe there'll be money in it, too, Saprillo. That's it. That's it. Money for you. Big money."

"There'll be money in it anyway. You've got the jitters, Chester. There's no other way. She's got to die."

"She won't." Chester was slightly surprised at his own courage in making the statement flat like that.

"So that's how it is." Saprillo didn't jump at him; didn't threaten him.

Arnold Chester straightened slightly. He guessed Saprillo needed a man like him. He guessed that Saprillo realized that he was a big shot. It made him feel cocky. He said, and meant it:

"That is just how it is!"

"Maybe you're right." Saprillo stroked his chin. "But

we'll have to talk it over and make plans. Come upstairs, where I can show a light. Come on!"

11

YELLOW

ON THE STAIRS Chester wasn't quite so sure of himself, and said: "I knew you'd see it my way, Augie. But I was careful." He tried a laugh, but killed it at once; it didn't sound as light and easy as he meant it to. "I thought of you like I'd think of others. I left a note behind in case anything happened to me. I put it in my safe. That would be the first place opened if—if anything happened to me."

"Now, that was clever," Saprillo said in admiration. "Watch that top step. Come on! The back of the house."

"Where's the—the child?"

"In the front."

"I should think you'd keep her in the back. That storeroom with the window high up."

"No. That's where we're going. I covered that window so I can have a light to read by. I've got to have some recreation."

Arnold Chester followed the dark shadow of Saprillo down the narrow hall. He saw the sliver of light beneath a door and heard the key turn in the lock. August Saprillo stood back for Chester to enter as the light splashed into the hall. He said:

"There's a couple of chairs and a bed I carted down from

the attic." He followed Chester into the room, the door swinging open behind them.

Arnold Chester was staring at that bed, his beady eyes popping; his breath coming in quick, uneven gasps. Plainly he saw the frail body of the child crouched in fear upon the bed; plainly he saw the cruel, tight ropes that bit into the flesh of her wrists. He saw, too, the swollen ankles that were bound tightly together, and the rope which held them fast to the heavy iron supports of the bed.

"No, you don't." Saprillo grabbed the stuttering Chester by the back of the neck as he turned toward the door. "Come over and have a look at our little playmate." He forced Chester across the room and to the bed, holding his head down close to the child's frightened brown eyes.

"Sit up and give the nice gentleman a smile, kid." He leaned over and cruelly struck the child across the mouth with the back of his hand. "This is the gent who lent us the house. This is the gent who wants you to stand up in court and put the finger on me. Tell him about your boy friend, Satan Hall."

"He'll come. He'll come!" the child cried out, more in fear than in defiance. "He won't forget me. He won't let you; he won't let you—" And then, in almost a shriek, "I want my mother."

"Well"—Saprillo pushed the speechless and trembling Chester back across the room and into a corner—"it's a different story, isn't it, when it's your face she looked at. What do you think of taking her home to her mamma now? What do you think of getting them to promise not to—to tell on us?" He lisped the last three words sarcastically. "Well—what do you say?"

And Arnold Chester didn't say anything. Mechanically he thrust a hand into a pocket, and taking out a handkerchief wiped the beads of perspiration from his forehead. He was breathing heavily and looking at Saprillo.

Saprillo stepped back a pace and stared at the man. He looked long and steadily at the pasty jowls, the frightened eyes, the trembling lips.

"By God!" he said after a moment. "You ain't much better than Frank Delanto. You're yellow as hell."

"No, no. I'm not!" Arnold Chester straightened slightly and tried to laugh. But it cracked in his throat. Then, as Saprillo's hand shot under his coat he screamed out, "What are you going to do? What are you going to do?"

Chester grabbed frantically at the wrist of that right hand; was flung against the wall and almost sank to the floor in fear as he saw the black gun; felt the nose of it pound hard against his stomach.

"I have a good mind to pump it into you."

"Not me, Augie. Not good old Chester. We've been friends too long. I came here tonight to help and advise you. Now I see it your way. You're right, as you're always right. But I thought—"

"YOU THOUGHT YOU'D lay the rap on me. You thought you'd see yourself clear if Satan got me. Well—that kid's threatened me with Satan enough. Every other word's been about him, and it's cost her many a slap in the mouth." And suddenly pressing the gun tighter, "I could give it to you right now and none would be the wiser. The shot would never be heard through these thick walls. I could do for you and the kid, and they'd think—they'd think—" Saprillo stopped talking. Up to that moment he had thought only of trapping Arnold Chester into his own position. The child should see him, too! Now, for the first time, he had thoughts of murder.

Murder! Saprillo's dark eyes flashed, his lips curled and he smiled. With Chester dead there would be no one to pin the job on him. Besides, there was a lot of sense behind it. If the police figured it out, they'd figure that Chester had as much interest in seeing Duffy free as he had. It would be a natural. They'd think Chester croaked the kid because she saw him, then lost his nerve and committed suicide. Suicide! He could make it look like that.

As the plan formed quickly in Saprillo's warped and twisted brain, he saw other good points in it. He'd kill Chester and the kid, then when Duffy was sprung he'd ring up the police; talk like a rat who had a grievance against Chester, and tip them off to where the kid was. They'd think Chester knew of the squeal, lost his nerve and shot himself. Fine! Great! It was Arnold Chester's own house. It was in the cards, else why was Chester so opportunely delivered into his hands?

Arnold Chester read murder in Saprillo's face. He didn't cry out for mercy now; he didn't plead for his life. He knew that death was sure and speedy unless—

"Don't, Augie." He shot the words out quickly. "There's the statement; the confession in my safe."

Saprillo laughed.

"That old crate! I'll pick up your confession on the way down town. There's still time, before dawn."

Arnold Chester's two hands shot out suddenly toward that gun. He opened his mouth to scream, but no words came. There was a single report.

Arnold Chester's mouth still hung open. Both his hands went to his stomach. He stood so, staring vacantly at Saprillo. Saprillo sneered and pressed the trigger again. This time Arnold Chester tumbled to the floor.

Saprillo shrugged his shoulders and looked at the dead man. "Maybe that ain't the way a suicide would do," he thought. "But that's the way he would have it and that's the way he got it." And turning to the child on the bed:

"Well, sister, how do you like— What the hell! The kid's out."

He walked quickly over to the bed and placed the gun close to the child's head. For a moment his finger tightened on the trigger, then loosened again.

"Where's your boy friend now?" he jeered. Then scowled when the child lay still, her eyes closed. "Where's Satan— Satan!" he said again; then grinned as her eyes opened.

"Satan. Satan!" the child called very slowly, as she lifted her bound wrists and cried out with the pain as she tried to spread her arms apart.

"You'll find him, kid. Don't you worry. You'll find Satan. Find him where he belongs—in hell. There—" Again Saprillo pressed the gun close against that little forehead; again his finger tightened upon the trigger. And again, he didn't fire.

A low voice spoke from the open door.

"I wouldn't do that, Augie," the voice said.

12

GUNS FOR TWO

THE GANGSTER RAISED his black eyes and looked straight into the green ones of Detective Satan Hall.

August Saprillo's first thought was that a gun covered him and that he was about to die. He'd take the kid with him. Then his eyes opened wide and his lips curled evilly. Satan Hall was standing there with both his hands at his sides, and both his hands empty.

August Saprillo didn't think any more. He just jerked his gun from that little curly head. Almost the moment he raised it he wished that he hadn't. While he held it against the child's head he had some chance to bargain with Satan. Now he knew the truth; knew it the very moment that right hand of Satan's moved, for that hand which had been empty a split second before, now held a gun. Satan had been afraid that he would kill the kid. Satan had trapped him into raising his gun.

They fired together. Just a single deafening roar. Satan's right arm dropped to his side; his right hand opened and his gun pounded to the floor.

But his left hand shot beneath his right armpit, and stayed there.

Saprillo clicked his heels together, spun around and crashed forward on his face.

Two minutes later Satan had cut the ropes with his left hand, and Connie was in his arms. Soft hair brushed his face; his cheeks were wet with her tears as she clung to him.

"Satan—Satan," she sobbed, "you took so long to come."

But he didn't mind the reprimand as he held her tightly with his left arm. What made his heart beat with a thrill he had never experienced before was the fact that she never once doubted that he would come.

Mrs. Colby opened the door as Satan staggered up the front steps with the child clasped in his arms. He knew that she took Connie from him and for the first time gave way to her emotion. He knew that Jackson Colby stood behind his wife, his dull eyes growing brighter; the former assurance creeping slowly back into them. He knew that bent shoulders straightened; that a flabby chin seemed to recede and tuck itself away beneath a loosened, wilted collar.

But it was Mrs. Colby who first saw the blood that dropped from the end of Satan's fingers and splashed upon the rug. Then fogginess, that Satan had difficulty in throwing off.

The doctor came, and almost on his heels the commissioner himself.

"You see," Satan told the commissioner, as he lay back on the bed in the guest's room, "it isn't because I'm not able to move that I'm staying here. It's because of Connie. I've got to go in every so often and see her. She's rather fond of me, you know."

"Yes—" said the commissioner. "A remarkable piece of

work, Satan. But how did you know she was a prisoner in
that house?"

"Partly luck. But mostly, picking out the weak link in
the chain, that every racket has. That weak link was Arnold
Chester. I thought he would know; that he had arranged
that Saprillo alibi. And I decided to find out from him
where Connie was. If he wouldn't tell me, I was going to
kill him. I know that doesn't sound right, Commissioner,
but it's just how I felt. Then I got the first break in the case.
While I was standing on a barrel, ready to force open a
window and climb into Chester's house, he came out the
back door. I thought that he had heard me, but he hadn't.
I followed him then, had a bit of trouble getting quietly
in a basement window of the house where he went, and—
Saprillo wasn't such a bad shot."

"You see," Dr. Thomkins, who stood by the open door,
finally got his words in, "the wound itself is nothing to
worry about. It's the loss of blood. A good sleep will help
that."

"No sleep for me." Satan tried to speak with assurance,
but the doctor, who was now at the bed, lifted Satan's
eyelids and smiled to himself. The hypodermic was already
beginning to take effect. And Satan slept.

Satan was not in court that morning when Jackson
Colby, correct and somber of attire, dignified and domi-
neering in bearing, stepped upon the witness stand and
swore to tell the truth, the whole truth, and nothing but
the truth—so help him God.

It was with dramatic effect that he spoke of his public
duty in identifying Duffy as the man with the gun who had

stood beside the murdered body in the park. If not able to take it, Jackson Colby was again able to give it.

It was the former self-assured and commanding Jackson Colby who, after the quick verdict of murder in the first degree, waved aside his protecting body of police and spoke with feeling and authority to the reporters.

Dr. Thomkins talked plainly to Mrs. Colby when she wanted to keep Constance in bed.

"The physical discomforts are nothing as compared with the mental agony she has gone through." He was very emphatic. "We must make as little of her terrible experience as possible. It's not her body that is in danger, but her mind. Let her go to this—this Satan Hall if she wishes. Let her feel that she is taking care of him. Give her a responsibility. This fear of hers that he is dying is bad for her."

So it was late afternoon when Satan opened his eyes and saw Connie sitting on the end of his bed. Her brown eyes sparkled when his green ones appeared from between blinking lids.

"Oh, Satan—" the words just burst from her. "Look; you're not The Man Nobody Likes any more." She flashed an evening paper before his eyes. He read the headlines across the top; looked at his cold, sinister face on that front page. He shook his head and frowned.

"It was father," Connie explained. "The commissioner told him you wouldn't like it, but he insisted. He said it was a public duty to let the taxpayers know the protection and— and bravery of—of— I don't know, exactly, Satan—but they were big and lovely words and made me very proud."

But this time Satan smiled as he stretched up his right hand and ran his fingers roughly through the tousled hair.

www.ingramcontent.com/pod-product-compliance
Lightning Source LLC
Chambersburg PA
CBHW020639030726
47498CB00002B/282